STARLING

STARLING

LESLEY LIVINGSTON

HARPER TEEN

HarperTeen is an imprint of HarperCollins Publishers.

Starling

Copyright © 2012 by Lesley Livingston

www.epicreads.com

Library of Congress Cataloging-in-Publication Data is available.

ISBN 978-0-06-206307-6

Typography by Cara Petrus

12 13 14 15 16   LP/RRDH   10 9 8 7 6 5 4 3 2 1

❖

First Edition

For librarians. Everywhere.

ACKNOWLEDGMENTS

This book marks the beginning of a brand-new adventure, a new journey. Some of the people who've stepped onto this road with me are familiar traveling companions; some are new. I would fold you all into the biggest group hug *ever* if I could get you into the same room at the same time. Insofar as that's looking unlikely, I'll just thank you all here.

First, as always, my profound gratitude goes to Jessica Regel, my agent. I continue to not be able to say enough about the depths of my appreciation—just please continue to rock on. Next up is Karen Chaplin, my wise, patient, much-smarter-than-me editor—thank you for taking such good care of me and of this series; you're a delight to work with. And a third thanks goes to Laura Arnold, who is also delightful and who acquired this series in the first place.

Thank you again to Jean Naggar and the staff of JVNLA for continuing to be outstanding. TimBits for you all again next time I'm in the office.

Thank you to the industrious, creative crew at HarperCollins: my editorial director, Barbara Lalicki; Maggie Herold, my production editor; and Cara Petrus, my designer. You've all made me, and this book—and Mason Starling—look so ferociously good! Thank you also to everyone at HarperCollins Canada for continuing to make me feel like one of the cool kids—especially my Canadian editor, Hadley Dyer, who indulges me in ebullient, mythology-laden, shop-talk lunches.

Now, as ever, I send massive love and gratitude out to my mom and my wonderful family. And to my friends. Because you all put up with me when I'm on deadline, and this just wouldn't be any fun if you guys didn't think it was kind of cool.

Of course, my most important acknowledgment/respect/ declaration of undying love/debt of gratitude and/or frosty beverages goes, unsurprisingly, to John. Again. None of this happens without you. None of it. You are the Gene Hackman Character to my Panicky Idiot Number One in *The Poseidon Adventure*.

Finally, thank you to my readers. To those who've followed me here, and those who've just joined me on the road. I hope you enjoy the Ride—watch out for stray Valkyries!

"C'mon, Mase! Where's that killer instinct?"

Calum Aristarchos bounced lightly on the balls of his feet, the tip of his fencing saber tracing tiny, taunting spirals in the air.

"En garde . . ."

Mason Starling's gaze narrowed behind the wire mesh of her cage mask, and she sank lower into her stance, thigh muscles searing with fatigue. She shook her head sharply to clear her mind as the sweat dripped, blinding, into her eyes. *Concentrate . . .*

The blade in her hand wavered, dipping as if in uncertainty.

She retreated a half step. . . .

And Calum Aristarchos made his move. Feet crossing over each other in a blur, he ran at her and thrust for her heart, his left arm flung back, spine arching like a dancer's, only *slightly* overextending himself. . . .

Mason dropped into a deep, leg-punishing lunge, scooped her blade back up and—

"A hit!"

"No!"

Toby Fortier—fencing coach drill sergeant, and *not* someone to argue that kind of point with—snorted and marked the practice score sheet. "She tagged you good, Aristarchos. Which also means she wins, again. Whining about it just makes you look like a girl." He glanced up at Mason as she pulled off her headgear and grinned. "A girl who can't fight like Mason."

Calum took off his own mask and flipped his practice foil around in the air, catching it by the blade, just under the guard. He sauntered back over to where Mason stood, his green eyes flashing and a wry smile bending his mouth up at one corner. Mason noticed that his face still glowed with the remnants of a deep summer tan. Part of what made him look like a magazine model.

"Okay," Calum said, nudging her with his elbow. "I guess you found that killer instinct."

"Sure," she agreed. "Or you just got cocky. That lunge left you wide-open."

"Not for everybody, Mase." He winked and plucked the sword out of Mason's hand. "Just for you."

Mason felt her heart flutter for an instant. "Does that mean you're gonna help me prepare for the Nationals qualifiers?"

"You bet." Cal wrapped one arm loosely around Mason's waist and whispered in her ear, "I always back a winner."

Mason's cheeks grew warm as she blushed fiercely. Then she felt another kind of heat—like a laser beam focused on the back of her head—and she glanced over her shoulder to find Heather Palmerston staring at her from across the gym. The tall blonde turned away when Mason's eyes met hers, and she slapped her fencing glove into the palm of one hand, the sound of the leather cracking like a whip. Mason was reasonably certain that Heather had only taken up fencing to stay close to Cal, even though the two of them had recently broken up.

Heather was an indifferent fighter—not bad, just not committed—and she really didn't seem to enjoy it all that much. Unlike Mason, for whom fencing wasn't a pursuit so much as a passion. *She* was shooting for a spot on the national team. And after that? Maybe even the Olympics. Heather . . . not so much. Even less so after she and Cal had broken up. Mason wondered why Heather hadn't dropped out of the fencing club then, but for Heather, everything was about appearances. And quitting would have made it look like she'd lost something. The thing she *did* seem to enjoy about it, though, was the way all the guys looked at her as she walked by dressed in her tight fencing whites.

Like Rory Starling, the younger of Mason's two older brothers, who was gawking at Heather that very moment. As she sashayed past where he was working out, punching the heavy bag in the far corner of the gym, Rory's jaw went so slack he was almost drooling. Mason rolled her eyes.

"She'd be a decent fighter if she gave a damn," Toby rumbled from right beside her. Mason hadn't realized he was standing there. "Couldn't hold a candle to you, of course, but she'd certainly hold her own." He grunted and ran a hand over his face, smoothing his finely trimmed goatee.

"D'you want her on the competition's team?" Mason asked. She'd meant the question to be a neutral one, but that wasn't how it came out sounding. Across the gym, Heather said something that made Calum laugh . . . and Mason felt an envious twinge in her chest.

Toby looked down at her and shook his head. "No, Mason," he said. "And you *know* your spot on the team is locked up."

"That's not what I meant—"

"I know. Just understand that it's not something you have to worry about. Not if you keep fighting the way you have been." Toby's gaze drifted back to where Heather stood shaking out her wheat-gold hair from its ponytail. It fell across her shoulders like spun honey. Lookswise, she was the exact opposite of Mason, with her black hair, winter-pale skin, and blue eyes. "Anyway," Toby was saying, "Palmerston's too high maintenance. I just hate wasted potential, that's all."

Mason nodded silently as Toby wandered over to where a couple of boys from the wrestling club were seeing just how hard they could peg each other in the head with a volleyball. Mason fished her aluminum water bottle out of her gear bag and took a long swallow to quench her thirst brought on by the long practice. She was tired, but not exhausted, and that was a good sign. Cal was a tough opponent—the toughest, in fact. He was still better than her, in spite of what Toby had said, and Mason was inwardly thrilled that not only had she been able to hold her own against him, but he'd actually seemed to appreciate it. She liked the idea of being appreciated by Calum Aristarchos. A lot.

Trying not to glance over to see if he was still chatting with Heather, Mason stuffed her water bottle back in her bag and gathered up the rest of her gear. As she did so, she became aware of a subtle shift in the quality of the light streaming in through the high, arched windows. Mason peered up through the construction scaffolding that had been erected all along the south wall of the hall that housed Gosforth Academy's new athletic center, startled to see that the previously clear blue vault of the sky had descended like a dark, heavy blanket, blotting out the sun.

Through the windows, Mason saw thick, bruise-black clouds boiling over one another, moving with a swiftness that was almost frightening. She glanced at her watch. It was only early evening—just before dinner—but it suddenly seemed much, much later. The light outside dimmed to an ominous purplish wash.

If the sky was going to open up, Mason thought, at least it wasn't anywhere near as far to get back to her dorm as it had been when the fencing club had had to use the Columbia University gym. That was a good six blocks away. Now she just had to run the length of Gosforth's quad in order to get home. It was one of the perks of the new facility. The building used to be the academy headmaster's residence, but the old gothic structure had recently been gutted and redesigned, turning it into a multipurpose center to be used by the gymnastics club and for dance classes and wrestling and—most importantly, as far as Mason was concerned—the fencing team. The sprung wooden floors had been installed only the week before, and the whole place smelled of lumber, varnish, and paint.

It was a gorgeous facility, with state-of-the-art equipment wrapped in the antique charm of the building's gothic architecture. There was even a little raised stage at one end for dance recitals and presentations, and the old stone walls had been left exposed along one side. Midway down the long north wall, double doors set into a high glass partition led to a soaring vestibule. It was an oddly extravagant feature for an athletics facility, but it was triple-glazed safety glass and probably could have withstood even a hard-flung basketball. It was there to showcase the high stone arch that had once housed a plain leaded-pane window, which Mason's father, as a benefactor to the school, had ordered replaced with a magnificent stained-glass masterpiece. Even on the dullest day the window caught the sun and shattered it into a million shards of rainbow-brilliant light, casting it across the dark wood-paneled foyer of the new gym, where glass cases stood displaying an abundance of sports championship trophies.

Mason smiled as she stared up at the stained glass. She was proud of her father and his commitment to the school, but sometimes she wished he would choose *slightly* less ostentatious ways to commit.

Outside, she saw that the shadows cast by the branches of the old oak tree in the school's quad had begun to wave wildly in the gathering storm. The tree was enormous—it had been planted when the school's original buildings had been constructed in the late 1700s on Manhattan's Upper West Side—and the gusting wind sent showers of leaves, twigs, and acorns clattering against the window and the old slate roof. The overhead fluorescents hanging from the hall's exposed beams flickered and dimmed. When they returned to their normal brightness, the gymnasium seemed to have taken on a slightly sepulchral air.

"Whoa," Mason heard Calum say.

She turned to see him gazing up at the gathering storm, his eyes wide and forest green in the uncertain light that filtered down through the tall windows.

"Hey, Toby?" he called. "Maybe we'd better head back to the dorms—that looks like some pretty serious weather rolling in."

"Sure," Toby agreed. "We've done enough work today. And it'll save *you* from getting your ass handed to you again by your partner." His mouth quirked upward, and he slapped the folder with the scoring sheets inside closed. Then he picked up his travel mug—his constant companion; the guy was a total caffeine junkie—and turned, bawling to the other student athletes to pack it in. He barked at the fencing club members to hand in their gear to Mason so that she and Cal could check the weapons for loose hilts and burrs and then return them to their proper places in the storage cabinets.

"Hey, Mouse, catch," Rory said as he tossed an extra practice foil carelessly at her, and Mason had to dodge or risk getting the tip through one eye.

Damn, he's annoying, Mason thought. She hated it when he called her Mouse. He knew it, too.

7

Heather, of course, just strolled right past Mason and handed her foil directly to Calum. They were still cordial, but since their breakup Cal had been pretty clear in his intentions to keep it that way—cordial. Not that Mason had made a point of noticing that or anything. . . .

"C'mon, Mase," Cal said, smiling at her.

He handed Heather's foil to Mason, shrugged out of his fencing jacket, and threw it over onto the pile of his own gear. Underneath, he wore only a thin T-shirt with the school logo stenciled on the back. "We should hurry to beat the storm or we're gonna get drenched on the way back to the Res," he said to Mason over his shoulder.

Calum in a wet T-shirt wasn't such a bad idea as far as she was concerned, but he had a point. She hurried toward the storage cabinet at the far end of the gym, but it became suddenly apparent that they weren't beating anything. Through the windows, she saw a blaze of lightning fork across the sky with a sizzling, ear-shattering crack that made her jump.

Is it a bad sign when you can actually hear *lightning?* she wondered. But she didn't really have time to ponder the physics of it because the sound was drowned out almost immediately by a cannon-roar boom of thunder so loud it felt as though it had come from inside her head. The air in the hall quivered with the shock wave, and the new gym floor felt as though it had actually heaved upward. Mason yelped and ran for the cabinet. Outside, the rain started to fall in fat, splattering drops and the wind moaned loudly.

Mason juggled her armload of whip-thin aluminum blades, trying to open the metal door without actually having to stop and put anything down. She was surprised when Heather appeared at her elbow and pulled the door open for her.

"Thanks," Mason gasped, struggling to untangle herself from the forest of swords.

"Hold still," Heather said. "You're gonna stab one of us." Together, the two girls struggled to disengage the weapons and stow them on the rack on the cabinet wall.

"Be careful with that épée!" Mason warned. "You're gonna snap the tip!"

"Yeah, yeah. Let *go*, Starling. I've got it."

By the time they got everything stowed, the sky had turned to shades of deepest midnight and lightning lashed the underbellies of black clouds. The lights flickered again, and Mason felt the breath stop in her throat for an instant.

"Jeezus." Cal snorted. "Who ordered the apocalypse?"

As if on cue, another magnesium-bright flash of lightning blazed, and the lights in the hall flickered and died. The entire gymnasium went suddenly, completely, dark. Mason sucked in a sharp breath, and her heart started to rabbit in her chest. She quickly grabbed her gear bag and hurried toward the door.

"Let's get out of here," she said.

She thrust through the double glass doors into the foyer and leaned on the main door's push bar—and nothing happened. She shoved it again, harder, but the heavy carved-wood door remained shut.

"What's wrong?" Heather asked from behind her.

"It's jammed or something," Mason said, and tried again.

"Let me try." Calum nudged her over to one side. He used both hands to push against the bar. He kicked the door's brass footplate and tried shouldering it open, but it wouldn't budge.

"Hang on, Cal," Toby called. They could hear him walking across the gym floor toward them. His worn, heavy combat boots made a steady *thump-thump* in the darkness. His bulky form suddenly loomed up in front of them, and he jiggled the door bar and pushed sharply on it a couple of times. Then he stepped toward an alcove at the side of the door. "Hunh," he grunted. "Weird."

"What's going on?" Rory asked, showing up with his gym bag slung over one shoulder.

"I think the power outage screwed up these new electronic locks," Toby answered. "The control panel's dead."

"Shouldn't there be a backup system or something?" Calum asked.

"Yeah." Toby punched at the panel and jiggled the door bar again. "But there should also be emergency lighting, and I don't see that it's come on, either. Could be that they just haven't got the bugs worked out yet. . . ."

Outside, it sounded like the world was coming apart. Mason could hear the old Gosforth oak creaking in protest at the punishing winds.

"I'm gonna go check out the fire exit door," Toby said. "Sit tight until I get back. Don't wander—there's still construction equipment lying stacked near the walls and I don't want any of you accidentally kicking a circ saw and amputating a toe."

Even in that pitch dark, it didn't take the fencing master long to travel from one end of the gym to the other and back again. And Mason knew, just from the sounds of his measured tread, that they weren't leaving anytime soon.

"We might as well make ourselves comfortable until the juice comes back on," Toby said, confirming her suspicions, and Mason heard him swishing around the dregs of whatever was left in his travel mug. "Fire door's sealed tight, too."

"That's not supposed to happen, is it?"

"No, Mason. It isn't." Toby sighed heavily. "And damned if I'm not out of coffee. *That's* not supposed to happen, either."

Look, Mason told herself sternly, *it's not as if you're in a small space or anything . . . you're not trapped. There's plenty of room.*

She could feel the airiness of the vaulting hall all around her, even if she couldn't actually make out the ceiling, but it wasn't that. It was more just the thought of being locked in with absolutely no avenue of *escape* that bothered her. That, and the darkness. It was so complete. So absolute. Shouldn't there have at least been some light spill from surrounding buildings or the street? The school was in the middle of freaking Manhattan, for crying out loud. . . .

"Toby," Mason said quietly.

He didn't seem to hear her. Probably because her throat was so dry her voice had barely come out as a whisper.

"Toby." She tried again.

"What's wrong, Mason?"

What was *wrong*? She was going to lose it any second—*that's* what was wrong. She was going to blow a mental gasket right in front of the hottest guy in school and his ice-queen ex and her stupid selfish brother and by the time first period rolled around tomorrow, everyone at the Gosforth Academy would know she was a claustrophobic freak. "Toby? I . . ."

"What is it?" he asked again. "Mason, we're stuck here until the power comes back on, so we might as well all just relax."

"I can't."

"Aw, hell," Rory muttered. "Here we go."

"Shut up, Ror," Mason said tightly.

"Mason, what do you mean?" Toby asked.

"I mean . . . I . . . I'm not exactly good with confined spaces." Mason could hear the panicky rasp in her voice. "I'm not good with being locked in." She knew that Toby had shifted forward, and that he was probably peering at her, trying to make out if she was kidding or not. Or if she was, in fact, on the verge of losing it. But she couldn't see his face. Zero ambient light filtered in through the windows. It was starting to feel like being trapped down a well or sealed in a coffin.

"*How* not good?" Toby asked quietly.

"Sweating-barfing-screaming-uncontrollably-psychotic-episode not good."

Toby blinked at her. "When?"

"Soon . . ."

"Well, that's just marvelous," Heather said in tones laced with disgust. "You puke on me and I'm punching you in the face, Starling."

"Not a problem," Mason said through her teeth. Her fists

were tight, sweat-slick knots of bone and muscle, and she couldn't seem to make her fingers unclench. "I'm not really gonna care *what* you do to me if it gets to that point—"

Suddenly there was a loud thump against the heavy double doors—as though something heavy had run into them at high speed—and even Toby jumped at the sound. In the silence that followed, Mason could hear her heartbeat pounding in her ears.

Then the howling started. Eerie and keening and somehow . . . inhuman.

"What the hell *is* that?" Heather said sharply. Even in the darkness Mason knew the other girl was staring accusingly at her, as if it might somehow be her fault. "Is this some kind of joke?"

"C'mon, Heather," Calum said. He also seemed to sense the accusation in her tone. "Mason has nothing to do with it. And it probably *is* a joke. Some jerk-ass freshmen are probably running around in this stupid storm, pretending they're ninjas. It's nothing to worry about."

"Cal's right," Toby said. "And anyway, nobody's getting in here anytime soon—ninjas or not. Just like we're not getting out. Sorry, Mase."

There was another loud thump on the roof, followed by a frenzy of hammer blows at the front door and the sounds of shrieking.

In the darkness, Calum stalked over to the door and hammered back, shouting, "Knock it off, you losers! We're stuck in here! Go make yourselves useful and get a freaking crowbar!"

The noise stopped. They all listened for what must have been several minutes, but all they could hear were the sounds of the storm. And Mason, panting for breath. In the darkness, even with her eyes squeezed shut, all she could see was red. The back of her fencing jacket was soaked with cold sweat and her stomach was churning. Mason was pretty sure that what they'd heard had *not* been pranking students. But she was also starting to think that she'd be perfectly willing to take her chances outside in the storm rather than spend another five minutes locked in with no escape.

Restlessly she retreated back into the gym and made her way carefully across the too-dark space toward the scaffolding under the tall windows set high in the wall. Originally they had been the second-story windows. The lower ones had been bricked over and, once the gym was finished, the long wall would hold athletic apparatus like a ballet barre and rigging for hanging indoor archery targets and practice fencing dummies. But for now, there was just the painter's scaffolding, and Mason reached out a hand and grasped one of the metal bars. She had to do something to keep herself occupied or she was truly going to lose it.

"Mase?" Calum called. "What are you doing?"

"I just want to check on something." She put a foot on a crossbar and pulled herself up to the first level.

"Mason," Toby said in a warning voice. "I'd rather not have to tell your father you broke your neck playing monkey bars in a blackout. Please consider the fact that he would probably feel obliged to break mine just to make it even."

"I'm being careful," Mason said as she pulled herself up to

the next platform, the one that would let her look out of the window. Mason edged over to the closest window and peered out into the storm. She could see the rain falling torrentially and could make out the dark shapes of some of the closest Columbia buildings, dark against a dark sky. But there were no lights. Anywhere. No emergency lights, no streetlights . . . nothing even powered by backup generators, it seemed. Mason swallowed against the constricting lump of fear in her throat. This just wasn't *normal*. She glanced back down at where the others huddled in the darkness.

"Looks like there's a power outage everywhere," she said.

She thought she might have heard the distant wail of a police siren over the noise of the storm, and she turned to look back out the window. Suddenly Mason screamed in terror and threw herself instinctively backward. She shrieked as her foot slipped off the platform edge and she fell, only saving herself from plummeting fifteen feet to the floor of the gym by catching one of the scaffold struts with the crook of one elbow. She hung in midair, thrashing and kicking her feet while Toby and the boys shouted her name and reached for her. They managed to grab Mason's legs and take her weight, and she let go of the scaffold bar. Once her feet touched the ground, Cal wrapped her in a fierce, totally unexpected embrace.

"Don't scare me like that!" he said as he held her close.

"I'm okay—"

Suddenly Rory shoved Calum aside. He grabbed Mason by her shoulders and shook her. "What the *hell* is the matter with you?" he screamed in her face. "You coulda killed yourself!"

Mason shrugged angrily out of her brother's punishing grip as Toby dragged him back a few steps.

"Back off, Rory," the fencing master said as calmly as he could. "Mason, what happened?"

"I . . ." Now that she was safely on her feet, the horrible image flooded back into her mind. "I saw something. Out in the storm. It was hideous—a face—all eyes and teeth and it was screaming. . . ."

"Bullshit," Rory scoffed. "First you freak out and now you're making things up. You're always making stupid shit up—"

"Toby said back *off*, Rory." Calum stepped in front of him and put a hand on his chest. "You can't talk to Mason like that."

"Screw you! She's my sister and I'll talk to her however I damn well want!"

"Stow it, both of you!" Toby finally shouted.

In the silence that followed, a sudden frenzy of sound came from overhead, like scrabbling animal claws and ear-splitting keening, somewhere high up on the roof. Mason flinched and looked up, even though she couldn't see anything in the darkness. The unearthly howling floated over the rattle of the rain.

Toby pushed the two boys out of the way and stood peering down at Mason. He took her by the shoulders and made her look at him.

"Mason . . . are you sure?" he asked. "It wasn't just the trees moving in the wind? You saw somebody out there?"

"Some*thing*. Eyes . . . and teeth," Mason said again. She

clenched her hands together when she realized she was shaking. In the darkness, she could just see Toby glance hesitantly back over his shoulder, toward the window. He thought it was her claustrophobia talking. "There *was* a face out there, Toby. I'm not crazy."

"Maybe we should break a window or something," Calum suggested. "Get the hell out of here—"

"No." Toby shook his head. "Nobody is breaking any windows."

Which was exactly when the tree in the quad came crashing down.

II

As if in mockery of Toby's proclamation, Gosforth's ancient oak smashed through the heart of Gunnar Starling's shining contribution to the brand-new gym—the new rainbow-glass window. The crowning branches of the venerable old tree looked like a hundred reaching arms, all ending in grasping, black-taloned hands. Sharp, glinting shards of colored glass flew through the air, and Toby and the students screamed with one voice, scattering for the far corners of the gym's long hall.

The tree's huge branches tore a gaping hole in the front of the athletic center, scattering leaves and heavy, splintered limbs . . . and a screaming horde of nightmares came pouring through.

Mason was the first to see them—dusky-skinned monstrosities, only vaguely human shaped, with slack, rubbery flesh. "Toby!" she shrieked in a warning. The creatures were the same as the one she'd seen outside the window, only there had to be a dozen of them at least, struggling to free themselves from the tangle of the fallen tree. Lightning flashed, illuminating the gym clear as day through the jagged opening in the roof, and the rain poured down in a chill deluge. Mason scrambled behind a stack of lumber in the far corner and watched as the apparitions untangled themselves from the oak.

Did those things bring the tree down? she wondered frantically, remembering the enraged screaming and the pounding at the door. *What are they? What do they want?*

The shadowy things wrenched at the branches, disentangling themselves and heaving aside debris with inhuman strength. They moved in a disconcertingly staccato fashion—arms and legs bending at odd, sharp angles—but they were fast. Bluish-purple skin, like drowned-corpse skin, stretched from bony frames, and lank hair hung from their scalps, tied back in long, ragged braids and rattails. The creatures looked like something out of a big-budget Hollywood horror movie—zombies with eyes that glowed with a sickly, milky-white light. Open mouths displayed ivory teeth bared in grimaces of madness and rage. Bloodlust.

This isn't happening.

This was the psychotic episode Mason had warned Toby of earlier.

This is it. Her mind was broken. . . .

Then, for a moment—a frozen instant in the chaos—Mason saw what she thought, at first, was an angel. A winged figure appeared in the darkness, outlined in coruscating, iridescent light, an ethereally beautiful woman with long silvery hair and blazing eyes. She hovered in the air, high above the gymnasium floor, limned with eldritch fire, and pointed some kind of spear or staff at something Mason could only half make out in the storm: a pale tangle of lean-muscled limbs, splayed among the tree's grasping branches. . . .

The dark, horrible creatures writhed and skreeled and drew back, scattering. But just as suddenly as the star-bright apparition had appeared, she was gone—taking the light with her—and the monsters regrouped and advanced again. And Mason saw that they had weapons, dark iron blades with battered, battle-worn edges and wicked sharp points.

Toby shouted, waving his arms to draw their attention, and one of the things sprang at him. He snatched up a spare piece of scaffolding pipe and wielded it like a broadsword, smashing one of the creatures in the side of the head, and there was a sickening sound of breaking open an overripe pumpkin.

The creatures howled in outrage and advanced on the fencing master. Until one of them swung its head in her direction . . . and Mason suddenly found herself locked in the beam of its baleful gaze. The creature's lips peeled back from its teeth in a horrible grin, and it barked out what sounded like some kind of command to the others. The things abandoned Toby and started to move toward Mason in a loose circle.

She backed farther into the corner, almost whimpering in terror.

Suddenly a full-throated roar of rage cut through the din of the storm. As wide as Mason's eyes were already, they got even wider. The pale shape she had seen earlier in the tangle of the oak wasn't another monster. It was a man—a young man—rising from the wreckage in between her and the shambling, gray-skinned apparitions . . . and he was stark naked.

As naked as the shining blade he held in his fist.

He thrust out his free hand at Mason, warning her to stay back, and then turned and lifted his blade to defend as the creatures attacked again. Mason didn't move. She couldn't. Even in the depths of blind panic, she couldn't help but watch in amazement as the strange young man turned and ran straight for one of the gray-skinned apparitions, sword held high over his head. He brought the blade down in a vicious arc and severed the arm of one of the creatures as if he were no more than chopping wood for a fire. Black, stinking blood erupted in a geyser from the terrible wound, painting an arc of darkness on the gymnasium wall. Another slash of the blade, and the horrible thing's head toppled from its shoulders.

Heather screamed, and Toby and Cal suddenly sprang to life, closing ranks behind the young man so that the monstrous attackers couldn't flank him. Cal, Mason saw, had a death grip on a two-by-four, and Toby hewed about with the length of pipe, striking blows—mostly glancing ones—and keeping the creatures at a distance.

But they just kept coming.

In the darkness, it was almost impossible to keep track of the things. Mason heard Rory cry out and Heather was screaming in terror. Toby shot a glance at the stranger, who nodded tersely at him and snarled, "Go!"

The fencing master whacked one of the shambling

creatures out of his way and charged over to Rory and Heather, over by the heavy bag that Rory had earlier been halfheartedly trying out his sparring skills on. Mason noticed, with the kind of detachment that was probably brought on by shock, that Rory was rather impressively holding his own against one of the monsters. He'd picked up an aerobics stacking step and was using it alternately like a shield to fend the thing off or to slam the creature repeatedly over the head with the hard plastic.

Mason felt useless just standing there. She looked around and saw a length of two-by-four stacked with the construction materials. She lunged for it. But the second she did, one of the monsters darted forward and made a grab for her arm. Lightning arced—flash after blinding flash, waves of white light rolling over each other like pounding surf—and Mason saw everything play out as if in a series of overexposed photographs.

The stranger and Cal leaped to tackle the creature that was on her heels.

Cal got to it first, bodychecking the thing away from her.

The blond guy shoved her behind him, snarling, "Stay back!"

Mason landed on her shoulder against the stacked lumber, fear and rage sparking behind her eyes. She sprang back up to her feet and charged forward again, determined to enter the fray, but she froze when she heard Calum shout a warning. She saw him pointing at the ceiling as one of the creatures dropped from the rafters, straight toward her. If she'd still been standing there, it probably would have broken her spine.

But instead, another sharp shove sent her sprawling, and the blond guy took her place. The creature hammered him to his knees, and Mason heard the *whuff!* of air as all the breath was driven from the young man's lungs and she saw his head smash into the floor. The sword flew spinning from his grasp, and he sprawled, dazed, in the middle of the gymnasium.

The creature threw back its head in a howl of glee, ropy arms thrown wide in a triumphant gesture that left its flank wide-open.

Diving for the dropped weapon, Mason scooped it up and ran forward, the blade held out in front of her like a lance. She was screaming in terror and, distracted, the creature rounded on her with vicious speed—only to drive itself accidentally onto the point of the blond warrior's sword in Mason's hand. The blade was so sharp it slid deep into the creature's flesh, and the thing writhed and screamed on the point of the blade, reaching to tear at Mason's face and hands even as it died. The screams stuck in Mason's throat as she saw the stranger rise up behind the thing to grab its malformed head with both hands. A sharp twist, a snapping sound, and the thing slumped to the floor, dead weight, sliding off the end of the blade in her hand.

Mason heard Cal's scream again—only this time, it wasn't a warning.

She heard Heather cry out, "Cal!" and Mason turned to see him caught in the gnarl-fingered grip of one of the creatures about five feet from where she stood. Mason dropped into a ready stance, looking for an opening, but the monstrous thing had Cal by the throat. Its sickly white moon-glow eyes locked with hers, and it grinned hideously, cruelly.

It hissed at her through jagged teeth—a single word that echoed in her mind. She didn't understand it. Couldn't hear it properly over the raging storm. But it somehow still terrified her to her very core.

The sword in her hand wavered.

She stood there, frozen, as the creature's ropy arm rose and then slashed down through the air, its talons tearing through Cal's flesh. His face and chest suddenly bloomed crimson as Mason watched, horrified.

Cal's howl of pain blotted out the sound of the phantom word locking up her brain and freed her muscles to move once again. The creature looked as though it was moving in for the kill on Cal, but before it could sink teeth or claws or blade into him, Mason reared back with the sword and charged forward again, yelling incomprehensibly as she swung hard at the exposed flank of the monster. She felt a fierce moment of savage elation as the edge of the blade bit deep into the horrid thing's withered flesh. The creature hissed wetly in pain and scrambled back into the darkness as another of its kind advanced from behind Mason. The momentum of her first blow carried Mason around, and she struck out wildly again—a glancing blow this time, but enough to make her assailant skitter back into the ink-black shadows beneath the fallen oak tree.

"Sword!" the stranger shouted, having regained his feet. Without thinking, Mason tossed it to him. He caught the heavy blade one-handed and swung it up and over his head. Then he proceeded to give the terrified fencing students and their teacher a master class in swordplay.

Mason grabbed for Cal's arm and struggled to haul him out of harm's way.

"Run for the cellar storage!" Toby croaked, appearing at Mason's side out of the darkness.

"You mean . . . underground?" Mason's stomach lurched.

"*Now*, Mason," Toby barked. "While he's got those things occupied!"

Following at Toby's heels, Rory didn't have to be told twice. Still clutching his gym bag like it was some sort of security blanket, he sprinted across the gym. Mason and Heather ran after him, and Toby followed, half dragging Cal, who was doubled over in pain. Rory grasped a metal ring recessed into the gymnasium floor in front of the stage and heaved open the trapdoor, which led down to what used to be an old cellar but now served as storage for stacking chairs and old gym equipment. As the others ran past her and descended into the darkness, Mason hesitated, her claustrophobia threatening to overwhelm her fear of their attackers. She glanced back at where the young man stood poised to defend against the next surge. She could barely see him in the gloom, but she knew when he'd turned his head and was looking directly at her. She knew in that moment that his eyes were ice blue.

"Go!" He urged her on.

"I can't," Mason whispered, her gaze locking with his.

His sword arm dropped to his side and he stood there, still as a statue, sculpted by the white-gold flashes of lightning. The sudden calm at the eye of a maelstrom.

"Yes," he said quietly. "You can."

She glanced back at the hole in the floor. "I *can't*. . . ."

"You'll be all right. I *promise*."

She looked back at him. Somehow Mason had heard his voice over the cacophony of the storm, and she felt, very suddenly, like she stood in an empty house with all the windows open. A comforting, imaginary breeze told her that there were escape routes. Ways out. Freedom. Peace and protection . . .

"Go," he said again.

She nodded and spun on her heel, ducking down into the storage cellar. Toby reached up behind her and pulled the trapdoor shut. A fraction of a second later, something heavy slammed onto it, and they heard howling. The stranger had bought them time to make it safely down into the storeroom. And now he was out there defending them.

She turned her back to the door and tried to block out the sound of the fighting. The darkness was suffocating. Mason heard one of the others scrabbling around and suddenly the screen of Rory's cell phone lit up. He held it above his head, the thin blue glow pushing feebly against the blackness of the storage space. Huddled behind a rack of shelves, Heather was wild-eyed and panting like a scared animal. Mason had never seen Heather Palmerston afraid of *anything*. Then again, she doubted Heather had ever watched a man behead someone. Some*thing*. Then again, neither had Mason.

Toby jammed his scaffold pipe diagonally through the ring handles on the door, effectively barricading them in. The sounds of fighting continued above them for several long minutes, and then stopped abruptly. They waited, but the only things they heard were the wind and the rain that poured straight down in through the gym's roof. Toby wordlessly held out his hand for the cell phone. Rory handed it over, and Toby felt around on one of the shelves and found a flashlight. He clicked the switch and a pale beam of light rendered the details of the cellar in stark black and ash gray and turned their faces ghastly white.

For a moment, everyone just stood around. Then a heavy knock on the door overhead made them all jump.

"Let me in," came a gruff voice.

"No way, man!" Rory exclaimed.

Toby hesitated.

"Let him in, Toby!" Mason said. "He just saved us!"

The fencing master stood there, torn.

"Toby?" Heather looked at him.

"Aw, hell . . ."

Toby wrenched the pipe out of the door's ring handles as Rory shook his head in disgust. The stranger heaved the door open and climbed down, pulling the door shut behind him. At the bottom, he leaned heavily on the stair ladder for support, breathing harshly. In the beam from Toby's flashlight, all of the contours of his body stood out in sharp relief. He looked like a Michelangelo sculpture, Mason thought.

"Bar the door," he said.

"Do it," Toby barked at Rory, handing him the metal pipe. "And somebody else find Beowulf here some pants."

"It's *Fennrys* Wolf," the young man rasped. "And yeah . . . pants would be nice."

III

N obody moved.

Mason turned her head from side to side and saw that both Heather and Rory sported identical deer-in-headlights facial expressions. Heather's chest was rising and falling in rapid, gaspy breaths that whistled raggedly in the darkness. Rory didn't look like he was breathing at all. The blood had drained from his face, leaving his complexion ghostly in the light of Toby's flashlight.

"Oh, come on . . ." Mason shook her head sharply and pointed to his gear bag where it lay on the ground beside him. "Rory—do you have any extra gym clothes in there?" she asked.

"What? Oh, uh, yeah. I guess . . ." He kicked the bag over to her and went to bar the door, moving as if in a daze.

She knelt down and rooted through the bag, pulling out a pair of sweats and a hoodie. She took them and walked over to where the stranger stood, keeping her gaze focused somewhere over his left shoulder. Out of the corner of her eye, she saw his mouth quirk upward in the shadow of a grin.

"Here," she said, handing them over.

"Thanks."

Mason nodded and turned away, walking swiftly back to stand just behind Toby as the guy put his sword down long enough to pull on the sweats and shrug into the shirt—both of which were too small for him and only served to emphasize his physique even more.

"Are those things gone?" Toby asked.

"Most of 'em are dead," the stranger grunted. "The rest are gone. For now." Once he was dressed, the stranger turned to face them, the sword hilt once again clutched tightly in his fist. "Where am I?" His voice was a low, husky growl. "Who are you people?"

"This is a school," Toby answered, shifting his bulk so that he stood in front of Mason and the others. "They're students."

"A . . . school. Where? What realm?"

"Realm? What are you talking about?" Rory asked, looking at the young man with extreme suspicion. "You on foreign exchange or something?"

"From a country where they don't wear pants?" Heather murmured, recovering a small measure of her usual self-possessed snark.

"Maybe he means borough," Mason suggested, ignoring Heather's comment. She turned to the stranger. "This is Manhattan. Uh . . . New York City? You know?"

A fleeting expression of recognition flashed across his

angular features. "New . . . I remember . . ." Then it vanished. "Something."

"Hey." Rory crossed his arms over his chest as if he'd decided that enough was enough and it was time for him to play tough guy. Mason hated it when he got like that. "What the hell kind of name is Fennrys Wolf?"

"I don't know. And it's *the* Fennrys Wolf, actually. I think—"

"What the hell is that supposed to mean?" Rory asked. "Who are you, really?"

The young man looked back and forth between them and said quietly, "I was hoping you could tell me."

There was something so naked in his expression, Mason thought. And then she started to actually blush at the memory of what he'd looked like just a few moments ago. *Okay, not naked . . . more like raw—uh, no.* That wasn't helping either. She winced inwardly. *How about . . . vulnerable?*

Yes. That was exactly it.

Whoever this guy was, in spite of his sheer brute strength and fighting skills, there was an almost fragile quality to him. As if he was barely holding it together. Mason frowned, staring at the handsome blond enigma, and wondered where in the world he'd come from.

Suddenly a sound caught Mason's attention—a low groan, coming from the corner where Calum had gone from leaning against the wall to slumped in a heap on the floor, semiconscious. Heather ran over and knelt beside him, and Mason heard her gasp.

"Guys," she said. "Guys . . . he doesn't look so good. I mean . . . he's—oh, shit. *Shit.* Cal?" She shook his shoulder, but there was no response. "Toby?" Heather looked up, and there was a shine of tears in her eyes.

Toby pushed Rory and the stranger aside and went to go look at Cal for himself. "Aw, damn . . ." Mason heard him mutter.

"What is it?" she asked. "What's wrong?" *Aside from the obvious . . .*

"His skin is getting streaky around the wounds and he's burning up," Toby said, sounding really worried. "It looks like he might have some kind of sepsis developing."

"Sepsis?"

"Blood poisoning," the Fennrys Wolf said.

"And it's spreading fast, from the looks of it," Toby muttered. "Too fast. That shouldn't be possible. Those . . . *things* out there must have been venomous."

Mason and Heather exchanged a stricken glance.

"Do something!" Heather exclaimed. "Help him! Where's the first-aid kit?"

Toby huffed in frustration and stood. "It's in the gym office. Out *there*." He glanced at the door. "And Band-Aids and iodine aren't going to do a lot of good for him if he goes into septic shock."

The stranger's brow creased in a deep frown. He stepped forward, as if he meant to push past Toby—who put out an arm, barring his way. Wordlessly, Toby eyed the sword in the young man's fist.

The Fennrys Wolf looked down at the weapon, then he spun the blade expertly in his palm and handed it over, hilt first—to Mason, who was too surprised to do anything but take it. His mouth ticked upward again in that half grin. Mason got the feeling that he didn't ever actually smile.

"I think I should take a look at your boy there," he said to Toby.

Toby stared at him for a moment, then took a step to the side. The strange young man kneeled down beside Cal and carefully pulled the torn edges of his T-shirt away from his shoulder wound. Mason saw Heather turn away, a sickened expression on her gorgeous face. There were three ragged parallel slashes across Cal's pectoral muscle that seeped blood but looked—hopefully—like they weren't too deep. The worrying thing, though, was the spidery network of angry dark lines that had begun to spread outward, creeping just under the surface of Cal's skin on both his face and chest.

The Fennrys Wolf sat back on his haunches and, for a moment, looked lost. Confusion chased through his gaze, but he shook his head sharply and his nostrils flared. His eyes fell closed, and one hand reached up and his long fingers closed around an iron medallion that hung from a leather cord around his neck. It was the only thing he'd been wearing. Mason watched as he began to murmur under his breath, his other hand hovering over Cal's prone form.

"Toby," Rory said behind her in a low voice, "what are you doing? Why are you letting that guy anywhere near Cal?"

"If he'd wanted to harm any of us, he could have just left us out there, Rory," Toby answered quietly. "With those things. As it stands right now, I don't have any way to help Calum. Maybe *he* does."

The strange young man hunched over Cal. "I could use a little light," he said.

Mason took the flashlight from Toby and held it out. The Fennrys Wolf reached back and positioned her arm so he could see better but, whatever it was he was doing, it was blocked from Mason's line of sight. All she knew was that he was concentrating very hard, muttering just under his breath. She couldn't quite make out the words, but Mason had the feeling that, even if she could have, she still wouldn't have been able to understand them.

Slowly, like an invisible ground mist seeping up out of the floor, Mason felt the air of the storeroom begin to change character. As if it was becoming electrically charged. Her feet and then her legs began to tingle slightly, like a current was running through the floor. Mason's stomach tightened, and she could hear the beating of her heart.

And then she thought she could hear Cal's . . .

Then the Fennrys Wolf's . . .

What is *this guy, like some kind of shaman or something?* Mason wondered. That was ridiculous. But then so was the idea that they'd been attacked by monsters. *I do* not *believe in supernatural creatures,* Mason said to herself firmly. *There has to be a rational explanation for all of this. There is no boogeyman.*

Finally, after several long, anxious minutes, the stranger's shoulders slumped, and he sat back against an equipment rack. The lines of his face were drawn with exhaustion, and the long columns of muscle down the sides of his neck stood out like cords. Mason could see the pulse beating just below his jaw, but she couldn't hear his heart now. The sound had faded, along with the feeling of electricity in the air. Outside, in the far distance, she heard a rumble of thunder. Maybe the storm—and all its horrors—was moving away.

"Has anybody got any water?" Fennrys asked, climbing to his feet.

"Yeah." Mason dug out her water bottle and started toward Calum with it. "Here . . ."

Fennrys intercepted the bottle and twisted off the top. "Not for him. For me." He threw back his head and swallowed the contents in one long gulp.

"Uh. Yeah." Mason took back the empty bottle when he handed it to her. "Okay . . ."

She shone the flashlight back at Calum. The telltale threads of blood poisoning seemed to be fading, even as Mason stood there looking at him. The bleeding had mostly stopped, too. Toby had folded Cal's torn shirt into a square and beckoned Heather over to hold it against his chest. Before she did that, she stripped out of her fencing jacket, took off the tank top she wore underneath it—defiantly daring them with her gaze to stare at her in her bra—and shrugged back into her jacket. She used the thin material of the tank to press gently to the wounds on Cal's face.

Mason looked over at the Fennrys Wolf. "Is he . . ."

"He'll be fine, eventually. I think. Maybe not as pretty as he once was." He staggered a few steps past Mason and stopped, bracing himself against the wall. He was almost as gray as the concrete bricks that supported him. He wiped a sleeve over his haggard face. "But then . . . who of us is?"

IV

Mason felt odd. She wasn't freaking out about being trapped in a cellar, and that just didn't seem right to her. They'd been down there for almost half an hour now, sharing the darkness in an uneasy silence ever since the Fennrys Wolf had done . . . whatever to Cal.

Now Mason stood behind a shelf stacked with old practice archery targets, just out of Toby's line of sight, and listened. Heather was sitting with Cal's head in her lap and appeared to be dozing. Cal was still unconscious. Rory had retreated to the very back of the storage cellar and was huddled against a stone wall. He was acting like a sulky kid, and considering the circumstances, it made Mason want to punch him. More than usual. Toby had drawn Fennrys away from the others to speak with him in private, but Mason's burning curiosity got the better of her and she crept silently closer to hear what they were saying.

"Look . . . Mr. Wolf, is it?" The fencing master's rumble of a voice carried over to where Mason stood, partially hidden behind a wire shelving unit, even though he was obviously trying to be quiet.

"No," Fennrys said. "It's not. It's just . . . I don't know." From where she stood hidden, Mason saw him shrug his broad shoulders. "Just call me Fennrys."

"Okay. It's . . . an interesting name. How do you spell that?"

"F-e-n-n-r-y-s," he said flatly. "I think."

Toby took a deep breath, and although she couldn't see his face, Mason could picture him tugging on his goatee, trying to figure out the best way of saying what was on his mind. "All right then. Fennrys. My name's Toby Fortier. And I'd like a few answers."

"I don't have any to give you."

"So you said."

"It's true."

"All right." Toby huffed and shifted his bulk restlessly. "Look . . . it's not that I don't appreciate what you've done here. I mean, I'm grateful. These kids are my responsibility and, well . . . that's just it." Toby's tone was carefully neutral, but even Mason could tell what he meant by that.

"Right." Fennrys laughed a little—not a happy sound. "I get it. They're your responsibility. And you don't trust *me* not to harm them any more than you trust whatever it is that attacked you outside."

"Not exactly. I'd much rather have them in here with you than out there with . . . whatever the hell they were."

Toby took a step toward Fennrys. His shadow wavered on the wall, a huge dark shape, and his boots crunched on grit on the floor.

"But I'm a fighting man," he continued. "And I *saw* what you did out there."

"Did you."

Toby got really quiet for a moment. Then he said, "Yeah. I did."

"And what, exactly, did I do, Mr. Fortier?" Fennrys's voice was strangely flat and tight. As if Toby's words were making him angry, but he was trying hard to leash that anger in. "Beside save all of you?"

"You did, at that. What I'd really like to know is how."

"I'm not sure I know what you mean," Fennrys said, offering nothing.

Toby grunted, and even though she couldn't see him, Mason imagined him crossing his arms over his barrel chest and pegging Fennrys with one of his laser stares. "I've made my living training people in the martial arts. I know how to handle myself with swords, small arms, advanced hand-to-hand combat . . . I've got buddies who are Navy SEALs."

That's a lie, Mason thought, frowning. Toby didn't just have Navy SEAL buddies. Toby *was* a SEAL. Ex, maybe. But he was the real deal. She'd heard her father talking about it one day to his butler, just after Toby had been hired at the school.

"Guess you're a regular expert there, Mr. Fortier," Fennrys said.

"I'm enough of one," Toby answered, ignoring the baiting, "to know that you could probably tear the hide off some of my friends without breaking much of a sweat."

"I don't pick fights with the fairer sex, sir," Fennrys said drily.

Mason had to cover her mouth to keep from snorting with laughter.

"Son . . ." Toby sighed in frustration. "You're not even old enough to have developed those skill sets."

Through the wire shelving, Mason saw Fennrys's eyes grow dark with confusion at the mention of his age. From what she could tell, Toby was right. The strange young man wasn't much older than she was. Nineteen, maybe? Twenty at the most. With a body that looked as though he'd spent every single one of those years in serious training.

Fennrys swallowed and remained silent.

"I also noticed those marks," Toby said, dropping his voice even further. "The ones on your wrists and ankles . . ."

Mason had noticed them too. Bands of bruising and abrasions, layers of them—new welts on top of old scabbing—as though he'd been kept in restraints for a long time.

"Are you in some kind of trouble, Fennrys?" Toby asked. "Running from something, maybe?"

Fennrys uttered a shaky laugh. "When I figure that out for myself, Mr. Fortier, I'll let you know. Listen. Why don't you go back there and ride herd on your flock, okay? I'll stay over here by the door. Out of the way. I won't bother you. I won't bother them. I think you'll agree that going back out into that storm isn't an option—even if the draugr are gone. We should wait until sunrise to be sure."

"Wait. What did you call them?"

"Sorry?"

"You gave those things out there a name."

"I . . ."

Mason leaned forward, peering intently through the metal grating of the shelf. *There's that look again,* she thought. The one that made this Fennrys guy seem as though the things that came out of his mouth were as much of a surprise to *him* as to whomever he was speaking to.

"Draugr," he said again, rolling the word over his tongue as if trying to identify its taste. "You're right. I did." His gaze flicked back up to Toby's face, but his blue eyes were hard, cold. He put up a hand, forestalling Toby's next question. "Don't ask. I don't *know* how I know. I don't *remember.*"

Toby was silent for a moment, and then he said, "But you know that they'll be gone at sunup."

"I *don't* know that." Fennrys shook his head.

"But you just said they would. You said—"

"I *said* I thought it would be safer if we waited." Fennrys ran a hand through the dark blond hair that stood up in tousled spikes from his head. He looked both very young and immeasurably old in that moment.

"And?"

"And it will." Fennrys offered Toby a weary grin. "Things always appear different with the coming of the light, Mr. Fortier. Sometimes darkness is better, but I don't think that's the case here."

Mason was a little surprised that Toby didn't just grab this guy by the front of his borrowed sweatshirt and shake him until some answers fell out. But he didn't. He just stood there.

And Fennrys stood facing him.

It was like some kind of super-tense Mexican standoff, except neither of them had a weapon pointed at the other.

Mason held her breath. Just then, something seemed to spark in Fennrys's gaze—a thought, or maybe a memory—and his hand drifted slowly toward the iron medallion at his throat, as though pulled upward by an invisible puppet string.

"I think we could all use some rest, Toby," Fennrys said after a moment, and there was a quality to his voice that was . . . strange. Almost hollow, like an echo. "Don't you?"

Mason shook her head. There was a sudden, subtle pressure in her ears, like she was on an airplane taking off and needed to pop them. She looked back at Fennrys and realized with a start that his eyes were now fixed on her. She felt her breath stop in her throat.

"We could *all* use some rest," Fennrys said again. "Couldn't we?"

Mason felt a strange tingling near the base of her skull. Fennrys's words echoed even more strangely. Mason heard Toby yawn. He mumbled an agreement, and she heard him start to head in her direction, his footsteps heavy and shuffling. Mason turned and stumbled back to where the others huddled in the darkness. Her eyes were so heavy by the time she got there that she was almost asleep on her feet. Heather and Rory were already out— Heather was snoring softly and Rory's head was tipped back, his mouth wide-open. Mason sank to the floor beside Calum's outstretched form, dimly aware of her relief at realizing he was breathing deeply, normally. He was sound asleep.

And then . . . she was, too.

V

The boots were a size too big and, without socks, they chafed at his ankle bones, but it was going to be better than walking the city streets barefoot. Fennrys straightened up from tying the bootlaces tight, stretched, and rolled his shoulders. His sword shifted on his back, concealed in a canvas bag designed to hold fencing gear. Fennrys had found it on a shelf and decided to borrow it along with the boots he now wore. In the glow of the dying flashlight, he gazed down the row of sleeping bodies. The girl with the dark hair and startlingly blue eyes was curled on her side, still deeply asleep.

Fennrys had allowed himself to indulge in a few much-needed hours' worth of sleep as well, but it was now time for him to go. Past time. Before he did, though, he knelt beside the handsome student who'd almost gotten himself killed during the fight with the draugr and carefully turned his head to the side. The kid—*he's not a kid any more than you are, pal,* said a voice in his head; *you're probably the same damn age—* was pale, his breathing fairly regular but shallow. Fennrys ran a fingertip lightly over the livid marks on the boy's face. The bleeding had stopped, but the angry, purplish lines that had begun to fade were starting to reappear under the skin and his flesh was still warm to the touch. Too warm.

"Damn . . . ," Fennrys murmured to himself. The poison of the draugr's claws was stubborn and strong. Fennrys hesitated for a moment, then reached up and worked loose the knot of the leather cord that held the iron medallion around his throat. It took awhile, as though the knot hadn't been undone in a very long time—but when it finally came loose, he tied the medallion around the injured boy's wrist. Pressing his fingers to the symbols inscribed on the metal surface of the disk, Fennrys felt it pulse gently, with a cool, cleansing energy. Satisfied that he'd done what he could, he stood and looked down.

The kid stirred in his sleep, and then settled with a sigh. He would probably carry the scars for the rest of his life, but at least Fennrys had seen to it that his life didn't end there on the floor of the storage cellar. He felt a twinge of regret as he stared down at the ruin of the young man's handsome face.

Big deal. What are a few scars?

What indeed? When he'd dressed in the borrowed sweats that the girl had given him, Fennrys had noticed that he himself carried more than a few—a *lot* more than a few—on his limbs and torso. Where did he get that kind of collection? Why had he been naked? In the midst of his confusion, he half smiled to himself when he remembered the vibrant pink flush of the girl's pretty face when she'd glanced at him in his altogether state. Not the other one—the gorgeous blonde was used to the contours of the male body. Or at least she made a really good show of pretending she was.

But the dark-haired girl had been sweet. Kind of shy, but brave enough to approach him when the others had hung back. Strong and swift enough to handle herself in a fight. She reminded him of . . . of what? Who? No one he could remember.

His mind was a total blank.

Well, maybe not a *total* blank. He *could* remember darkness . . . the feeling of cold stone against his bare, shivering flesh. Damp. And a stench like wet earth and rot. A voice. And then light—so bright that he flinched and closed his eyes even at the mere memory of that brilliance. It hurt his mind to think of it.

After a moment, the fragmented memory faded and Fennrys opened his eyes again. He looked down at the dark-haired girl where she lay on her side, one arm flung out. The sleeve of her fencing jacket was pushed up and the skin of her arm shone pale in the gloom. As pale as Fennrys's own flesh—which bore an unhealthy pallor, as if he hadn't seen the sun in a very long time—only hers glowed like an alabaster sculpture lit from within. Fenn traced the path of a blue vein on the inside of her wrist, like following the course of a river on a map. Then he ran his fingertips over the roughness of his own wrists. Toby was right. Fennrys had been chained. Recently and for a long time.

What the *hell* was he?

The question framed itself in his mind that way . . . not "who" but "what." Maybe he didn't want to know. Maybe he'd be better off if he never found out. . . . He could just disappear into the world and . . . what? Start a brand-new life for himself? He couldn't even begin to imagine what the old one had been like.

Swords. Monsters. Danger . . .

The dark-haired girl stirred in her sleep and made a small sound, almost like a whimper. Her hands floated up in front of her face, as if she fought against something in her dream. Gently Fennrys took her hands and lowered them to rest at her sides. He lightly stroked her forehead until she settled back into stillness and the shadow of a frown on her brow smoothed.

In the silence and the darkness, he turned and listened for a long moment. No rain. No thunder . . . even the wind seemed to have died to nothing. And there were no sounds of the draugr now, either. Had he killed them all in those few frantic moments, hours earlier? He wasn't sure. Maybe there were others still out there, lying in wait. Waiting for him . . . or for these kids and their teacher? Fennrys considered that an unlikely possibility. They were nothing. Nobodies. A bunch of absolutely normal teenagers.

While *he* seemed to be . . . something else. Something dangerous. He didn't want the dark-haired girl in danger because of him. He stood and turned away from her. A small, single action that made him feel unutterably alone.

Once outside, Fennrys picked his way through the wreckage of oak tree roots and torn earth and headed across the otherwise manicured lawn of a courtyard toward the stone arch that led out onto the street. The pale, anemic gloom of predawn told him that sunrise was still a good hour or two away as he left the grounds of the Gosforth Academy—that was what the sign out front told him the place was called— but he hoped it was enough to give him a margin of safety. Fennrys headed south for several dark, silent blocks until, eventually, he looked up at the street signs to get his bearings. Broadway and West 110th, Cathedral Parkway.

So . . . Upper West Side, then?

Yeah. He knew what that was. Where it was. And he also knew that a large expanse of Broadway played host to a famous theater district, although that was much farther south than he was now. He was, it seemed, very familiar with New York City. He knew streets and neighborhoods, directions, destinations . . . the only blank on the map of his mind was himself. It was as if he was an empty space drifting around the city, untethered. Detached from his surroundings instead of defined by them, by what could have been a life's worth of experience accumulated on these streets. The harder he tried to relate to the landmarks around him, the slipperier every-thing seemed. Anything that might have pertained directly to him just twisted away and was lost to a vacuum in his mind.

"That's great," Fenn muttered to himself. "I know where to go to catch a musical, but I have no idea where I live. Not an ideal situation." He twitched up the hood of his borrowed sweatshirt. "Especially considering that I have a sneaking suspicion I'm the kind of guy who hates musicals."

Even in his present state of what seemed like some kind of amnesia, Fennrys knew that the broad-bladed sword he'd been carrying when he'd found himself naked in a tree in a rainstorm wasn't something a normal person would carry around on the streets of . . . *New York.*

Why did he have a sword? Why was he in New York? Did he, in fact, live there?

If so, where was his place? His clothes?

Why did he bear those marks on his ankles and wrists?

Who was he?

Who am I . . . ?

The question pounded in his brain in time with his footsteps, and he turned east and broke into a loping jog, the sword slung on his back bouncing gently against his spine with each step. A fine mist now hung in the dim air, thickening at ground level to a rolling fog. The buildings on either side of him were dark, the streetlights were out, and no one—absolutely no one else—was around. That struck Fenn as . . . strange. A blackout in the middle of a city like New York, and nobody was taking advantage of it? No mayhem, no mischief . . . it was as if even the unsavory elements of society knew better than to venture out on a night like the one that had just passed.

He headed farther east, skirting the southern edge of Harlem. As he ran, the lights in the buildings and on the streets began to slowly, one by one, blink and flicker back to life. Silhouettes in doorways, eyes in shadowed faces peeked out at Fennrys as he passed. On his right, a long stone wall ran alongside him for blocks. Behind it, through the curtain of rain that fell gently now, softly, he could see trees. A lot of trees . . . a park.

Central Park.

A violent shiver ran up Fenn's spine. He knew, instinctively, exactly where he was now. And he knew that, unless his life depended on it, the park was the one place he wouldn't—shouldn't—go. What he didn't know was *why*, but the feeling in his gut was enough to make him just keep running.

Finally, far in the distance, he could hear the sound of wailing sirens. Fennrys kept running. It was the only thing that felt right at the moment—the pounding of his feet on the pavement in the fencing master's stolen boots, the feel of the rain-wet air stinging his face, and the sound of his breath and heart, loud in his ears.

But then he heard another sound, a different rhythmic pounding, and looking up, he saw two massive shapes in the middle of the road, moving swiftly toward him.

Horse cops, Fennrys thought. *NYPD. About bloody time . . .*

A pair of them, armored and helmeted men perched on the backs of huge, heavy beasts—Hanoverians or a similar breed, horses with hooves the size of dinner plates. Fennrys tucked his head farther down between his shoulders and tried to make like he was just another jogger, out in the middle of a citywide, blackout-making torrential downpour.

For reasons he couldn't quite fathom, Fennrys really wished he still had the iron medallion with him that he'd left with the injured kid at the school. He also knew he'd left it there for a good reason. Instinct was the only thing he had to go on at the moment, but it was everything. Instinct . . . and the reassuring weight of the sword in the canvas bag slung across his back.

The echoing *clop-clop* of the horse cops' passage rang in his ears, weirdly amplified by the wet, shimmering air.

The sound chilled him to the bone. *Jog casual,* Fenn thought, trying not to glance back again in their direction. There was nothing about him to attract their attention. Almost nothing. Maybe it was the combat boots that gave him away. Maybe it was the undisguised fighter's physique that the school-logo workout gear did nothing to disguise. He didn't know. But something did . . .

He heard a murmured, guttural exchange and the sound of those enormous hooves clattering on the asphalt as they accelerated from walk, to trot, to gallop. Fennrys glanced up and felt his heart leap into his throat. *Those are no cops!* he thought as two magnificent figures thundered toward him through the rolling banks of fog. Now he saw high-crested helmets with noseguards and cheek plates covering the planes of their faces. Longbows and arrow quivers carried crisscrossed over the bare-chested torsos of men. Torsos that flowed seamlessly down, melding with equine musculature. The mirage image of New York City cops astride their mounts shimmered and dissolved, revealing the strange, mythic, *impossible* creatures beneath: centaurs.

Okay. Now I know I'm crazy, Fenn thought.

And then he thought, *Run!*

VI

"Damn his eyes!"

Toby's roaring jolted Mason from sleep and a strange, tangled dream where she was falling through darkness and then light and then darkness again, through a storm-ridden sky and then a vast underground cavern riddled with masses of tree roots and then the sky again—and she'd been on fire. At least she'd woken before she'd hit the ground. Her brother Rory, taunting her about a falling nightmare when she'd been just a kid, had told her that if you hit the ground in one of those falling/ flying dreams, then you die in real life. That your heart would stop from shock. Mason didn't believe him, but she still wasn't anxious to test the theory.

Toby was waving around the now-sputtering flashlight and swearing a blue streak—something he usually tried to keep a lid on, with varying degrees of success, in front of the students—and Mason pushed herself to her feet and went to see what had gotten him foaming at the mouth.

"He stole my damned boots!" Toby growled before she even had a chance to ask him. Toby was something of a freak of nature in that he could fence in combat boots—thick, heavy-soled things that he'd lovingly broken in over a couple of decades—but now he stood there, sock footed and outraged on the cold concrete floor, looking slightly comical.

And the young man they knew only as the Fennrys Wolf was gone.

Over near the wall, Rory snuffled in sleep and shifted as if swimming back toward consciousness. Mason noticed that one of his running shoes was untied and lying on the floor beside his foot. She knew what must have happened. Rory had little girly feet and Fennrys had obviously not been able to fit into *his* footwear.

She turned back to Toby and had to stifle a laugh at his expression. "How deeply asleep do you have to be for a guy to be able to steal your boots?" she asked.

"I can't even believe I fell asleep in the first place," Toby muttered. "It's like someone slipped me a mickey or something. One second I'm standing there talking to the guy, next thing I know is I can feel a cold breeze up my ankles. Something very weird just happened here."

"You think?" Heather said, a little blearily, as she walked up to stand beside Mason. Heather was calm and her eyes looked a little vacant, as if she'd been given a sedative. Mason felt a little like that herself. She searched inward for the panic she would have normally experienced full bore under the circumstances and found it—but it was a distant, muted thing. Still . . . better not to push her luck.

"Toby." Mason checked her watch by the flashlight's pale glow. "It's morning. Can we please get out of here? He said we could."

"Yeah, I . . ." Toby stopped, eyeing her sharply, and Mason realized that she'd basically just told him that she'd eavesdropped on his conversation with Fennrys. To her relief, he decided against calling her on it. Instead he just said, "Yeah. I think we're probably okay now."

"Why hasn't anyone come to find us?" Heather asked quietly. "Where *is* everyone?"

Mason had been wondering that herself. It had seemed pretty unlikely that anyone would have been wandering around in that storm, but surely someone would have noticed that the oak tree had come crashing down. Heard it? Maybe not. Not above the noise of the storm. But now . . .

Toby eased open the storage hatch and climbed up out into the gym, the girls following at his heels. The light coming through the shattered window could barely be called that. It was still murky predawn. And the place looked like a bomb had hit it. A section of the roof had caved in, and there were branches and bricks, shattered slate roof tiles, and shards of rainbow glass everywhere. The new pine floor was soaked and warping already, and there was a gaping hole where the main entrance used to be.

There was no sign of the . . . what had Fennrys called them? Mason frowned, remembering. *Draugr.* That was it. But there were none to be found. Not even bodies, or any signs that there had ever been a fight, let alone a small-scale battle. No blood—black *or* red—and no tell-tale marks to show they'd been dragged off somewhere. . . .

It was like the whole thing, except for the storm, had been nothing more than a terrible dream.

"Toby."

Calum's ragged-edged voice made Mason jump. He stood there, bent inward and holding his left arm tightly against his body. The sound of his breathing rasped through his teeth, as if every breath hurt. He was deathly pale, Mason thought, but still so handsome. . . .

Until he turned toward her.

And she saw the parallel claw marks that ran from his hairline to his chin on the left side of his face. It *hadn't* been a dream. But it had definitely been a nightmare.

"Toby," Cal said again, and Mason saw that the left side of his mouth was twisted upward in pain. "What are we gonna tell people when they ask what the hell happened here?"

Mason couldn't keep from wincing at the sight of the gashes on his face. Cal's green eyes flicked over to her as she did so, and his gaze went ice cold under the gloss of pain. He turned his face away from her and looked back to where the fencing master stood in silent thought. The furrows on Toby's brow were etched deeply, and his eyes moved back and forth over the ruined state of the Gosforth gymnasium. Finally he turned back to Cal, his expression carefully neutral as he looked at him. She wished she'd been able to do the same a moment earlier.

"What the hell are we going to say, Toby?" Calum asked again.

"It was the tree," Toby said quietly. He gestured with one hand at the gashes on Cal's face. "And the broken window glass."

After a long moment, Cal nodded faintly. Standing on Mason's other side, Heather shifted back and forth, the hint of a troubled frown shadowing her brow, but she kept quiet.

"Wait a minute," Mason said. "What?"

"The tree falling, Mason." Toby's voice was flat. "The branches and the glass. That's how Calum got hurt. That's what we're going to say."

"I don't get it. That's not what happened."

Beside her, Heather shifted some more but still said nothing. Rory, who'd finally dragged himself out of the storage room and stood listening, shrugged and said nothing. Toby set his jaw stubbornly, as if daring Mason to voice an objection. But it was Cal who really surprised her. He crossed his arms—at least, he tried to, but it was obviously painful—and glared defiantly at her.

Mason took a step backward. "Are we just going to ignore what happened here?" She looked back and forth between the faces of her fellow students. "Are we just going to lie and forget it ever happened?"

"What do *you* think we should do?" Rory scoffed. "Hold a press conference and tell the world we were attacked by . . . what? Storm zombies?" He gestured around to the wreck that was, quite obviously, lacking any proof of the attack. "*Disappearing* storm zombies? I mean, you're obviously okay with being labeled a freak, sis—that's situation normal for you—but me, not so much."

"But it's what happened! We should tell people—"

"What?" Calum's voice was like a lash. The sound of it spun her back around to face him. "The truth? Is that what we're gonna tell people? Jeezus, Mase, *look* at me. I don't want that. This . . . *this* is bad enough as it is."

He turned away, and Mason saw him wince again in pain. Or maybe shame. She wasn't sure exactly what he had to be ashamed of. Calum Aristarchos had never struck her as the kind of guy who was overly concerned with his looks. But, then again, when you grew up looking the way he did, you probably didn't have to be. And now . . .

Heather was staring at Cal, but he turned away from her too. She shook her head and muttered something to herself that Mason couldn't quite hear.

"Heather?" Mason asked. "What about you?"

"I dunno, Starling." She shrugged a bit helplessly. "I mean . . . how the hell would we explain those things? And that *guy*. Who is also inconveniently missing in action."

"I don't know how to explain any of it. But something happened here." Mason pressed the other girl, sensing that Heather was almost as uncomfortable as she was with covering up the truth. "A *lot* of somethings, actually. Do you want us to lie too?"

"As opposed to telling the truth and having everyone think we're either stupid, crazy, or pulling some jerk-ass stunt?" Heather shook her head. She was silent for a moment, and then she nodded her head once, decisively. "Yeah, Mason. I think I want us to lie."

"I—"

Rory finally rounded on her. "Mouse, *shut* up for a second!"

Mason's mouth snapped shut. She thought he was going to ridicule her again, but he surprised her by taking her—gently—by the shoulders and looking her in the eyes, his expression serious.

"Listen to what we're saying," he said quietly. "Listen to what *I'm* saying, for once. Imagine telling Dad what you think happened here."

"I don't think, I *know*. And so do you."

"Okay. Still. Imagine telling him that story." Rory stared at her, and she stared back. His eyes were shades of hazel that constantly shifted with his mood. At the moment they were a stormy gray-green. And they were worried. "What d'you think Gunnar would do? Hmm? Do you think he'd leave you here at Gosforth for another second? Me, sure. Dad doesn't give a rat's ass what I say or do. But if he thinks there's something weird going on here or—God forbid—he thought *you* were in any kind of danger? Well, I can guarantee you Top Gunn's little girl is gonna get yanked back to the estate for some good old-fashioned home schooling and a sundown curfew. Let's see you compete in the Nationals if that happens, sis."

"He wouldn't."

Toby made a rueful sound that wasn't quite a dry laugh. "Yeah, he probably would, Mason."

As much as she didn't want to believe it, she knew they were probably right. Toby had known her father a long time. It was Gunnar Starling who'd gotten him the job at Gosforth—a job Mason had the feeling Toby wasn't going to

55

jeopardize with wild stories. Stories about things that they had absolutely no proof of. She gazed around bleakly at the damage to the gym.

"Okay," Mason said in a near-whisper voice. "I won't say anything." Mason looked up through the hole in the roof. "I promise. But I'm also not going to just forget about what happened here. And I think—no, I *know*—that we're all going to have to deal with it at some point."

VII

Howls of laughter rang out, telling Fennrys that he'd been spotted again by the nightmares hunting him.

He'd done his best to lose them by dodging down alleys and cutting through apartment complexes and tenements at the southern edge of Harlem, running, hiding, heading east as he zigzagged from one block to another until he'd crossed Park Avenue and was only about three long blocks from the East River.

But every time he thought he'd eluded the centaurs, they would appear out of a drift of fog at the end of an alleyway and howl for his blood. Just like they were doing now. Fennrys swore and rolled out from behind his latest hiding spot—a thicket of tangled bushes in a vacant lot—as the horse-men rounded the corner of a building and reared in tandem, lashing out with metal-shod hooves. The pair accelerated into a gallop, and Fennrys knew, once they got up to speed, they would run him down.

They were close enough this time for him to hear one of them roar something about "worthy prey" and the "glory of the hunt." In the instant before he turned and made a run for it, he saw one of them draw from a holster and, like a double-exposed image of cop and creature, Fennrys saw, not an NYPD standard-issue sidearm, but rather the image of one, wrapped around the real weapon like a tangible shadow—another mirage. He heard a sharp *twang* and dodged sharply to his right as a crossbow bolt sang past his head like a ferocious, deadly bird.

Fennrys knew perfectly well that a crossbow like that could fire a projectile that would punch through plate armor. He didn't bother to question why he possessed that kind of knowledge—rather he just accepted it, took a sharp right, and pounded south, cutting through the grounds of a couple of blocks of housing complexes before turning east and then south again. A dark stairwell behind a Dumpster in a narrow lane gave him a chance to catch his breath.

After the silence had stretched out for a good few minutes, Fennrys crept slowly from his hiding place. He saw the FDR Drive running past in front of him—and a switchback ramp that led up to the narrow pedestrian bridge that spanned across to Wards Island. Fennrys glanced around, and it seemed as though he might have lost his pursuers. But if he hadn't, the bridge looked as though it might actually be too narrow to accommodate the massive bulk of the creatures—the horse halves of them were like Clydesdales on steroids, almost more bull-like than equine. Fennrys took a chance and darted up the ramp, sprinting across the long, slender span of the bridge.

When he got to the island, he just kept running. He scaled the fence surrounding the tennis courts and ran across them at full speed, feeling terribly exposed in the predawn light. He was about halfway across the open expanse when arrows started slamming into the ground on either side of him. Fennrys flinched and threw his arms up over his head and cut sharply right, continuing to run in a zigzag pattern toward the trees at the north edge of the tennis courts.

Suddenly one of the crossbow bolts hit the center of Fennrys's back, and the power of the shot punched him to his knees. He hit the ground and rolled, assuming for the moment he'd probably just been killed. But then, through the pain of the impact, he realized that the stout, deadly bolt had glanced off the broad blade of the sword on his back.

In his head, he heard a woman's voice whisper, "Do not lose this sword. Do not let it far from your hand. It will be your companion and your comfort in days to come as only a good blade can be to the warrior. It will save your life, hopefully as many times as need be."

How many times would that be? Fenn thought a bit desperately as he rolled and scrambled to his feet, arms windmilling as he struggled to regain his balance and then plunged on.

From behind him and above, he heard a roar of outrage as the centaur realized he'd been denied his kill. They were shooting at him from the raised deck of the Triborough Bridge—far enough away that the power of that shot hadn't been enough to shatter the sword blade and sever his spine. Fennrys was astounded that they'd been able to move that fast—the on-ramp to the Triborough was north of 120th Street. His decision to cross over using the footbridge had given him time, but probably not enough of it.

But then he heard one of them shout to the other. "Shoot him! He's on Dead Ground—we cannot follow! Shoot him now or he is lost to us!"

Hope bloomed in Fennrys's chest, and he jagged sharply left and crashed headlong through a cluster of whippy saplings that slapped at his face and arms. Then the shadows swallowed him up and he was safe from the monstrous archers, for the moment. Maybe, judging from what they'd said, they wouldn't follow him down onto the ground of Wards Island itself. But he wasn't going to take chances. They'd seen him head into the trees, but the trees weren't thick enough to hide him for long if the horse-men did come looking for him. He headed east, following the shoreline of the island where it bordered the river. Ahead of him, looming like the sentry tower of a medieval castle, was the soaring concrete support pylon of another bridge—a massive, red-painted, iron-girdered arch that gracefully spanned the frothing white waters of the river like a huge bow. The shadows beneath the concrete tower were impenetrable and the vantage point unobstructed. Fennrys would be able to see anything coming from almost a mile in any direction while remaining unseen himself. Good enough.

The wet, heavy air wrapped itself around him like a cloak as he settled down to wait for morning. If this so-called Dead Ground could keep those things from following him, then he could just bide his time until sunrise. And a return to some kind of sanity or normalcy.

Or maybe not.

A flicker of movement in the gloom caught at the corner of Fennrys's eye. He went stone still, held his breath as an enormous shadow loomed on the concrete bridge support in front of him. Fennrys dropped into a deep crouch, reached over his head to grasp the hilt of his sword, and spun around. The blade hissed as he drew and snapped it straight out in front of him. A large, shabby figure of a man froze instantly, the sharp point of the weapon hovering less than an inch from the center of his chest. Beneath the wide, chewed-up brim of an old leather hat, his eyes glinted in the darkness as he stared, unblinking, at Fennrys. One rag-wrapped fist held a length of lead pipe.

"Drop that," Fennrys said quietly.

The man was big—huge even—but, as far as Fennrys could tell, human. He couldn't even believe he was framing his thoughts in that way, but after the things he'd seen and done that night . . . of course, who knew? Maybe he'd been drugged. Possibly he was just—and Fennrys kept coming back to this possibility with a knot of fear in his throat—delusional.

"I said . . . *drop* that." With barely a twitch of his arm muscle, he sent the point of the sword jabbing forward. Just enough to sting.

"Ow! Hey!"

The bulky shape dropped the pipe and backed off, putting a hand to his chest. Fennrys kicked it out of easy reach. The man glowered at him and pointed at the iron span overhead.

"My bridge, brother," he rumbled in a voice like a rock slide. "I been here longer 'n you. Longer 'n most. Show a little respect."

"I'm not your brother and I won't be staying. But I'm also not going anywhere until after sunup. So you can either sit over there—*way* over there—and behave yourself, or go find another bridge to lurk under. Like that one." Fennrys nodded to where he could see the elegant swooping lines of the bridge the centaurs had been shooting at him from.

"The Triborough?" The enormous rag-and-blanket-clad bum snorted. "That's just a *bridge*."

Fennrys glanced quizzically at the guy and rolled his eyes at the span above their heads.

"Not all bridges are created equal, brother." The man backed off and sat with his broad, hulking shoulders against the soaring concrete arch. "This"—he knocked on the concrete bridge support behind his head with one enormous knuckle—"is the Hell Gate. And this"—he put his hand flat on the ground—"is Dead Ground. *They* won't follow you down here."

"Really." Fennrys was too weary to be surprised by the fact that the guy had seen a pair of centaurs shooting arrows at him and didn't seem to think it was anything out of the ordinary. "And why's that?"

"Here's Dead Ground." He shrugged again, as if that explained everything. "Unquiet at that."

Dead Ground. That was what the one centaur had said to the other, Fennrys realized. What on earth was that? Before he could ask the question, the big man was speaking again, patting the packed earth beside him with his baseball-glove-sized hand.

"Many dead, many many, lie under this land," he rumbled. "Makes this place safe for some. Not so safe for others." He turned toward Fennrys, his shiny bead-black eyes gleaming in a face defined by bulky, misshapen features. "I wonder . . . which one are you?"

Before Fennrys could ask what he meant by that, the guy lurched to his feet and shambled around to the other side of the massive concrete bridge trestle, laughing quietly to himself.

VIII

As Toby and the students moved cautiously through the gym, Mason kept surreptitiously scanning the wreckage, searching for anything that might give her a clue as to what those things had been. Or some kind of proof that they had even existed at all. But there was nothing. Not even a tuft of hair or a broken fingernail left behind—let alone the arm or head that Fennrys had so expertly severed. Fennrys, who, for all intents and purposes, was just as much a phantom as the draugr. Aside from the theft of Toby's boots, there really was no evidence he'd ever been there either.

Almost no evidence . . .

"Cal . . ." Mason reached out suddenly and touched something hanging from his injured left wrist, which he cradled with his other arm. Her fingers closed around the gray metal disk tied there with a leather thong, and it felt hot. Mason jerked her hand away as if she'd touched a live wire, and her arm tingled almost up to her elbow. She rubbed at it and stared at the iron medallion. It was *his*. The Fennrys Wolf's. She'd seen it hanging around his neck, and she felt almost irresistibly compelled to reach out for it again, in spite of the shock it had just given her.

But Calum lowered his arm to his side, almost as if he was trying to hide it behind his back.

"That's *his*," Heather said. "The wolf guy's. I saw him wearing it."

"I can't see how you could have missed *any* detail of his wardrobe, with the way you were staring," Rory said drily, ignoring the dagger glance she shot him in return. He turned to Cal. "Wonder why he left it with you."

"Maybe he thought I was hot," Cal said, equally drily.

"Children." Toby rubbed at the bridge of his nose. In the gathering light he looked terrible, gray and worn. "Can we please dial down the bullshit and maybe take a minute to get our stories straight? Before the Headmaster wakes up and looks out his window into the quad?"

That might have already happened, Mason thought as a siren started to wail in the far distance.

Closer, she heard a voice, someone shouting, and then another. Gosforth Academy was waking up to find its venerable oak tree felled and its brand-new gym demolished. What it *wouldn't* find were the creatures that Mason was almost sure had been responsible *for* the devastation.

And now . . . now that they had all agreed to remain silent . . . there was no one to tell of their existence.

★ ★ ★

Emergency personnel and school administration descended on the scene within minutes, along with a crowd of gawking students from the dorm, most of them still in sweats and sporting bedhead. Mason was led, under protestation that she was fine, to sit beside Heather Palmerston on a bench while a paramedic examined the small collection of cuts and bruises the girls had sustained.

"Mason!"

She glanced up in apprehension as she heard her name called out in a familiar voice. Gunnar Starling came striding across the quad, a thundercloud frown on his brow. Mason felt her heart lurch a little—whether in fear or relief, she wasn't really sure—at the sight of her father. His custom-tailored overcoat flowed cloaklike in his wake, and his thick silver hair was like the mane of a lion. His elegant Nordic features were drawn, and his pale blue eyes dangerously alight with anger.

Maybe not anger, Mason thought. Maybe it was . . . worry.

Which was worse. If Gunnar Starling was angry about something, he dealt with it swiftly, surely, and permanently, and that was that. If he was worried about something—some problem that he couldn't immediately solve, make better, or make go away—then Gunnar was someone to be avoided at all costs. Mason hoped he was just really pissed about the rainbow window.

Her father bore down on her where she sat huddled under an emergency blanket. Heather seemed to have lapsed into a kind of dull stupor, unaffected even by the sight of buff firefighters—until the moment two of them rounded the far side of the building, supporting Calum between them. Mason, Heather, and Rory had all been able to clamber over the trunk of the fallen oak tree in order to get out into the quad. But not Calum. Toby had made him stay put inside the ruined gymnasium until the firemen could go around and force open the jammed emergency exit door. It was a decision that had quietly infuriated Cal, Mason could tell, but it was also a moot point. In the state he was in, he hadn't had the strength to climb over the twisted, massive bulk of the fallen oak, in spite of the Fennrys Wolf's mysterious ministrations. Which, Mason suspected, had probably saved Cal's life.

She wished there was some way she could thank Fennrys for what he'd done for them, but she feared she'd probably never see him again. It made her unaccountably sad, but she had more immediate problems to deal with at the moment. Like her father switching course in midstride when he spotted Toby talking to the fire chief. Gunnar looked like he was going to rend the fencing instructor limb from bloody limb.

Mason jumped up off the bench and ran straight toward her father, heading him off at the pass.

"Dad!"

"Mason! Honey . . ." Gunnar Starling wrapped his daughter tightly in his strong arms and kissed the top of her head. "What in hell happened to you?"

"Nothing." Mason tried to sound convincing. "I'm fine. It was the storm. I guess the old oak just couldn't stand against it. . . ."

Her father pushed her to arm's length and bent down to peer into her face, his stare almost palpable in its intensity.

"You shouldn't have been in the gym."

"Dad, I had practice—"

"And you shouldn't have been alone like that with no one to protect you."

"I *wasn't*—"

"Hey, Pop," Rory said, wandering up next to them, hands stuffed casually into the pockets of his jeans. Mason noticed, though, that they were balled into tight fists.

"Rory. Damn it!" Gunnar rounded on his younger son. "You should have been looking out for your sister."

"I'm *fine*, thanks," Rory muttered acidly.

"Rory was great, Dad," Mason pulled at her father's arm, ignoring the pointed glare her brother gave her. Mason had learned early in life that Rory did *not* exactly appreciate anyone standing up for him. "And Toby was awesome, too—he totally took care of us!"

Gunnar's glance flicked over to where a paramedic had bandaged Calum and was leading him to an ambulance. Cal shrugged angrily away when the woman tried to support him under his arm.

"Yeah," Mason continued, trying to recapture her father's attention. "I mean, poor Cal got pretty banged up, but that's because he was just in exactly the wrong place when the oak came crashing down."

Gunnar turned back to his daughter, frowning.

"But nobody panicked and Toby made sure we all knew what to do and we're all okay." Mason tried to smile brightly. "He made us stay in the storage cellar overnight, until the storm passed, just in case and . . . and . . ." She faltered to a stop, willing her father to remain calm and not kill anyone on her behalf.

"The car's around front of the academy," Gunnar said. "Go wait for me."

"What? Why?"

"You're coming home with me for a few days until I get to the bottom of this." He glanced at Rory. "Both of you."

"Dad—no! It's the middle of the semester." Mason was horrified. "I have exams. And practice. The national qualifiers are coming up. I can't leave."

"Mason—"

"It was just a *storm*." She glanced at Rory, who frowned deeply at her but stayed silent. "That's *all*. It could've happened anywhere. It could've happened on the estate."

"Where I could have taken care of you—"

"I can take care of myself. *Please*. I'm really, *really* okay."

She watched anxiously as Gunnar exchanged a long, laden glance with Toby. She was doomed, Mason thought. Her father was going to drag her out of there kicking and screaming—because that was the only way she was going to go—and she'd be locked up in the gloomy, gothic Starling estate for who knows how long. Rory had been right.

But then suddenly Gunnar's arm muscles seemed to relax a bit beneath Mason's fingers. His glance had shifted and he was looking over her shoulder. Mason followed his gaze and relaxed a little, too.

Roth. Oh, thank god, Mason thought. *Saved.*

Her other brother, Rothgar—except nobody really got away with calling him Rothgar except their father—had arrived, dressed head to toe in the motorcycle leathers that made him look armored. He stalked through the quad archway and headed toward them, his gait relaxed, casual, supremely confident. He would keep her father calm.

Roth's presence had a way of acting like a mute button or a freeze frame. Everyone always seemed to get very quiet and still around him. Mason was used to it, but it always secretly amused her. He was only twenty-two years old, and it wasn't like he was some huge, muscle-bound biker dude or bouncer or something. And yet people always tended to behave themselves around him.

With Gunnar, he was simply a calming influence, because anything the elder Starling required, Rothgar Starling would simply make happen. He was the epitome of the strong, silent type; usually the only thing anyone heard out of him was the sound of his thick-soled, steel-toed boots as he stalked into a room. Rory had once secretly referred to Roth as their father's errand boy, but really it was more like he was Gunnar's second-in-command.

"Hey, Mase." Roth held out a hand as he walked toward her. Mason took it, and he drew her into a quick embrace. "I heard you had an unscheduled sleepover in the gym last night, little sister."

"Yup. Complete with light show and bonus random acts of God. Or Goddess. Apparently it's not nice to fool with Mother Nature."

"Better believe it." Roth bestowed a grin and wink on her. "She has a temper."

"Hope Gosforth has insurance."

Gunnar Starling's expression darkened, and he turned and glanced over his shoulder at the gaping hole on the athletic center's outer wall, framed as it was by shattered rainbow shards.

"I'm really sorry about the window, Dad," Mason said. "It was so beautiful and I know how proud you were of it. . . ."

"Don't you worry about that, honey," he said without turning back to look at her. "It was only a thing. Things aren't important. Possessions are fleeting. . . ." He trailed off before he could really heartily launch into one of his signature "material things are of no consequence/life beyond this life is what's important" lectures. It was a fave theme of his. Which always struck Mason as kind of funny. Her father was one of the wealthiest men in North America, and yet he was always telling her how unimportant it all was. From anyone else, it probably would have come off as disingenuous. But coming from Gunnar Starling, they seemed like words to live by. Mason wondered if any of Gosforth's other wealthy patrons thought that way. Patrons like the tall, striking woman who walked through the archway at that very moment, pausing with one hand on her angular hip to scan the assembled crowd with a sweeping gaze.

Daria Aristarchos. Calum's mother.

Her dark brown hair was caught up in a messy bun and she wore yoga pants and designer sneakers, and yet somehow she still managed to convey an air of movie star or post-career runway model. It was easy to see where Cal got his looks from, although Mason wondered if his father was even half as good-looking as his mom. She had never seen him. Cal's parents were divorced and his dad lived somewhere on the other side of the Atlantic. It hadn't been a very pleasant parting, Mason gathered, and Cal had adopted his mother's last name in the wake of the split.

Mrs.—*Ms.* Aristarchos, Mason mentally corrected herself—looked like she was barely managing to contain a simmering rage as she pulled Gosforth's headmaster over to a corner of the quad for a private discussion.

Mason turned to see her father looking in Cal's mother's direction, and his expression had hardened again. "Honey," he said without looking at Mason, "get your things and meet me at the car."

"Dad—"

He swung a blazing glare on his daughter, and Mason's mouth snapped shut. Then he stalked across the lawn to join the headmaster and Daria Aristarchos. Interrupt was more like it, Mason thought as she watched Cal's mom turn to her father with a look on her face that might have turned a lesser man to stone. She couldn't hear what they were saying, but it seemed to be a bit of a heated exchange.

Roth rolled his eyes and took Mason by the arm. "Come on," he said. "I'll walk you to your room and you can grab a few things. It's Friday. There probably won't be any classes while they're doing cleanup anyway. You can spend the weekend at home, and I'll talk Gunn into letting you come back in time for class on Monday morning. Deal?"

"You will?"

"Trust me, Mason." Roth gave her one of his rare smiles and led her toward the door into the res wing, past where

Heather still sat on the bench, looking just a little lost.

"Hey," Mason murmured as they passed.

"Hey." Heather nodded back, and then seemed to notice that Mason's brother was there. "Hi, Roth." She turned on a bright smile and tossed her thick blond mane over her shoulder.

"Hello, Heather." Roth's mouth ticked upward in a half smile. He was pretty used to that kind of thing from girls, and Mason had never once seen him fall for it. "Are you okay after last night? Do you need anything?"

Heather looked on the verge of making a flirty comment but then seemed to rethink the idea, realizing that it wouldn't do her any good. Or maybe, Mason thought, she really was just too shaken up by things to actually make the effort. Whatever the case, Heather slumped forward a bit and shrugged a shoulder, saying, "A new gym would be nice."

"Pretty incredible." Roth shook his head. "You know, there were blackouts over half of Manhattan last night. But I didn't see anywhere on the news that took as big a hit as this place. . . ." He glanced back at the gym and the grotesque tangle of oak tree roots that stuck up into the air like so many grasping fingers. "That's a lot of damage."

"Yeah." Heather traced her thumb over a bit of graffiti carved into the wood of the bench: H+C, surrounded by a heart. "Well, the tree falling did most of it," she said absently.

"Most of it?" Roth asked sharply.

Mason and Heather exchanged a look.

"Uh . . ." Heather shifted on the bench. "I mean, all of it. I mean . . . what *else* could it have been, right?" She laughed, and it was an awkward, shrill sound.

Roth blinked at her and then glanced back at Mason, who shrugged and tried to look nonchalant.

"Why don't you walk with us back to the dorm?" Roth asked Heather. "You look like you could use some sleep. You both seem a little on edge."

"A tree almost killed us, Roth. You probably would be, too." Mason smiled wanly at him. "Or not. Knowing you. C'mon, Heather. Roth's right. It's only quarter after eight, and I've already had more than enough excitement for one day."

They dropped Heather off in front of her door on the second floor, and then Roth escorted Mason down the long hall toward her own quarters. He put an arm around her shoulders, and Mason leaned wearily against her big brother as they walked.

"So," Roth said quietly as they left Heather behind in her room. "You and Heather Palmerston. Pals?"

"Hardly." Mason snorted at the very thought. "It's more like . . . temporary bonding through shared adversity. I predict that by Monday morning, she'll be back to wanting to duct tape me upside down to my locker."

Roth chuckled. "Just as well. Her whole family is whacked, y'know."

"Really?" Mason stopped in front of her door and fished around in her bag for her key. "And here I thought Heather was just a natural-born bitch."

Roth answered his sister with a grin. He leaned against the door frame. "I hear the Aristarchos kid got hurt," he said.

"Yeah." Mason dug harder through the depth of her bag and avoided making eye contact with her brother.

"I also heard he's gonna be okay. Basically."

"I really hope so."

Mason could feel Roth's keen gaze on her, and she struggled to keep from blushing. The last thing she wanted Roth to know was who she was crushing on. She also didn't need him to suspect that Calum hadn't, in fact, been injured by the tree falling through the gym window. She hated the fact that she had agreed with the others to keep the details of their terrifying ordeal secret. But she had, and she would. And even if she hadn't, she wouldn't have even known where to begin to tell Roth the truth of the matter. Thankfully, her fingers brushed her key ring in the corner of her bag, and she opened her door and gestured Roth inside.

The room was cold and smelled of rain. Mason glanced over at the open window and saw that the sill, along with a circle of carpet directly beneath it, was soaking wet from the storm. She ignored it. Mason never closed her window, and a little dampness was a small price to pay for her mental and emotional stability.

She'd suffered from claustrophobia ever since she was a little girl and a game of hide-and-seek had gone horribly awry. At six years old, Mason had thought herself very clever when she'd hidden in the abandoned garden shed on the edge of her father's rambling Westchester estate. But Rory had seen her pick her hiding spot, and he'd thought it would be a big joke to lock her in and leave her there for a while. Except that . . . about an hour after sneaking up on Mason and sealing her into the tiny shed with the slid-bar lock, he'd forgotten all about their silly game—mostly because he was already in a car, on his way to a two-day sleepover at a friend's cottage . . . a cottage in the Hamptons that had no phone and no way to contact Rory to find out if he'd happened to have seen his baby sister before he'd left. Mason had blocked out most of her memories of the experience, but she'd been told that they still hadn't found her by the time Rory got back.

Roth glanced at the window but didn't say anything. After it had all happened, they told her that Roth was the one who'd found her. She didn't remember that. She didn't remember any of it—except as distorted night terrors. All she knew was that Roth never bugged Mason about her claustrophobia, and she appreciated it enormously.

She dropped her gear bag on the bed and yanked open the zipper. Then she rummaged through her dresser, tossing her makeup bag and toiletries and a couple of favorite T-shirts into the bag, along with her laptop and a few textbooks she needed for homework. The thought of having to go home made her angry and anxious, but if Roth said he'd get her back to school for Monday, she'd go. Roth never went back on a promise.

She glanced over to where her brother perched on the edge of her desk, arms crossed over his broad chest. The gesture made his arm muscles bulge and Mason grinned a little, remembering how lucky she had considered herself when she was a kid, to have such a big strong brother to take care of her if she ever got into trouble.

She wondered silently what Roth would have done if he'd been in the gym with her only a few hours earlier. She wondered if he would have fared as well as the mysterious Fennrys Wolf. She felt her cheeks grow hot at the thought of the gorgeous, lean-muscled blond guy, and she looked away from Roth and cast around for something to say before he asked her why she was suddenly blushing.

"Hey, um . . . so what's the deal between Dad and Cal's mom?" she asked. "They sort of seem like they hate each other or something."

Roth frowned faintly. "Yeah. There's a bit of history there."

Mason gaped at him. "You're kidding. You mean, like . . ."

"No, Mase." Roth shook his head and laughed. "Not *that* kind of history. Just Gosforth interfamily crap. You know."

She nodded. Mason tried to avoid anything to do with it, but it wasn't easy in a place like Gos. The Gosforth Academy had been founded in the late 1800s by a handful of extraordinarily wealthy, extremely influential "Founders," men and women who had decided that public schools—even other private schools—just weren't good enough for their little darlings. Gosforth, they claimed, would be a haven. A super-elite sanctuary, as well as a place of exceptional learning and culture. Mason had always been a little embarrassed by the entire situation and had routinely petitioned her father to let her go to a regular school, with no success.

Descendants of the founding families had been attending Gosforth for so many generations that there was a whole tangled mess of feuds and bad blood—and alliances and pacts—that no one could really sort out to any great degree. As far as most of the conflicts went, no one could even remember the origins or reasoning behind them. But it still sometimes made picking where to sit in the dining hall difficult to negotiate. Mason did her best to stay out of it all.

"I don't know the whole story," Roth was saying. "All I know is that she and Mom were best friends when they were young."

"Daria Aristarchos and Mom? *Our* mom?" Mason's jaw dropped. That was something she couldn't fathom. Not from everything she knew about Calum's mother. And everything she knew about her own, which admittedly wasn't all that much. "You're kidding. I thought Mom went to school somewhere else. Somewhere *not* Gosforth."

"She did. Mom wasn't part of all this." Roth smiled, rolling his eyes at the room and, Mason got the impression, the school at large. "She never had to deal with being a Gosling. With all of the impossible expectations and the 'hallowed histories' of a bunch of deluded, spoiled aristocrats who think they're above everyone else and hold the fate of mankind in their greasy palms—"

He broke off when he realized that Mason was staring at him. She didn't think she'd ever heard him string that many words together in a sentence before.

Roth chuckled and shook his head. "Mom was normal. That's all, Mase. And *that* is why she was so much cooler than any of us have any hope of ever being."

"I wish I'd known her," Mason said quietly, feeling the familiar ache of her mother's absence. Yelena Starling had died in childbirth, and it was a hard thing for Mason to think about—without thinking about that fact that *she* was the reason her mother was gone.

Roth pushed himself away from the desk and walked over to where Mason stood by the bed. "C'mon," he said, holding out his hand for her bag.

She zipped it shut and handed it over with a sigh. "Right. Home sweet home, here I come."

IX

Fennrys crouched on his haunches, huddled under the Hell Gate Bridge trestle waiting for the dawn, or his sanity, to return. He needed one or the other, something that would shine a light on his darkness and banish the things that went bump—and thrash, and chase, and kill—in the night. He squinted into the east, where the horizon was finally brightening. He'd made it. At the very least, he seemed to have—hopefully permanently—ditched the marauding horse-men that had been hunting him.

Centaurs.

He must be in some kind of serious trouble.

Or—and this was far more likely—clearly insane. As the rose-and-gold light of predawn crept toward his shadowed hiding place, Fennrys stood and peered around the corner. Nothing. The big homeless guy had disappeared, as if into the morning mist, and Fennrys was alone.

He remembered that he had told the fight guy at the

school—what was his name? Toby?—that they would be safe with the coming of the dawn. That the draugr would be gone with the morning light. He knew that to be true. He knew, in all probability, that it was true of the centaurs as well. He did *not*, however, know *how* he knew that.

When the sun finally lifted above the horizon, he waited for at least a whole hour, just to be sure, before he left the safety of his hiding place and made his way back over the pedestrian bridge to Manhattan. Once there, he began to walk south.

When he reached Ninety-Fifth Street, where the shoreline of the river bent east again, he turned right and headed deeper into the heart of the city. The wind off the water was starting to give him a chill down one side of his body. He shivered and shoved his hands into the pockets of his hoodie. And felt something tucked away in one of them.

Curious, Fennrys fished the object out of his pocket. It turned out to be a large wad of bills, and he stared at them for a long time. That, at least, solved *that* problem. He glanced to the east, where the sun had climbed well into the sky, and wondered if the clothing stores on Fifth Avenue were open yet.

The saleslady in the upscale clothing store was delightful and helpful and never for an instant indicated that the Fennrys Wolf was dressed inappropriately when he walked through the doors of the shop . . . wearing sweatpants that were two sizes too small, a hoodie emblazoned with a private school crest, and a pair of combat boots that looked as though they'd been run over by a freight train.

"I'd suggest the dark wash jeans in the slim fit," she said, handing him another stack of pants to consider. He'd already had her put the socks and underwear on his bill and was in the dressing room trying on shirts and jeans. "They'll go well with that tailored button-down. I've also got a few outerwear pieces I can bring you to try. There's a soft canvas jacket in hunter green—"

"Leather," Fenn said. It was harder for teeth and claws—and swords—to get through leather. Not that he was going to tell the salesgirl that. "I'd like a leather jacket, please, if you have one."

"Of course," she agreed. "I have a nice piece left over from last season that's marked down."

"And boots."

"I already have a pair ready out here for you to try, sir." When Fennrys finally emerged from the dressing room, the saleslady cast an approving eye over him. "You'll be wearing the items, then?"

"Yes."

"Shall I burn the ones you came in with?"

He grinned at her. "Thank you, no. Just put them in a bag for me." Fennrys had an idea. He hadn't been able to stop thinking about the girl from the school. Her face, the memory of those deep blue eyes, was the only thing that had kept him focused instead of disappearing into a mental tailspin as he'd sat under the bridge, waiting for the morning. Fennrys didn't know why, but he knew he needed to see her again. And returning the borrowed items was the only excuse he had. Fennrys paid for his new wardrobe and, as the saleslady handed him his shopping bags, asked, "Know any good hotels around here?"

The escalator carried him up a chartreuse neon-lit corridor and out into the expansive, fantastical lobby of the River Hotel with its vaulting, vine-covered ceiling and sparkling chandelier. There was a long wooden check-in desk carved with the spreading branches and roots of a massive, twisty tree. It reminded Fennrys of something, but he couldn't, in that moment, think what it was. Behind the desk, soaring windows looked out onto a terrace that was a secluded oasis in the middle of the city—a profusion of greenery scattered with teak chaises and banks of cushions for lounging. It was early for check-in, and the girl behind the counter was giving him an apologetic hard time about the fact that he would need a credit card as a damage deposit to secure the room. All Fennrys had was Rory's wad of cash.

He was about to abort the attempted check-in and walk away when he saw a tall, model-gorgeous woman in an elegant, figure-hugging suit signal to the girl he was speaking to.

"Will you excuse me for one moment, sir?" the girl said, and slipped away to confer with the other woman.

Fennrys sighed and figured that he was on the verge of being tossed out of the hotel. He pushed away from the desk and turned but paused when the girl hurried back to him with a sunny, slightly anxious smile pasted on her face.

"If you can wait one moment, Mr. Wolf, I'll just check to make sure your accommodations are fully ready for your stay. I've upgraded you to our penthouse suite, and the lounge will be pleased to offer you complimentary refreshments, once you're settled." She slid a key card across the polished surface of the desk toward him.

Fennrys glanced back over to where he'd seen the woman in the suit standing, but she was no longer there. "The upgrade . . . is there an extra—"

"No. The same price as the regular room. For you." She paused as he looked at her, confused. "Everything is taken care of. Please enjoy your stay."

There's got to be a mistake here, Fennrys thought. *A nineteen-year-old nobody—literally—does not get this kind of treatment in a swank hotel.*

He slowly picked up his two shopping bags and nodded at the clerk. He wasn't going to push his luck. He just took the room card and walked casually to the bank of elevators. The door to one of the cabs glided open, and Fennrys stepped inside.

As the elevator began to rise, he pulled what was left of the money roll out of his pocket and fanned the bills with his thumb. He felt a twinge of guilt and wondered idly why a high school student would be wandering around with that kind of a stash. But then again, he'd seen enough of the school to know that it was populated by the abnormally rich. That made him feel a little less bad—that, and the fact that the kid had seemed like kind of a jerk anyway.

Fennrys shoved the money back into his pocket. It had started out as a small fortune, but at New York prices it would dwindle rapidly. At the hotel's regular rate, he could afford maybe a couple of nights. Time enough for him to figure out what the hell he was going to do with the rest of his life. Maybe even time to remember what he'd already done.

The water in the penthouse suite's shower ran hot and for a long time. Fennrys stood there, palms pressed against the glass-tiled wall, letting the water drive the chill from his bones and muscles that seemed to have always been there—as if he'd spent a long time in a very cold place and it had become a part of him. He closed his eyes and tilted his face up toward the spray, his mind a strange, empty place. Memoryless. Almost.

There were flashes. Images.

Blinding light reflected off burnished, shimmering rooftops. Green fields. Clouds *beneath* him . . . then the light and the brilliant colors shattered, like someone taking a hammer to a rainbow, and he was plunged into suffocating darkness. That particular image carried the bonus feature of smell with it. Dank, earthen. Heavy and cloying, the odor of graves and of rain-wet ashes in long-dead fire pits. The smell of death. And, echoing in his head, the sound of a woman's voice telling him to remember. *Remember your promise,* the voice said. Fennrys turned off the shower and reached for a towel. He had to see that girl from the school again.

X

The trip home to their estate in Westchester County was, as usual, via Gunnar's private train. Her father didn't like driving and hated sitting in traffic, but he was a mad rail-travel enthusiast—the result of having been raised from a long line of shipping magnates. Boats and trains were Gunnar's great love, as they had been his father's before him. It was, apparently, a familial thing, although Rory seemed to be the only one from Mason's generation who had inherited the gene. Roth's preferred mode of transportation was his Harley, and Mason was indifferent.

She had a suspicion that her claustrophobia was the main reason her father used the train to take them home, even though he would never draw attention to the fact. In truth, she appreciated the gesture, but she still felt uneasy as their chauffeur dropped them off at the small outbuilding in the uptown Manhattan rail yard that had been converted to an elegantly appointed executive lounge where her father's clients could wait in comfort for his private train to pick them up for business trips.

When she was little, it had been fun riding around in a private train car decked out with antique Waterford crystal chandeliers and Italian leather banquettes and burled oak paneling. She'd actually felt like a princess in a fancy carriage. Now it just made her feel like the proverbial bird in a gilded cage.

In the train car, it was deathly quiet except for the low strains of classical music: Puccini's *Turandot*. Roth had left Mason back at the school and gone to get his Harley, saying he'd see her at the estate. Mason wished she had his kind of freedom. Her father sat in the front of the car, which had been partitioned off and turned into a high-tech mobile office, and that left Mason alone with Rory to share the ride. And he was lousy company, more so than usual, sprawling in one of the sleek swivel chairs and staring out the window at the passing scenery. And ignoring his sister as if she wasn't even there.

Mason didn't push him. Even though she was dying to talk about what had happened in the gymnasium, she wasn't dying to talk to Rory about it. Rory dealt with things in a weird way, and she figured that's what he was doing now. Dealing. So she let him brood. She just wished he wasn't such a shithead.

She never used to think that about him. She used to adore him, like she still adored Roth. Like Roth, he had once been kind to her. Now he was just kind of an ass. He was popular and handsome, like Calum, but he was also callous, pompous, and way too full of himself.

And Mason suspected that, deep down, he hated her.

It all stemmed from that stupid game of hide-and-seek when she and Rory were kids . . . and from the fact that Mason had forgiven Rory for the utter stupidity that had put her in such danger. She'd even stood up for him against the wrath of their father; she remembered her six-year-old self asking Gunnar to please, *please* not be mad.

It was only her pleading that kept Mason's father from tearing the hide off her brother's back. But he never played hide-and-seek with her again. In fact, Rory had never really talked to her much at all after that.

Roth had once told her that the reason Rory had become so distant—so antagonistic, in fact—was that he couldn't forgive himself for putting his baby sis in danger. Mason knew better. The problem was that Rory had never forgiven *her*. She had pleaded for clemency for her brother, and in doing so she had spared him a whipping and shamed him instead. At the time, Mason had been too young to realize that her brother would have much preferred the beating.

Weakness didn't go over well in the Starling clan.

An hour later, they arrived at the Starling family estate, just outside the tiny township of Valhalla, New York. Gunnar's private coach had dropped them off at the little rural station in town, and their driver had been waiting with the Rolls to take them the rest of the way through the gorgeous Westchester countryside, along winding roads and down a long private drive that led to the rambling gothic mansion situated between the shores of Lake Kensico and Lake Rye.

When they pulled up in front of the house, Rory was the first out of the car. He threw open the door of the Rolls and stalked into the house, but Mason knew he wouldn't be there long. In a few minutes, she would hear the engine of the vintage Aston Martin DB5 convertible Gunnar had given him for his seventeenth birthday roar to life, and he would take off down the road.

Mason's father watched Rory stomp into the house, with a tight, unreadable expression. Then he reached in a hand and helped Mason out of the car. He grabbed her bag out of the trunk and walked her up the front steps of the imposing, grandly gothic mansion. Once inside, Gunnar gave his daughter a gentle push toward the curving staircase. "I want you to go lie down."

"Dad, it's not even the middle of the day yet."

"And you spent last night in a storage cellar. Don't tell me you actually got any quality rest."

Well, no . . . not with the storm zombies and all . . .

"Go on. Get some sleep, honey." Gunnar kissed his daughter on the forehead and aimed a pointed glance at her. "*Just* sleep. No dreams. No nightmares. Okay?"

Mason liked that idea. A lot. Her father rarely mentioned her bad nights—the ones where she would shake the house awake with screaming—but he knew all about them. Once she'd climbed the stairs and made her way down the long hall to her room at the very end of the north wing, she put her bag down and closed the door, turning the deadbolt and strangely reassured by the solid clack of the latch.

First things first: she went directly to the tall window and opened it, letting the breeze spill in and breathing the cool air of the countryside. And then, after untold hours spent wearing it like a shirt of protective chain mail, Mason shrugged out of her fencing jacket, leaving it in a heap on the floor beside her bed. She kicked out of her shoes but didn't bother changing out of her tank top and leggings before she flopped down face-first on top of her comforter, and she was sound asleep in moments. She didn't even hear Rory's car as it roared out of the garage and sped past, underneath her window.

Rory's hands were white-knuckled on the steering wheel as he jammed his foot on the accelerator and blasted down a twisting road. When he reached a barely discernible side road, Rory turned and slowed down enough so that the rutted dirt surface wouldn't take out the DB5's undercarriage. The narrow lane, shadowed by a high green tunnel of overarching tree branches, came to an end at a little gravel clearing at the edge of Lake Rye, and Rory stomped on the brakes just in time to keep the car from rocketing into the water. The dust cloud from the car billowed past, out over the still surface of the lake. Rory watched it dissipate as he slowly forced his fingers to unclench the wheel and his breathing and heartbeat to regain a steady rhythm.

The train trip had been agony. Having to sit there the whole time with his father ignoring him—as usual—and Mason staring at him and trying not to. Having to pretend he didn't know anything more than she did about what had happened to them in the gym. He'd felt like he was going to burst open, and all of the precious secrets he'd accumulated over the years would come spilling out.

Rory glanced in his rear- and side-view mirrors, just to make sure he was alone on the road, and turned off the car's ignition. Then he unzipped his jacket and pulled out an old, thick leather-bound book he'd stopped at the house to collect and hidden under his clothing. The leather was dark with age, embossed with a knot-work scroll that was worn almost smooth. The pages within were yellowed, the ink faded in places.

And the handwriting was Gunnar Starling's.

When Rory was young, he'd learned that the most interesting things in life were almost always kept hidden. Locked away in dark places. And the harder it was to break the locks, the better the prize inside. He'd been overcome with a fervent, abiding desire to ferret out those treasures, so he'd developed a talent for listening at keyholes and finding ways into places he was forbidden to go.

It had been over a year since Rory had last read through the diary pages. He'd almost convinced himself that it was best just to leave it alone. To forget about all the things he'd learned. But now, after the storm—after the attack by the draugr—he felt a savage anticipation. Maybe all the things he'd dreamed about would finally have a chance to come true. He flipped the diary open and began to read from the very first pages once again.

Gunnar Starling had begun to keep a diary after he had first stumbled across a trio of women who called themselves the Norns in Copenhagen.

If I am to be honest with myself, I must admit that this was no accident. I suspect they had been hunting me, though who knows for how long . . .

Rory ran his fingertip across that line on the first page of the diary, even though he almost had the passage memorized.

The Norns.

Three beings, clothed in the guise of mortal women, who—according to Norse mythology—were responsible for deciding the fate of men.

Rory's father had been in Copenhagen on a business trip with *his* father, Magnus Starling; a young man learning the ropes of the family shipping business. One night, Gunnar had gone out into the city on his own. He'd been looking for something, anything, to alleviate his restlessness brought on by the tedium of the past few days.

And he found it.

As he walked through the front door of a dark, cavernous bar down near the canal, heavy velvet curtains parted and a man appeared: impeccably dressed, with deeply tanned skin, dark glittering eyes, and a head of perfectly coifed dread-locks that fell uniformly to brush his shoulders.

He grinned at me—a gleaming, pointed grin—and said, "Welcome, Mr. Starling. You can call me Rafe. I'll be your host for the evening."

I cannot remember having given the man my name. He showed me to a table in a private alcove that was set with four chairs, as if he thought I might be expecting company. I wasn't, of course. But company found me, nonetheless.

At first, Gunnar thought they must be "working" girls by the way they were dressed, with their wild hair and heavy makeup and tight, revealing black clothes. He was about to wave them away. But then the man returned, bearing a tray of four stout clay mugs full of something pungent and murky—mead, maybe? The three women sat down at his table without invitation.

"On the house," Rafe said, nodding at the mugs. Then he gestured to the women. "Gunnar Starling, meet Verda, Skully, and Weirdo."

The women turned as one and glared at the man, and I felt a surge of apprehension. But he just grinned at me and said, "Not their true names, of course, but they insist on dressing like a Berlin dive-bar punk band."

His mockery of them struck me as reckless. Dangerous. But then the woman he'd called Verda turned and gazed into my face with pale yellow-green eyes and said, "This is the one."

"Sure he is." My host laughed cruelly. "I've heard that from you before." Then he turned to leave us alone. "Don't take too long," he said. "And don't wreck the joint."

He closed the curtain, leaving me alone with the strange trio, but at that point, I'd had enough. I swallowed the drink in one mouthful, fully intending to leave. But then something . . . extraordinary happened. And even though my eyes will be the only ones that ever read these words, I am almost afraid to write them. . . .

Rory let the leather-bound book fall open in his lap as he leaned his head back and pictured the scene. . . .

The women reached into small leather pouches that hung from their belts and spilled handfuls of tiny golden acorns, each one carved with a mark—a rune—out onto the table. Gunnar tried to pull his hands away from the table but suddenly found that he couldn't. His fingers felt as though they were rooted to the surface. He felt the wooden chair beneath him shift and ripple, bending toward his spine, wrapping around his torso. . . .

Rory opened his eyes, and his gaze drifted back to the page.

My feet felt as if they were spreading out across the floor, sending roots into the ground. I looked down at my hands, horrified—they were gnarled and barklike, and when I struggled to break free, my arms only creaked like tree branches in a storm wind. I opened my mouth to cry out but could utter only a thin, wailing moan.

"Let go of your fear, Gunnar Starling," the three women said in unison, their voices echoing like thunder in my head. "You are at the heart of Yggdrasil, the world tree. You will know your destiny. You will fulfill it."

The acorns lying at the center of the table began to spin like tops, emitting rays of golden light, and I could not tear my gaze away. The world blurred all around me and I saw my life—branching out into several different paths like the limbs of a tree, each decision taking me in a different direction.

One of those paths led to my most closely held, most sacred soul-deep desire. . . .

The dearest wish of Gunnar Starling's heart, Rory knew, had never been that of a normal young man. Most normal young men didn't yearn to bring about the destruction of the world. They didn't think that humanity was beyond redemption—had been for centuries—and didn't seek an end to mankind so that the world could start over again from scratch. But that exact thing was the one singular ambition Gunnar had been nurturing secretly since he was a child and his own father had told him who—and what—he was. The secret history of the Starling family was a legacy that had been passed from generation to generation. Since before his ancestors could write down the stories of their gods, they had served them. The Aesir. Thor and Odin and Loki; lovely Freya; fearsome Hel, Mistress of the Underworld; and Heimdall the Bridgekeeper . . . the gods and goddesses of the Vikings were the guiding stars in the skies above the Starling clan's heads. The prophecies of those gods demanded an eventual, catastrophic ending, and it was the duty of their devotees to help bring that about.

Until my own father betrayed that sacred trust, Rory thought bitterly, his hand clenching into a fist on top of the diary page. But that was much later.

On that night in Copenhagen, Gunnar had found himself at the head of the path. He followed that path in his mind and was rewarded with a glimpse of the glorious horror he would bring down upon the world . . . but then, suddenly, everything went dim. A thick fog rolled across his mind, and the images were swallowed up in uncertainty. But it was enough. He knew what he must do.

When I came back to my senses, I was alone. I swept up the acorns that lay scattered on the table, put them in my pocket, and left the bar. The night air was cool and soft, and everything around me was brighter and sharper than it had been before. Down in the harbor, I stopped to gaze out over the dark waters. It was late enough that there were only a handful of people around, and no one paid me any heed. No one—except the famous bronze statue of the Little Mermaid, who sat out on her rock in the middle of the bay. As I gazed out at her, I swear I saw her lips curve in a wicked, beckoning smile as she flicked the tip of her tail fin.

I nodded politely and continued on my way. My own eyes have been opened, and now I can see . . . but I realize also that such visions hold dangers of their own. I must be careful. But I must be brave—

Rory was jolted out of his immersion in his father's story by the sharp, insistent ringtone of his phone. He looked at the number and decided not to answer it. His "business transactions" could wait. He turned his gaze back to the last lines of the entry.

This morning, Father asked me what I seemed to be so very happy about.

"I have met my future," I said. "I have met the woman I will marry, and she is wonderful. Her name is Yelena Rose. She lives in New York City. And she is as beautiful as I knew she would be."

With her at my side, I will do what must be done.

It is my destiny. Mine . . . and Yelena's.

"And mine, Top Gunn," Rory murmured as he closed the diary in his lap and stared out over the lake. "Only I won't give up on my destiny like you did, old man. . . ."

If he was to believe any of what his father had written, then he knew that his ancestors had dedicated their lives in service to the Aesir—the gods of Norse legend—and awaited their return to the mortal realm.

Rory had also learned that there were other pantheons of gods, all with devoted clans of mortal followers. He knew that magick existed. He even knew how to use it after discovering the golden acorns hidden in Gunnar's study.

Perhaps most surprising of all the things Rory had discovered was that Gosforth Academy wasn't *just* a school. It was a safe house. Neutral ground. A place where the influential families—rival clans serving rival gods—could keep their children safe under the same roof. It was both a fail-safe situation and an insurance policy.

According to what Rory had subsequently learned about the school history, it had worked extremely well from the time the school was founded. No single family had ever gone out of its way to make trouble. Rites were kept, rituals preserved, but so far none of the old gods had come thundering back—either as nuisance or outright threat to humanity.

Gunnar Starling, however, had formulated other plans.

Rory glanced nervously at the clock on the dash. He would have to return the diary soon to the brass-bound lockbox on the desk in Gunnar's study. He didn't like having it in his possession for more than an hour or two at a time. Rory was already worried that his father might one day notice that a few of the handful of gilded acorns were missing from the box. But before he returned the diary, he opened the leather book back up and flipped to the one page he'd spent the most hours staring at.

The words of the prophecy were scrawled across the page, as if Gunnar had still been caught in the throes of the vision when he'd written them.

One tree. A rainbow bird wings among the branches.
Three seeds of the apple tree, grown tall as Odin's spear is,
gripped in the hand of the Valkyrie.
They shall awaken, Odin Sons, when the Devourer returns.
The hammer will fall down onto the earth to be reborn.

Even if Gunnar hadn't spelled out the meaning in the diary, Rory would have figured it out. His mother's maiden name had been Rose. Apple trees were part of the rose family, and apples held all kinds of significance in myths and legends. Starlings were birds noted for the iridescent rainbowlike sheen of their feathers. And Norse mythology was predicated on an end-of-the-world scenario—Ragnarok, when a monstrous giant wolf named Fenris would devour Odin, the father of the gods, and a great war, fought by the souls of the dead, would destroy the mortal realm.

The prophecy, as Gunnar had understood it, meant that he and Yelena would have three sons who would become "Odin Sons," leaders of the warrior host of Asgard, an army of fallen heroes. The Devourer, the Fenris Wolf, would appear. Then Thor, the god of thunder, would be reborn into the mortal realm.

When Gunnar met Yelena, it was the start of the end of everything.

Except that their third child born turned out to be a girl.

And Yelena had died bearing her.

XI

Mason had promised her father no nightmares, but it wasn't a promise she'd figured she could realistically keep. Mason had been having nightmares since she was six. Most of them variations on a theme.

This time, when she opened the dream shed door she found a different twist to the old hide-and-seek scenario. Stepping inside the old forgotten gardening hut led, quite unexpectedly, to a dark, rough-walled cell. Like a medieval dungeon carved into the earth. Manacles hung from rusting chains. It was a place Mason had never been before—in dreams or otherwise—but it felt strangely familiar. In the corner, she saw a bench, once painted a bright sky blue with red roses on it. But the design was faded, the paint dull and peeling. *That* was something she knew. It was the bench in the garden shed where she'd gone to hide from Rory when they'd played a game. Where she'd become trapped. After her second full day locked in the darkness, her six-year-old self had lain down on that bench and cried herself to sleep. Beyond that, she couldn't remember what happened until after they'd found her.

Now, though, she knew she wasn't in a shed. She backed away, and her shoulders jammed up against iron bars. When she turned around, she saw that the Fennrys Wolf stood on the other side.

He held something in his hand that looked like a staff or a spear. And he was smiling. But his smile, Mason thought, was . . . strange. And when he opened his mouth to speak, his whole face distorted, jaws opening wider and wider until all Mason could see was a cavelike blackness in front of her. And all she could hear was the sound of the Fennrys Wolf's voice.

Telling her to run.

Mason's eyes snapped open and she lay flat on her back, staring up at her ceiling. Moonlight poured in through her open window and shifting, silvery patterns shimmered along the walls and ceiling, reflections from the pool outside below. She must have been asleep for hours. But she knew that there was no way she would ever be able to make her brain calm down so she could return to that state.

Fennrys . . .

The Fennrys Wolf . . .

What kind of a name was that? Well, she knew exactly *what* kind of a name it was. She just wanted to know the *why* of it. She rolled her head on her pillow and gazed over to where the messenger bag with her laptop in it lay on her desk in the corner of the room. She thought about getting it out and just calling up Wikipedia, but after a moment, she got out of bed and wandered instead down the long hall to her dad's study.

Stretching as she went, Mason padded on cat-silent feet, stiff from having fallen so instantly asleep. In her nightmare, she hadn't been able to run when Fennrys told her to, and she had awakened in the exact same position she'd fallen asleep in.

It was the thought of him that sent her now to the wall of books that covered one long side of the study, floor to ceiling. Mason had spent a lot of time here when she was a little girl, climbing like a monkey up and down the rolling ladder, running her fingers across raised letters on leather-bound spines. On one of the high shelves, Gunnar had a large collection of Scandinavian literature—histories and myths and folklore—and it was to those volumes that Mason climbed. She was careful not to make any noise. She didn't want anyone to know why she'd taken a sudden, fierce interest in the myths of the Vikings.

Mason had learned some of the stories of the Norse gods, but they had always struck her as just grimmer, colder, weirder versions of the same kinds of stuff found in Greek and Roman myths. Jealous gods, scheming and plotting against one another—only with the added bonus of a fatalistic rush toward the eventual prophesied annihilation of the world. Mason had never developed her father's fierce fascination with the myths. Still, she knew enough about the ancient stories of her ancestors to know that a wolf figured prominently in the lore.

She pulled down a large hardcover picture book that she remembered fondly from reading it repeatedly as a kid. It was full of brightly colored, fanciful illustrations of long-haired maidens and spiky-haired bearded warriors. A merry depiction of a fatalistic cosmology that was supposed to end—or already *had* ended; Mason could never get the whole Ragnarok thing quite straight—with the destruction of the world.

Cheery, she thought.

"F-e-n . . . ," she murmured to herself as she ran a finger down the index and remembered that the story of the Fenris Wolf—or Fenrir, as the creature was often called—was under the heading of "Loki's Monstrous Brood."

"Monstrous," Mason muttered, turning to sit on the ladder step with the book in her lap. "Well, *there's* a comforting adjective. . . ."

Even just flipping through the book brought back her dormant memories of the stories. She remembered that the wolf was the offspring of an occasionally mischievous, frequently downright malicious jotun, a giant, named Loki. She knew that, in the great apocalyptic Norse battle at the end of days, Ragnarok, the Fenris Wolf was fated to devour Odin, the one-eyed father of the Aesir, what the Norse called the good guys in their convoluted pantheon of gods.

Mason avoided turning to the page that she knew depicted Odin, in helmet and eyepatch, astride his eight-legged steed and with his mighty magic spear in his hand, riding full tilt straight into the giant wolf's slavering maw and down its gullet to his doom. She knew that all sorts of really bad stuff happened when he did.

What she *didn't* know was why some guy named after that particular monster had made such a bizarre and frightening entrance into her life. Or why she couldn't stop thinking about him in ways that weren't necessarily bizarre or frightening, but were nevertheless disturbing enough to keep her awake in the middle of the night.

Calum Aristarchos was having similar difficulties sleeping, jolted from restless dreams by the sound of voices wafting through his open bedroom window. At first he thought he was dreaming, or that his mother was listening to opera somewhere in the house. The voices were high and sweet, singing complicated harmonies that beckoned him.

Cal sat up, head fuzzy from his medication and muscles aching from the punishment they'd taken, and swung his legs stiffly over the side of the bed. Awkwardly, he pulled on a pair of sweats and, barefoot and shirtless, padded soundlessly across the thick carpeting of his bedroom to a set of French doors. They opened out onto his own private terrace overlooking the lawn that swept down to the waters of Long Island Sound. He stepped out into a night of velvet blackness and liquid silver moonlight and wondered if he wasn't still dreaming. Everything shone with a kind of surreal glimmer. Cal hadn't been home since the beginning of the semester and he had grown used to not being able to see the stars in Manhattan. Then again, he couldn't remember ever having seen that many stars at home either, but there they were: like handfuls of diamonds strewn across the night sky.

Outside, the music was . . . not *louder* . . . but more compelling. Irresistible. Cal felt an instant of searing electricity where the wounds on his face and chest tingled sharply, and then he was moving, striding down the immaculate landscaped path accented with classical Greek marble sculptures, down toward the landing where he usually tied up his jet-ski when he was home for the summer months. Cal had learned to swim almost before he could walk. The water had always been like a second home to him, and his mother and sister had always joked that he was half fish. One of the mer-folk. It was a joke.

Or maybe . . . it wasn't.

When he got to the bottom of the path, he crept around a stand of cedar trees, scarcely daring to breathe. For a brief instant, he thought he'd stumbled on some kind of sorority initiation week. Girls—really, *really* beautiful girls—sat on the shore and swam, frolicking and splashing, out in the Sound. They were all laughing and singing, and only half of them wore anything that could even remotely be considered clothing—filmy tunics and gossamer gowns that clung to lithe wet limbs—and they didn't seem to notice Cal spying on them. Or maybe they just didn't care.

He watched, mesmerized by the spectacle, when suddenly, out in the middle of the glassy black water, a pearly froth of foam bubbled up, as if churned by something below the surface. Cal squinted at the disturbance, struggling to make out what was causing it.

Suddenly a boiling geyser of white water burst high into the air and a massive silver horse—its hindquarters fused into a single muscular tail, finned like a fish's—leaped into the night. A girl of unearthly beauty rode upon its back, holding fast to the creature's sweeping sea-green mane and laughing with abandon.

She was followed by dozens of others, and they all rode upon the backs of monsters. Bulls and horses and snow-white leopards that leaped, breaching the surface of the water like dolphins so that Cal could see them clearly. Their back ends were uniformly scaly and had long, iridescent fins where legs and hooves should be.

"I'm definitely dreaming," Cal heard himself say.

Then one of the nymphs hoisted herself up onto the deck of the landing and turned toward where he stood hidden. She held out a delicate, web-fingered hand to him. Her eyes were black, glittering, and pulled at him like magnets. Her skin was silver-white, the color of driftwood, and glistened with phosphorescence beneath the transparent sheath she wore. She opened her full, berry-red mouth, and laughter like bells tinkling fell from her lips. Her teeth were sharp, narrow, and there were too many of them.

She sang his name.

Cal closed his eyes and swallowed the fear that surged up his throat. He put a hand to the side of his face, where the claw-marks were, and remembered other monsters. Other things that had no business existing in the world.

Then he turned and sprinted back up the path toward the house, covering his ears as he ran so he wouldn't hear the longing in the mer-girl's voice.

XII

By late Tuesday afternoon, Mason was seriously rethinking her decision to return to school so soon. A pop quiz in Latin class on Monday threw her for a loop, and an assignment she'd thought wasn't due until the next week was, of course, due that very day. She was starting to think Rory might have had the right idea when he'd begged off sick and stayed home.

Mason had known instantly that her brother was faking, and she'd been feeling fairly righteous about returning to school herself. On top of that, she'd looked forward to getting some real sleep. It was easier for her to sleep peacefully at Gosforth, for some reason. Like there was some kind of protective bubble around the academy grounds that kept the nightmares at bay.

Now, however, Mason envied her brother. She'd realized, late on Tuesday, that she had an interschool mini fencing competition scheduled that she'd totally forgotten about, and once she'd actually made it to the gym, things didn't exactly go swimmingly. "Craptastic" would be a more accurate descriptor.

The sword in Mason's hand whipped back and forth through the air like the tail of an angry cat. She'd just given up the winning point in the second bout in a row—to lesser fencers—and she was furious with herself. Heather sat on the bench watching her, having already fought her bouts. She'd won all of them but one and just shook her head as Mason stalked past.

"Well, that kinda sucked," Toby murmured drily as she shouldered past him on her way to the dressing room.

She rounded on him and actually had to count to ten because she was in serious danger of biting her coach's head off.

"I know," she said through gritted teeth.

She huffed in frustration. She'd tried to tell herself that it was just the fact she'd been home for the weekend and lost two days' practice that had thrown her off. But it wasn't that at all. It was just . . . the second she lifted her sword and faced off against an opponent, she didn't see another fencer in whites and a mask. She saw monsters.

"I know . . . ," she said again, more softly. "I'm sorry, Toby. I guess it's just having a sword in my hand again . . . I couldn't stop thinking—"

"No!" Toby's voice was like a whip. "We do *not* think about it, Starling!"

Toby turned a blazing glare on her, and Mason blinked up at him in surprise. The fencing master was one of the most even-tempered human beings she knew, and it was really unlike him to snap.

"It *didn't* happen." He took a large swallow from the coffee mug in his hand, his angry gaze still fixed on her. "Remember? That night was nothing but a storm. And it sure as hell is not going to become some kind of excuse for not producing when you're out there, Mason. Now pull your head out and get back in the race."

"I'm sorry . . . ," she said, her voice barely a whisper as her throat closed up, threatening tears.

He took a breath and seemed to calm down a bit. "The NACs are next week—*next* week—and you are not competing at a national level. Contrary to what I said to you the other day, Mason, I will have no qualms about replacing you on the team with Palmerston. I don't care if I'm already a fighter short with Cal out of the action. If you keep wussing out on matches like that, I'll bench you—permanently."

Mason swallowed the watery, burning knot that closed off her throat and nodded decisively. Toby didn't make idle threats. He was serious and he was right. She had been terrible. She'd done her best to forget all about it, but all she'd seen when she'd been out on the floor with a sword in her hand had been the shambling, gray-skinned apparitions from the night of the storm.

She knew it was just her mind playing tricks on her. Sure, she had every right to be freaked out by recent events. Her reactions were normal, anyone would tell her that—if she was actually allowed to talk about it. But of course that wasn't an option. She shook her head. Fine. She could wade neck deep into denial, just like they could. She could get on with her life.

"I'm sorry, Toby," she said, straightening up and looking him directly in the eye. "You're right. And I'll do better. I promise."

"I know you will, Mase," Toby said. His mouth curled up into a smile, but it was a weary one, Mason thought. "Now get out of here. Practice. A lot."

Mason packed up her gear, exchanged her fencing jacket for a fleece-lined hoodie, and left the Columbia U gym, letting the chill in the air cool the sweat on her skin. She'd shower when she got back to the dorm. She didn't want to be around a bunch of people waving weapons. In spite of what she'd said to Toby, even just walking the length of the gym, past the other bouts, made her mind flash back to that night.

Damn, I wish I could talk to someone about it. . . .

But there was only one person who hadn't sworn himself to secrecy about that night, and she didn't know if she'd ever see him again. She suspected not, although that made her heart clench a little every time she thought about it. Whoever the Fennrys Wolf was—*what*ever he was—Mason felt almost as though she would be somehow incomplete for the rest of her life if she never saw him again.

As she walked back to Gosforth, she noticed that there were still an abundance of college students sitting out on café patios, even though the weather was unseasonably chilly. The sky overhead was a bright indigo blue behind tumbling purple and gray clouds, and the wind kicked up eddies of road grit that stung Mason's cheeks and made her squint. She put her head down and stared at the sidewalk as she walked. Another strong gust of wind forced her to close her eyes— and she ran straight into a solid wall of muscle in a football jacket.

Mason bounced off his shoulder and almost wound up on her ass, but he caught her on the way down and steadied her. "Hey," he said, looking down on her from a positively Olympian height. "You're a Starling, right?"

"Uh. Yes?" Mason said, blinking up into the square-jawed face of Taggert Overlea. She was surprised he knew who she was. The college boys barely acknowledged any of the Gosforth crowd, with the possible exception of Heather Palmerston and one or two of the other girls.

"Yeah. Yeah, I thought so."

He grinned down at her, and Mason felt an uncomfortable twist in the pit of her stomach. There was something disconcerting about the big football player, like his eyes were just a little too bright or his smile too wide or something. Maybe it was all that posing for the cameras after winning big games. Tag and a couple of the other younger players had become CU heroes recently, dragging their team's sinking fortunes out of the abyss with berserker-like tough-guy play. At least, that's what Mason had heard around the gym. This guy was one of a handful of rising football stars. *Whoopee*.

"Hey. Can you tell your brother next time you see him that he's gotta call me? We were supposed to hang this week-end before the game, but he was a no-show and I gotta talk to him."

"Roth?" Mason blinked. She couldn't imagine a less likely

person for Taggert to "hang" with than Roth Starling. His letterman jacket would clash with Roth's head-to-toe leather. And she really couldn't picture Tag's meathead buddies sharing amiable conversation with Roth's legion of glowering biker boys.

"No." Tag shook his head. "Not that freak. Your other brother—Rory."

"Oh!" And that was somehow even *more* unlikely.

"Yeah."

"Uh, okay," she said, stumbling back a step as Tag leaned in closer. "Um. He's home sick right now—I mean, he's totally faking it, but whatever. He probably just forgot. If I talk to him, I'll tell him to get in touch."

"Cool. It's *really* important. Plus, tell him there's a bush party next weekend I can get him into—y'know, pull some strings and stuff, 'cause I know people, but he's gotta call me first. I need to talk to him."

"Right."

"You could come too, you know." Tag's gaze slid from her face to her chest. "It's a kegger, and I'm kinda guessing you don't have fake ID."

Mason resisted the urge to cross her arms in front of her. "You kinda guessed right."

"Yeah, but nobody'll mess with you if you're with me." He grinned wolfishly.

"Oh, uh, yeah. Sure." She paused awkwardly. "Well, gotta go," she said abruptly, spinning on her heel and taking off at a pace that was just short of sprinting. She could feel him staring at her for the better part of a block.

She shuddered. What was Rory doing hanging out with a creep like that, she wondered. Sure, Rory had his fair share of questionable personality traits. But he was also super-smart—top of his class smart—and a girl magnet with dark eyes and sleek black hair almost as lustrous as Mason's own lush mane. He was athletic. He could have made almost any of the school's sports teams. For a few years there, he even seemed interested in securing himself a place on the rowing team. But then something had happened, and he'd blown off practice permanently. She figured that it must have been something like they'd told him he couldn't be captain of the team after only a few weeks. Rory seemed to think that the world was a special place created for him and him alone, and everyone who didn't share that opinion was just in his way.

And strangely enough, it was Gunnar Starling who was chief among those who definitely did not share that opinion. Sometimes Mason thought her father hated Rory with a fierce passion. But then sometimes she would catch Gunn staring at his middle child with an expression of such longing and loss that it made her own heart ache. She didn't understand it. In some ways, she almost expected that he would have cast that kind of glance *her* way. After all . . . *she* was the one who had ended the life of Yelena Starling, Gunnar's beloved wife, through the simple act of being born herself.

Back at Gosforth, Mason felt her heart hop a little in her chest when she saw Calum's familiar golden-brown head of hair showing just above the heads of a group of students walking through the quad. She quickened her pace to catch up, trying not to seem like she was running.

She glanced at the gymnasium as she passed, which was once again hidden behind sheets of construction plywood and scaffolding, so soon after having been renovated. The venerable old oak tree had been chainsawed into logs and, at Gunnar Starling's request, transported in a truck to the Starling estate to be used for firewood. Appropriate revenge, Mason's dad had joked when she asked him about it, and she supposed it was—considering the tree had taken out Gunnar's beautiful, expensive window.

Ahead of her, Cal disappeared through an arched doorway. Mason caught up to him in the hallway in front of his locker.

"Hi, Calum," she said, quickening her pace to keep up with him.

"Hey," he said. He glanced back but didn't stop for her, or even slow down much at all.

"How are you?" He must have been late for an evening tutorial or something, because his stride seemed to be lengthening as he walked. "We missed you at the mini bout today. Of course, I'm kind of glad you weren't there to see me—it was pretty embarrassing—but, y'know, the team missed you. Are you going to come by tomorrow for prac—"

He stopped so abruptly that Mason ran into his shoulder with her forehead. She took an awkward hop step back and looked up at him as he turned. The left side of his face was covered with a white gauze bandage from hairline to jaw. It looked as though the healing scars beneath were pulling up the right side of his mouth into the shadow of a sneer. His left arm was in a sling because of the damage to his pectoral muscles.

"What do you think, Mason?" His hand, hanging limply against his chest, twitched slightly. "Does it look like I'm going to be fighting again anytime soon?"

Mason swallowed convulsively at the sight of his injuries. They really *had* been as bad as she'd thought. No. They'd been worse. Much worse . . . before the Fennrys Wolf had done what he'd done. Mason noticed Calum still had the iron medallion Fenn had given him. He wore it now around his neck—she could see the outline of it beneath the collar of his T-shirt.

"Right." Mason ducked her head and stared at her feet, avoiding the look in Cal's eyes. "Well, no. I mean—I knew you wouldn't be back to fighting yet. But you said that you'd . . . um. I mean, I just thought . . . never mind."

She was being selfish. Of course he wouldn't want to come to practice just to help her prepare for the upcoming competition. Even though he'd promised. Things had changed. Everything had changed. She glanced up at him and saw that he was staring coldly down at her. All the warmth that had been there in his gaze before the night of the storm seemed to have been snuffed out, and Mason felt her heart clench in her chest.

"I have a test to study for," he said. "I gotta go."

"Right. Sure. It's nice to see you . . ."

He turned and continued on down the hall.

". . . back."

He left her standing in the middle of the hallway, clutching the strap of her gear bag, her knuckles turning white with the effort to keep from shaking with anger and embarrassment. It wasn't as if she'd *done* anything to Calum. She felt the heat creeping up her throat and into her cheeks. A cluster of students standing by the lockers were staring at her pointedly, mostly smirking. Carrie Morgan was actually snickering out loud at her.

"Hey, Heather," Carrie called out suddenly.

Mason turned to see the other girl coming up behind her. She hadn't noticed her in the hallway, but she groaned inwardly, figuring that Heather would gleefully join the others in making fun of her.

"Did you see that?" Carrie said. "Starling here just tried to make a totally lame move on your ex, and Callie Boy shut her down. It was *cold*." She grinned viciously.

"Really, Carrie?" Heather said, tilting her head on her long neck and giving the other girl an appraising look. "Colder than your frigid butt? Or do you just conserve all your body heat for that geeky math TA who smells like a wet goat?"

A hollow, shocked silence descended on the corridor. Carrie's face turned a mottled shade of purple with barely repressed fury, and Mason thought she might pop an eyeball. The crowd of students standing around her drifted a few feet back and within seconds had collectively found something else to do or somewhere else to be.

Mason felt her fingers loosen their death grip on her gear bag, and she turned and continued down the hall without bothering to add anything to Heather's artful smackdown.

There wasn't anything she could say to top that, anyway. All she had to do now was not show any surprise at what Heather had done. Or the fact that she had fallen into step beside Mason. When they were far enough away, she glanced over to see Heather wearing a very slight grin.

Mason warily considered expressing gratitude, at the risk of having Heather turn it around on her. She was in unpredictable waters. But she felt she had to say something. "Thanks," she murmured casually. "Also? Nice one."

Heather shrugged an elegantly sculpted shoulder. "Carrie Morgan is a slag, and she's been asking for it for months now. She also neglected to mention that Calum stomped on *her* when she went after him right after we split. I should be thanking you for giving me an opening."

Mason felt her own grin spreading over her face. Three days since the night of the storm, and everything had changed. Everything.

Dammit. Calum cursed himself silently as he stalked down the hallway toward the library. *What the hell did you do that for, you ass?*

The hurt in Mason's gorgeous blue eyes haunted him as he took a seat in the far corner of the library, behind the stacks, where he could be alone.

Why had he been such a jerk to Mason? Cal wondered angrily. He liked Mason.

You more than "like" Mason Starling.

Up until the beginning of that school year, Cal had actually been blissfully unaware of that fact. All throughout the previous year, Calum Aristarchos and Heather Palmerston had reigned as the uncrowned king and queen of the school. Gosforth's ruling power couple. Then, at the beginning of semester, Heather had gone and—out of the frickin' *blue*—dropped a bombshell on Cal. She was breaking up with him. Her reason?

Cal was in love with Mason Starling.

News to *him* . . . until he actually thought about it.

Cal had, up until that time, been under the impression he'd never really spared the black-haired, sapphire-eyed, heartbreakingly lovely girl on his fencing team a second thought. Then, suddenly, she was the *only* thing on his mind. He'd actually been on the verge of asking her out on a real one-on-one date when . . .

Cal put a hand to the bandage on his cheek.

Well, that isn't going to happen now. Is it?

He'd seen the way she'd looked at him. Moreover . . . he'd seen the way she'd looked at *him*. That guy. The arrogant blond naked—what the *hell*—stranger who'd appeared in the middle of all of that stormy insanity and, like some kind of mythic hero, saved their necks. While Cal stood around and got his face shredded.

And now . . . everything was different.

Not just Mason, but the whole world around him had changed. After that first night back home on his mother's estate on Long Island, where she'd fumed and fussed over him in her elegantly awkward, distantly maternal way, Cal hadn't even wanted to return to Gosforth. Ever. All he'd wanted to do was wait for nightfall and the singing outside his window that made him forget about his failure in the gym and the wounds that marked his flesh. It also made him forget about Mason—almost. The doctors—there'd been more than one—had told him he'd need plastic surgery eventually. A few of them had seemed a little puzzled over the way his scars were healing.

Cal shook his head. He realized that he was clutching the medallion he wore under his T-shirt. It was *his*. . . . the Fennrys Wolf's. Cal felt a surge of something like static electricity wash over him, leaving the hairs on his arms standing up. He could sense the power contained in the little iron disk, and he had a sneaking suspicion that he shouldn't have been able to.

But what he had experienced, in the dark, under the moon . . . staring out over the black waters of Long Island Sound . . . had changed him. Maybe even more than the marks on his face.

You've been on some pretty heavy meds, you know. . . .

Sure he was. Not just for the pain, but to help drive back the nightmares and help him sleep. And if he hadn't been on those meds because he'd been attacked by *monsters*, then he might have been perfectly willing to believe the things he'd seen were just drug-induced hallucinations. Frankly, that would have been a whole lot easier to accept. He wished he could talk to someone about it.

No. He just wished he could talk to *Mason* about it.

XIII

The accommodations were fantastic, but the River Hotel's clientele was . . . disconcerting. It consisted mostly of European couples, or gatherings of beautiful young men and women who seemed to do little but drink from champagne flutes in the lounge and glance at him sideways as he walked past. Fennrys did his best to ignore them, but it had started to get to him after a couple of days. He didn't much like the idea of spending another evening hanging around in a place where the people looked at him as if they knew something about him that he didn't.

Instead, he went in search of a Laundromat he remembered seeing on his way to the hotel from the clothing store. After three blocks or so he found it, underneath an ancient, peeling sign that advertised WATERFORD LAUNDERETTE AND SHIRT SERVICE.

He pushed the door open and stepped inside the long, dingy room that was basically just an alley of front-loading washers and dryers facing off against one another. The Laundromat was deserted except for the bundled shape of a very old woman wrapped in shawls, sitting at the very back of the place on a plastic chair. It didn't exactly look like somewhere one went to get something cleaned.

He stuck a ten in the change machine at the front of the store and bought a soap packet from the vending machine. Then he wandered to the back of the Laundromat and chose a washer. He threw in the sweats he'd borrowed that first night, set the dial to the shortest cycle, and paced, waiting for it to finish.

When it did, he tossed the damp clothes into the dryer and slumped down on a bench to wait. In the heat, the drone of the machine was hypnotic, and eventually Fennrys found himself struggling to stay conscious. His body jerked as he forced himself awake, and he turned his head to find the old woman watching him from the back of the laundry. At least she seemed to be watching him. Her eyes were fixed in his direction, even though he could see that they were filmy with advanced cataracts—a shade of milky blue that reminded him, uncomfortably, of the eyes of the draugr.

He nodded politely, not even knowing if she could see him. But then she nodded back and raised a gnarled hand, knocking on the glass of the front-load washer beside her. Fennrys could see a load sloshing around inside it, but when he looked closer, he noticed that the soap froth was tinged a pinkish color. As he stared at the churning water, it turned steadily darker, becoming crimson. Then blood colored. Through the murky red water, Fennrys caught a sudden glimpse of an article of clothing within and was startled to see that, whatever it was, it bore an emblem that was strikingly similar to the Gosforth private school crest on the sweats tumbling in the machine behind his head.

Fennrys shot to his feet and spun around to yank open the door of his dryer. A waft of steam engulfed his face as he hauled out the still-damp clothes and shoved them in the bag along with Toby's boots. He turned on his heel and left the Laundromat, without so much as glancing back at the old woman. He walked for blocks before he finally felt like her rheumy white eyes were no longer fixed upon his back.

Fennrys's aim was outstanding, even in the uncertain light and deepening shadows of evening. He hit the dead center of the window with the pebble, first time. It just happened to be the wrong window. After a moment, the casement slid up with a grating noise and a blond head appeared, leaning out.

"Hey, hotshot," the gorgeous girl from the gymnasium said after a moment—the *other* gorgeous girl, not the one he had come to find. For some reason, she didn't seem surprised to see him again. Or maybe she just did a really good job of suppressing any reaction that would make her seem less than completely cool and in control. "Nice pants." She grinned wickedly. "Think I liked you better without them."

"Oh. Uh . . ."

"You're looking for Mason, aren't you?"

"I think so." He didn't actually know the name of the girl he was looking for. "She has, uh—"

"Dark hair, blue eyes," the blonde interrupted him. "Little

light in the bra-filling department. That the one? You know, the one you couldn't rip your *own* eyes off . . . even while you were killing monsters?"

Fenn frowned up at her. This wasn't going the way he'd planned. He nodded. "That's who I'm looking for. I thought I saw her in that window."

"She was here a second ago. I ditched class today and needed to borrow her poli-sci notes."

"Right. Sorry I disturbed you." He turned to go.

"Wait!" She stared down at him for a long moment and then shrugged. "Her name's Mason Starling. And her room is the south corner window, same floor. That's where she was headed when she left here."

"Thanks."

"Hey, hotshot." The girl called him back again. "We might not be best friends or anything, but Mason's okay. And I might feel obliged to hire someone to make your life particularly miserable if you bring trouble down on her."

"I don't think you have to worry about that, Miss . . ."

"Palmerston. Heather Palmerston. You can Google my family, and you'll see I have the means to follow up on my threat."

He grinned up at her. "Like I said—you don't have to worry about that. I won't. But if I do . . . you're certainly welcome to try." The way he said it didn't sound like a boast, even to his own ears. It sounded like a simple invitation, and an unself-conscious assessment of his own abilities.

"Okay then," Heather said, crossing her arms and tossing her hair over her shoulder. She glared fiercely down at him. "Just so long as we understand each other."

"I'm pretty sure we do."

"You were definitely more fun pantsless," Heather said, and slammed the window shut.

Fennrys shook his head and loped around to the other side of the stone building, where he could see a light glowing behind the curtained corner window on the second floor. The bottom pane had been lifted open, so he aimed for the center of the top glass square. As accurate as his aim was, it took three or four tries to get Mason to come to the window. When she finally stuck her head out, there was a look of confusion on her face as she glanced cautiously into the night.

"Evening," Fennrys said in a quiet voice, and stepped out of the shadows beneath the trees.

It startled Mason enough so that she jumped and hit her head on the casement. She swore and drew back, her eyes wide when she saw him standing there. He saw her breathing quicken, and he wondered if it was in fear. Not that he would have blamed her. Considering the circumstances of their last meeting.

"What are you doing here?" she asked in a hissing whisper, her hands gripping the windowsill with rigid fingers. "What do you want?"

"I just wanted to talk," he said. "Is that all right?" He considered telling her that he came by to drop off her brother's gear and the boots, but he was afraid she would tell him to just leave the bag on the sidewalk and get lost. "Just talk."

"Are you alone?" she asked. "Or did you bring zombies with you again?"

"I'm flying solo tonight."

Mason chewed on her lower lip as if trying to decide whether to believe him or not. Her gaze flicked to the trees and darkened buildings behind him as if looking for confirmation that he was truly alone. Then she looked back down at him, and he was struck again by how pretty she was. The orange glow from a streetlamp down the block highlighted the curve of her cheekbone and emphasized the deep sapphire blue of her eyes. And her black hair hung in a straight and shining curtain in front of her shoulder.

"Hang on a minute," she said.

Fennrys waited for what was probably five minutes but seemed a lot longer. In truth, he was actually surprised to see her walk around the corner of the building. Fenn had more than half expected her to either stay inside and wait for him to go away, or call the cops. He found himself almost smiling in relief.

She stopped a few feet away from him, looked up into his face, and said, "What do you want?"

"Hello again to you too," Fenn said wryly.

Mason stared at him, unblinking. "Hello. What do you want?"

"I wanted to . . ." *See you again. Speak to you. Make sure you aren't just another broken memory or piece of a dream.* "I wanted to return the gear I borrowed." He held up the shopping bag he'd brought along.

"Oh. Okay."

Did she look disappointed? His heart rate quickened for a brief moment at the thought she might have actually wanted to see him again. But then he took a breath to calm himself, afraid that he'd imagined the fleeting look. "And I wanted to say thank you," he added, turning away so that she couldn't read his thoughts in his eyes.

"Mister . . . uh . . . Wolf, was it?"

"Just call me Fennrys."

"Right. Okay." Mason nodded and kicked at the ground for a moment. "Well, Fennrys, you're welcome. Any time. Except for the never again part."

"I hope that's the case, yeah."

"Do you mind telling me just what the hell happened during that storm?"

"I would if I could."

"I don't know what that means." She straightened up and frowned at him. "Okay, look. What do you want from me?"

"What?" Fenn's gaze snapped back to her face. "Nothing. I don't . . . there's nothing—"

"Who are you, really?"

"If I knew that, you'd probably be the first person I'd tell."

"Why me?"

"Because you're the only person I know. Everything else is just a big blank."

"What?" She blinked at him.

He tapped the side of his head with a finger. "I don't seem to be able to remember. Anything. I mean anything about myself. Or my life before I crawled out of the tree that crashed through your gym."

Mason's mouth opened and closed a few times, as if she were trying to figure out what to say to that. Finally she settled on, "Did you ever stop to think that maybe you should go to see a doctor or something?"

"Sure. But there's probably a wait list. I figure the local emergency ward deals with naked amnesiac monster slayers pretty much every Saturday night."

"You're serious." Her eyes narrowed. "This isn't some weird cover story or something, is it? You're not, like, some kind of bodyguard or something my dad hired to keep an eye on me, are you?"

"Who's your dad?"

"The guy whose really expensive stained glass window you helped destroy."

"Ah." Fennrys winced a bit at the memory. "Wouldn't a guy like that have enough money to hire a guy with pants if that was the case? And maybe, I don't know, a machine gun instead of a sword?"

Mason crossed her arms over her chest. "I guess you're right."

"I wasn't hired by your father, Mason." He held out the bag, like some kind of peace offering or something.

Mason eyed it suspiciously. Then she reached out, her body language clearly conveying that she thought it was most likely filled with scorpions or incendiaries. When its contents didn't immediately leap out and attack her or explode, she looked at him and nodded once.

"Okay," she said. "Thanks. I don't think my brother cares about the sweats, but Toby was pretty pissed about the boots. . . ."

Silence stretched out between them. Fennrys didn't know what else to say.

Mason shook her head and started to turn away. "Well, good night then, man of mystery—"

"Mason." He stopped her with a look. "When I said that I don't know who I am or anything about my life, I *really* wasn't joking." He reached out toward her but stopped himself from actually touching her. "And I wasn't lying."

Fennrys's arm dropped back down to his side and he stood there, waiting and feeling very nearly helpless. If Mason turned around and went back inside, if she left him standing there, he didn't know what he would do. He wouldn't come to her again. He felt his heart beating loudly in his chest, but his breath was stopped in his throat. Mason's whole body was tense, poised for flight.

"That's . . . I'm sorry." Her fingers knotted in the strings of the shopping bag. "That must be horrible. It's just . . . so hard to believe." She put up a hand to stop his protests. "No, I *do* believe you. I think." Her words came haltingly as she tried to mentally work through what he'd told her. "It's just . . . I mean . . . I've heard of that kind of thing happening in movies. On TV and stuff. I didn't think it was really real."

"I wish it wasn't."

"So where have you been these last couple of days?"

"Oh . . . I'm staying in a hotel."

"Really." Mason raised an eyebrow at him. "How . . . I mean . . . I didn't think you were carrying a wallet when I first saw you."

"Yeah. Um. I kind of owe your brother." Fennrys grimaced and rubbed at the back of his neck. "Either he's selling hot electronics out of the back of a van or he's got a hell of a paper route, but I found almost two thousand bucks in the pocket of his hoodie."

"Ha!" Mason's laugh rang out into the night, and it made Fenn's heart leap a little to hear it.

"I mean—I'll pay him back," he said. "I'm good for it. You know. Someday. Probably . . ."

"Don't worry about it." She grinned. "Finders keepers, I say, and serves him right! I'm sure he probably pinched that bankroll from my dad or something anyway."

"Well. It'll be gone soon enough." Fenn sighed. "Manhattan's expensive."

Mason stopped smiling and looked at him. "What are you going to do then?"

He smiled slightly and shrugged. He didn't know. At the moment, it didn't matter. He would be content if he could just stand there staring at the girl in front of him, who actually seemed like she might just care what happened to him.

XIV

Mason stood on the sidewalk in the middle of the night, staring up at a guy she'd already seen naked but knew absolutely nothing about. She realized that this was the strangest possible situation, and she was perfectly aware of the fact that what she should do would be to thank him for returning Rory and Toby's property, wish him a pleasant rest of his life, and turn around and get the hell out of there.

Instead she looped the strings of the shopping bag over her shoulder and said, "Do you want to talk about it?"

The fleeting look of stark vulnerability—and gratitude— that crossed his face in the second before he was able to compose himself back to his guarded repose was all she needed to tell her she'd said the right thing.

"Come on," Mason said, and turned to head north up the street. "I know where we can go."

Mason led Fennrys north up Claremont Avenue and

turned left on West 122nd Street. She thought about taking him up the stone steps into Sakura Park to sit on one of the benches there but decided that it was too secluded a place to be alone with him. He might have seemed harmless, but she had seen him in a fight, and the new clothes didn't exactly disguise his muscled frame.

They crossed Riverside Drive and walked in silence until they came to a wide, paved open space, ringed around with trees. In the center was a stoutly impressive square stone building, complete with pillars and a tall cupola. In front of the monumental structure were wide stone steps bracketed by two huge, fearsome-looking eagle statues, wings spread wide, hooked beaks gaping.

"General Grant's Tomb," Mason said. "He's in there. Him and his wife, Julia." She hugged her elbows and gazed at the tall double doors. "Sealed away in these two huge caskets, like sarcophagi. Like they were royalty or gods or something."

Fennrys shrugged as they walked toward the monument. "I suppose there are worse ways to end up," he said.

Mason turned and gave Fennrys a long, unblinking stare. "I can't think of a single one."

Fenn looked down at her.

"I have spatial boundary issues," she said drily.

"Ah."

She led him over to the wide concrete ramp that supported one of the eagles and sat down, leaning back on the statue base and looking up at the wings that swept over her as if providing shelter from a storm. The place was almost deserted when they got there, with the exception of a couple of thuggish-looking guys in feature-obscuring hoodies lurking around the far side of the terrace. And they took one look at the Fennrys Wolf and made themselves scarce. Mason smiled to herself. With Fennrys at her side, she felt absolutely safe that night. He watched the lurking guys leave and muttered something under his breath that sounded like "hobgoblins," but Mason just let that slide. She settled herself more comfortably against the sharp angles of the marble and got right down to the heart of the matter.

"Tell me," she said softly. "What *do* you remember?"

He shook his head slowly from side to side. "I know which way is east and which is west. I know how to climb stairs and cross the street. I'm pretty sure I could make a wicked Florentine omelet if I was hungry and had eggs and spinach handy. I knew what to do to help your friend who got hurt . . . even though I'm not really sure what that was."

"Oh."

"I know my name."

"It's hard to forget."

His mouth bent in a fleeting grin. And then his expression hardened. "And I know how to fight. That's all."

"That can't be everything. I mean . . . you remember everything that's happened since we met, right?

He nodded. "Yeah. I do."

"Well?" she prompted him. "Anything super interesting, or did you just wander aimlessly around the city for three days?"

She watched keenly as his expression clouded over.

"No. Nothing."

He was lying. Or maybe he didn't trust her enough to tell her yet.

"It was a beautiful old tree," he said, trying to lighten his tone. And change the subject. "The one that took out your dad's window. I feel kind of bad about that."

"It's a pretty old school. It probably had termites. It wasn't your fault." She avoided mentioning again the things whose fault it had been. Even though Fennrys had been the one to put a name to the creatures, she believed him when he said he didn't know anything else about what they were or where they'd come from.

"How long has that place been there?" Fennrys asked.

"Gosforth? Almost as long as New York has been around. I mean, it didn't always look like that, with all the impressive, imposing Old World architecture and all. It probably started out as a wood-frame schoolhouse. But the Gosforth founding families have made sure over the years that the academy's facilities maintained a certain . . . standard." She sighed. "I find it kind of obnoxious, if you want the truth. All that conspicuous affluence on constant display."

"You don't like your school?"

"It's okay. It's got good programs."

"Good friends?"

Mason shrugged. "I do fine on my own."

"Yeah. Me too."

Mason could hear the aching loneliness in his assertion. She wondered if he'd heard it in hers. In the distance, the sound of traffic on Riverside Drive was a soothing hum. There were no sirens to be heard in the distance, which was rare. The sky overhead was a deep black, broken only inter-mittently by long thin streamers of clouds, shredded by an earlier wind, that glowed sepia orange with reflected city light. It was peaceful. It was beautiful. Mason had to stop herself from leaning into Fennrys's warmth and wishing he would wrap an arm around her shoulders.

"I should go," she said. "It's getting late and I've got prac-tice first thing in the morning."

"Practice?"

"Fencing."

"Right. I almost forgot—you're pretty handy with a blade."

She shrugged and pushed a silky black ribbon of hair that had escaped her ponytail back off her face. "I'm good. I need to be better. I'm trying to make the national team."

"Will you?"

"If I don't get distracted. If my practice partner doesn't go completely AWOL on me. Both of those things are looking pretty unlikely right now."

"Who's your partner?"

She turned her head and looked at Fenn for a moment. "His name's Calum Aristarchos. He's the guy you . . . saved. Fixed. That night."

It was weird how everything could seem perfectly normal between the two of them. Like they were just two regular young people talking to each other about regular stuff, until anything to do with that night filtered down into the conver-sation.

A small crease ticked between Fenn's dark blond eyebrows. "Ah," he said. "Right. Nice-looking kid."

"Kid." Mason snorted. "You're probably the same age, you know. Or close to it." And yet she knew what he meant. They didn't seem like they were the same age. Fennrys seemed so much more . . . worldly. Like he'd seen things and done things that Mason couldn't even imagine. Even if he had no idea now what those things were.

"How is he?" Fennrys asked.

"Avoiding me."

"Sorry to hear that." He didn't really sound sorry. Mason glanced up at him, but Fenn's expression was once more a carefully composed, unreadable blank. She wished he wouldn't do that.

"You'll be okay without him," Fennrys said. "I saw you fight."

"You saw me flail around in a state of panicky idiocy." She shook her head. "I got really, *really* lucky with one blind thrust."

"It wasn't just luck. Under all that flailey panic? Trust me. You're good."

"That's what I *used* to think." Mason suddenly found herself unexpectedly almost on the verge of tears. "I used to think nothing would distract me in a fight. Nothing could break my focus. Now all I see when I fight is those . . . *things*. Coming at me. And it's like I'm paralyzed and I don't know how to even hold my blade anymore, let alone use it. I mean, I lost a bout to Kristen freaking Denholm, and she barely knows which end of a saber is which. If I lose next week, I lose my shot at making the team. I lose *everything*."

Fenn shifted slightly so that he was looking at her and a

stray breeze wafted the scent of him toward her. She could smell the leather of his jacket and the warm scent of his skin. She closed her eyes and remembered vividly, as if it was happening right in front of her that very moment, how he had looked when he'd fought to save her life. The pure, savage grace of him. The way the muscles had moved under the skin of his arms and shoulders. The fierce, focused intensity of his glacial gaze. Everyone else that had been there seemed content to forget that night. Mason didn't want to. Mostly because of the way the Fennrys Wolf had fought. For her.

You're being stupid. He was not *fighting specifically for you. And how do you know that those things weren't there because they were after him in the first place? This guy is dangerous. You hardly know him. You should go. Now, Mason.*

"Right. So. Um . . . practice. I should . . ." She grabbed the shopping bag and started to slide her legs around so she could stand, but Fenn took hold of her arm.

She glanced down at his fingers and then up at his face.

He let go of her. "Can I see you again?"

Her heart skipped a beat. And then her head intervened. "I'm seriously not sure if that's a good idea."

"I need to see you again, Mason," he said in a low, urgent voice.

"Why?"

Fennrys took a slow breath, as if to steady himself, or give himself time to think. "Well . . . for one thing, I need to get my medallion back."

Oh.

"So talk to Calum," Mason said as she stood and hitched

the straps of the shopping bag up on her shoulder.

"Mason." His voice was quiet in the night. Almost a whisper. *"Please."*

"I . . . oh . . . ," she muttered. "All right. I'll see what I can do."

"Thank you." He almost smiled. It made him look younger. Almost his age.

Mason had to look away before that smile made her want to stay there all night.

"How will I be able to contact you?" she asked.

"I'll come to you," he said. "I have very high-tech methods of communication. Just don't bump your head on the sill next time a pebble hits your window." He stood beside her. "Come on. I'll walk you home."

XV

The bandage was smaller. It no longer looked like the side of his head was wrapped in a big white mitten. And it left both eyes completely unobstructed, so Mason got slammed with the full effect of Cal's glittering green-eyed gaze when he heard her call his name in the quad and turned around. For a fraction of a moment, she found herself comparing it to Fenn's winter-storm-blue stare. But just for a fraction of a moment.

She could still see the edges of the draugr's claw marks beneath the bandage, and she tried desperately not to let her own eyes drift in that direction.

She smiled her brightest possible smile and said, "Hi, Cal . . ."

"Starling."

Starling. He used to call her *Mase.* She felt the smile falter on her face.

"What d'you want?" Calum asked in the way he might ask

one of the math geeks looking to borrow a protractor.

She almost turned and walked away right then. But then she remembered why she was there. It wasn't for her. *"Mason . . . please."* The way Fennrys had pleaded with her—the way *he'd* said her name—made her hold her ground and stay standing in front of the boy who, only a few days earlier, had made her heart beat faster when they'd sparred but now just made her want to run and hide.

"Well . . . I was still wondering if you'd help me work on my defense strategies," she said, struggling to be casual. "Toby thinks I'm kind of plateauing, and you always seem to know how to get me through that stuff."

He frowned down at her and Mason looked away, but kept on talking.

"And I know that you're not a hundred percent yet, but I thought that maybe we could help each other," she said. "You could run me through drills, and I could help you if there was any—I don't know—stretching or anything you had to do. I mean, they probably gave you some rehab exercises for your arm and stuff, right? And . . . you know . . ."

She looked up to see that he was still there. Still looking at her.

"I miss you, Calum," she said. She meant it.

The line of his mouth softened suddenly, and a tiny bit of the spark that was usually there whenever he looked at her seemed to reignite. For a moment.

And then Mason said, "And, hey. If you still have that medallion thing . . . the one Fenn gave you? You could bring it to practice, and then I could give it back to him if you wanted."

The spark in Calum's gaze flickered and died as the planes of his face went hard and sharp.

His nostrils flared and he said, "'Fenn'? Psycho Viking is now 'Fenn' to you? And—what? He's back? Sniffing around Gosforth like some kind of dog? Or is it just you he's sniffing around?"

"What? No! He came by to return Rory's stuff."

"Came by from where? When?"

"Last night—"

"Last *night*. Of course he did. Who is this guy, Mason? Do you even know? Do you care? Or are you just a raging hormone for his hot blond bod?"

"Stop it, Cal!" Mason almost shouted, her temper flaring. "What the hell's the matter with you? You wanna know who he is? He's the guy who saved your life—*that's* who he is. I think you'd be a little grateful."

"Yeah? Well, it looks to me like I don't have to be," Calum said, reaching up and under the collar of his shirt to grasp the medallion. He pulled it off with a sharp tug that snapped the braided leather thong that held it around his neck. "Looks like *Fenn* is getting everything he needs already from you."

He threw the medallion to the ground at Mason's feet and stalked off. She stood there, shaking with hurt and rage. And disbelief.

The door opened, and Heather Palmerston stood blinking at Mason in confusion. Understandable—she didn't have any of Mason's borrowed notes to return. That wasn't why Mason had sought her out. Heather tilted her head, waiting.

Mason cleared her throat and said, "Hi."

"Hey."

"Can I talk to you?"

Heather cast a glance up and down the obviously empty hallway and reluctantly stepped back and let Mason into her room. Like Mason's, it was long and narrow, with a high arched window at the opposite end and a single bed and bookshelf. Unlike Mason's, it was crammed with stuff. The bed was unmade and the armchair and the desk chair—and the desk and several of the shelves and a good portion of the floor space—were buried under piles of clothes and books and random stuff.

She threw herself onto the bed. "Have a seat. If you can find the furniture."

Mason picked her way through the room as if avoiding booby traps. She made it over to the window without incident and perched on the sill, crossing her arms and shifting uncomfortably as Heather stared at her, waiting for her to say something. Mason thought for a moment and then decided to just come right to the point. Heather seemed to appreciate directness.

"Why did you and Cal break up?" she asked.

Heather opened her mouth, and she blinked at Mason. It was obvious that question wasn't what she'd been expecting from Mason. To her credit, she closed her mouth and shrugged. "I dunno," she said. "We just did. It was time, I guess. Plus his mother's an overbearing psycho bitch."

"Really? Why do you say that?"

"Just the way she acted around me. Probably couldn't

stand Cal dating someone who was prettier than he was." She rolled her gaze over Mason. "So, y'know, *you* should be okay there."

"Thanks."

"I'm kidding. Well, not really. I mean . . ." She shrugged again.

Mason shook her head and smiled wanly. The way Heather said it, there really wasn't an excess of ego involved. And she had to agree—Heather was, essentially, flawless. Much prettier than she was. She was all gold and honey and warm sugary blush tones. Mason's look was like ice—black hair and winter-white skin. Someone had once told her she looked like a magpie. Mason had laughed and said a starling could kick a magpie's feathered ass out of the sky. Starlings were fighters. Except now, where Cal was concerned, Mason felt like she was punching air.

Heather looked at her in the silence and sighed. "You're prettier than Calum, Mason. Okay?"

"Everyone's prettier than Calum now," Mason said quietly. "At least, that's what he seems to think."

"Yeah . . ." Heather frowned. "I went to see him at his house on Long Island yesterday. He's going back there every day after classes instead of staying in the dorm. He's not really dealing so well."

"Are you? I mean . . . about that night."

Heather turned a flat stare on Mason and said nothing.

"Yeah." Mason nodded. "Me neither."

"Look. I'm just trying not to think about it, okay?" Heather ran a hand through her hair, which looked like it could use a good brushing. There were circles under her eyes. She was still gorgeous. "Maybe you should do the same."

Mason was quiet for a moment. Then she just came out and asked the question that had driven her to Heather's door. "Why does Cal hate me, Heather?"

"Oh, boy." She shook her head. "Are you really that thick?"

"Uh. I guess so. What am I missing?"

"Oh, nothing." Heather rolled her eyes. "Just the fact that Calum doesn't hate you. Calum is horribly in *love* with you. And if you want the *really* real truth . . . that's why we broke up."

"You have got to be kidding me," Mason felt her jaw drift open. She knew that Cal *liked* her—before the storm, at least—because he wouldn't have asked her out if he hadn't. He wasn't the kind of guy who dated girls to make an ex jealous or any of that kind of juvenile crap. So, yeah. She knew he'd liked her. But "liked" was several thousand miles away from "horribly in love." And Mason couldn't believe that *she* was the reason he'd broken up with a girl like Heather Palmerston. "C'mon, Heather, you're joking, right?"

"Wish I was. Believe me. But I'm not. Our hero, Calum Aristarchos, carries a torch held very high for Mason Starling." Heather pronounced it like she was narrating a story. Some kind of twisted fairy tale. "And it looked as though he was just starting to get her to notice that fact when there was a little incident which shall remain unspoken of. Now . . . he's damaged goods."

Mason was shocked to her core by what Heather had just

told her. "I don't care about the scars. I really don't. Do you?"

"Of course not. It's not just the scars, though. It's how he got them." Heather shook her head. "Cal thinks he's hero material. And when you needed a hero, he didn't measure up. He got his ass kicked, his face chewed up, and then not only did a screaming-hot blond mystery man show up on the scene and save you instead of him doing it—*you* had to go and save Cal from further damage. You probably should have just left him behind to get eaten by the zombies."

"I wouldn't have done that. And I think that's all a bunch of bull."

"Doesn't mean it's not true. You're Gunnar Starling's little girl, for crying out loud. That makes you, like, royalty in this town. Boy's gotta measure up to court the likes of you, highness."

Mason snorted. "Cal isn't exactly descended from a long line of paupers, you know. And how do you know this stuff, anyway? Did he . . . *tell* you he likes me?"

"I didn't say like. I said love." Heather picked at a thread on a throw cushion, frowning faintly. "And he didn't tell me. I told him. Then we broke up."

"What?" Mason gaped at her. "That's crazy! What if you were wrong?"

"I'm never wrong. It's a gift. I just know when people are in love. You want to know the real reason Calum and I broke up? Well, that's it. He wasn't in love with me, and he never will be."

"You're awfully jaded for someone with such a keen insight into the romantic inner workings of the soul."

"Why do you think that's *not* the reason I'm jaded? I see people every day who are hopeless for each other. And most of them are too stupid to do anything about it. Either that, or they're in love with the wrong person and they can't see the right person standing in front of them because, you know what? Love isn't blind. It's blind*ing*." Heather had gone from picking at the cushion's stitching to punching it, like she was trying to soften it into shape. "It turns perfectly normal, rational people into drooling brain-deads. The whole Hallmark image of the chubby little naked kid with the blindfold and arrows? Seriously. I think the *real* Cupid is probably more like some psycho juvie with dark glasses and a Taser."

Mason grinned at the mental picture. It wouldn't sell as many cards in February, but it was pretty funny.

"Anyway, don't worry about Aristarchos." Heather sighed. "He'll get over himself eventually. Or he won't. And then he'll either get with you, or you will have moved on by then. Because *you* don't know what you want. Yet. And he's not worth pining over in the meantime."

"Are you?"

"What?"

"Pining over him."

"Why would I do something like that when I just told you that it isn't worth it?" Heather answered flatly.

"Right."

Mason stood and turned to leave. Then she stopped and asked, "Hey, Heather? You say I don't know what I want yet. Does that mean you do? Do you know who I'm in love with?"

Heather looked at her as if Mason had just asked a question in a foreign language. She stared blankly at Mason for a moment and then looked away. "I . . . no. I don't know. Probably nobody. Or . . . I don't know—you haven't met them yet. Or something."

"I thought you said you could always tell."

"I can. If it's a living, breathing person, I know. I've never met anyone who hasn't been in love at least once by the time they're twelve. You're an enigma, Starling. Or, possibly, you just don't have a soul."

Heather smiled brightly as she said it, but Mason felt a chill crawl over her scalp. She swallowed a tightness in her throat.

"Go to bed, will you?" Heather waved her toward the door. "But before you do, bring me back your chem homework to copy. Payment for Heather's Advice to Lovelorn Losers."

XVI

*T*ink.

Tink.

Afternoon sunlight poured through Mason's dorm room window, even as a shower of pebbles bounced off it.

Tink.

Mason blinked and shut the textbook she'd been reading without actually seeing any of the words or absorbing the information. She rolled off her bed and went to the window, trying not to already be smiling by the time she got there.

"You could get a cell phone, you know," she called down to Fennrys, who stood in the deep blue shadows cast by the trees on what had turned out to be a cloudless day.

"Why do I need to do that?" He grinned up at her. "As far as I can tell, you're only ever in one of two places. Either in your room, or at the gym. And you're the only person I know, remember? Who else would I call?"

"Right. Either I really need to broaden my horizons . . . or you do." Mason leaned on her elbows and felt a little like Juliet leaning over her balcony, bantering back and forth with Romeo in the garden below.

Fennrys stepped out into the sunshine—and for some reason, that single act reassured Mason enormously. It was silly, she knew, but thinking about it, she'd never seen him in broad daylight before. She'd begun to think, only half jokingly, that he was some sort of creature of the night. A vampire or—no . . . more like a werewolf. But standing there in a sunbeam with his dark-gold hair glinting in the light and the paleness of his skin not quite so pronounced as the first night she'd seen him, Mason began to think that maybe he was just a regular guy after all.

Oh, he is so *not regular and you know it.* Well, no. Not regular like any of the guys she went to school with. But regular enough that she could go for a walk with him. In the daytime. In populated areas.

As she was thinking that, Fennrys cocked his head and called up to her again: "It's a beautiful day, Mason. I would like to spend it with someone, and as I said, you bear the distinction of being the only person in the world who I actually know. So it falls to you."

"Well, so long as I'm your first choice, then. . . ." She rolled her eyes and ducked her head back inside. His attempts at suave kind of fell somewhere between stilted and goofy, but it was somehow borderline charming all the same.

She had his medallion in the pocket of her jeans. She'd taken it to a shop and had it restrung on a new braided leather thong with a silver clasp and silver rings knotted throughout the leather. She'd asked the guy to polish it up too, and the iron gleamed like new, almost silvery itself. But she didn't give it back to him right away, even though she knew that was why he was there.

Because she was afraid that the minute she did that, he'd be gone.

"So . . . how've you been?" she asked, turning to wander casually down the street, as if they were just heading out for coffee or something. As if they had met under normal circumstances in the first place and this was nothing out of the ordinary.

Fenn tilted his head and walked beside Mason down the sidewalk. "I've been okay. I guess."

She waited for him to elaborate, but he didn't. Small talk was not a forte of the Fennrys Wolf, she decided. It sort of reminded her of Roth, the way he only seemed to say something when he really figured it was necessary. Maybe they'd read the same handbook on mastering the arts of the strong silent type. Whatever. Mason already knew that it worked for her brother. Roth left scores of girls pining in his wake, even though he never seemed to notice. She wondered if it was the same with Fennrys.

"Have you remembered anything else?"

"No."

"Found clues?"

"No." He frowned.

"Any idea what you'll do next?"

"No."

Mason sighed. *So much for Conversational English 101.* Fennrys seemed to notice after a moment that she'd fallen silent.

"I don't know," he muttered in a tone that fell somewhere between annoyance and frustration. With a shading of utter bewilderment that, try as he might to disguise it, was the thing that Mason heard most clearly. "It would be a hell of a lot easier to find myself if I knew where to start looking, you know?"

He looked so forlorn for a moment. Mason wished with all her heart that she could somehow help him find his way home. Suddenly, in the depths of her pocket, where her hand was clutched around the iron disk, she felt a kind of spark— like an electrical shock. Her feet stuttered to a sudden halt in the middle of the sidewalk, and she closed her eyes. An image flashed into her mind. . . .

Mason's eyes snapped open and she stifled a gasp. For a brief second, it had seemed as though she stood in the middle of a dream, complete with vivid imagery of a place she knew perfectly well she'd never been to—but seeing it had drenched her with an overwhelming sense of déjà vu. And even though the exact spot where she'd been standing had been unfamiliar, landmarks all around her hadn't been.

"I have an idea," she said, turning abruptly and taking Fenn's arm with her free hand. "I think we should explore the city together. See if anything sparks your memory."

"Sure." Fennrys lifted a shoulder and looked at her, curiosity kindling in his gaze. "What the hell. I don't start my paper route until Monday."

Mason laughed, remembering what he'd said before about Rory's ill-gotten income. "Cool." She grinned, almost tingling with excitement. "Let's grab a cab."

"Where are we going?"

"South. Down around Chelsea."

"Why there?"

Mason shrugged. She didn't want to tell Fennrys that, at the *exact* moment she'd wished she could help him find his home, she'd had a kind of . . . vision. For one thing, it would make her sound like a flake. For another, she could be totally wrong. What was even scarier was that she might be totally *right*. Either way, she needed to know. "Gotta start somewhere. And Chelsea's nice. My dad used to take me there. A new park just opened up not too long ago called the High Line, and it's kind of cool. It's built on this old elevated stretch of railway track. You'll see when we get there."

She stepped out into the street to look for a cab, but Fenn pointed to the nearby subway station at 116th Street.

"If I'm a New Yorker—and I'm not saying I *am*, but I feel like I *might* be—wouldn't I take the subway?"

"Yup," Mason agreed, "you probably would. But not with me."

"Is this a private school thing?"

She rolled an eye at him. "It's a Mason Starling thing. I told you the other night, I have spatial boundary issues."

"I don't actually know what that means," Fennrys said, frowning down at her. "And the subway entrance is right there. Couldn't we just—"

"Spatial. Boundary. Issues."

Mason flung her arm in the air and hailed a yellow cab that was weaving its way through traffic on Broadway. She opened the door as the cab pulled to a stop in front of them and rolled the window halfway down before climbing into the backseat. Then she scooted over to the opposite side and did the same to the other window as Fennrys slid in beside her and closed the door behind him. His eyebrow twitched up at her as she settled back on the seat.

"You really like your fresh air."

She crossed her arms over her chest and gazed at him defiantly. "'Spatial boundary issues' is my way of saying I don't really do enclosed spaces very well."

"I sort of noticed that about you, yeah." Fennrys shrugged. "Hey. I don't blame you. I'm all in favor of exit strategies, myself."

"Is that what you think it is?" She cocked her head and looked at him sideways, trying to figure out if he was mocking her. "You think I need to have planned escape routes around you?"

But it seemed he wasn't actually kidding. "I think maybe, yeah. It's not a bad idea," he said flatly. "And not just around me."

It was the kind of statement that effectively killed the small talk between them for the rest of the ride. Mason told the driver where to let them off once they got down to Chelsea. He pulled over to the curb, and she ran her debit card through the reader—if she was going to force him to take cabs instead of the subway, the least she could do was pay for the ride. The cab drove off, and Mason was left standing on the sidewalk in a part of town that she was only vaguely familiar with, beside a guy she was totally unfamiliar with, and wondering what the hell had gotten into her. Her normally reserved character was noticeably absent. In truth, she barely recognized herself. And the same could be said for her surroundings.

"Wow," she said, looking around at all of the cafés and shops, at galleries that had sprung up like wildflowers in the old warehouse buildings. "Every time I come down here it seems like there's another half-dozen trendy art galleries that have opened up. This place has really changed a lot."

"You're telling me. I remember when . . ." Fenn faltered to a stop and frowned at a building in the distance as if it was an affront to his sensibilities.

"What?"

"That's not possible," he said flatly.

"What isn't?"

"That apartment complex there. The big one. When do you figure it was built?"

"London Terrace?" Mason asked, following Fennrys's gaze toward the stacks of redbrick buildings with the square-turreted towers. "It's pretty well-known. It was built sometime in the 1930s. At the time, I think it was the largest of its kind in the world. Why?"

Fennrys went a bit pale. "I remember when it wasn't there."

"Fenn, that's . . ."

"Impossible. Yeah. That's what I just said." He turned to face her and his eyes flashed dangerously. As if he thought maybe she knew something about him—something she wasn't telling him—and he was angry with her. "Why did you bring me down this way?"

Mason backed off a step. It was hard sometimes to remember that she knew virtually nothing about this guy. "I don't know," she said. Mason didn't want to tell him that it was because a spooky, premonitory feeling had led her to suggest they go to that part of town, and she felt her cheeks growing hot under his stare. "I . . . I had a flash. Like an idea, I guess."

"You mean like a vision?" he asked her in all seriousness.

"More like a mental picture. I just wanted to come down to this part of town with you all of a sudden. That's all. I swear."

Fenn turned back to glare at the apartment buildings in the distance, and Mason realized that he wasn't angry. He was frightened. His fists were clenched, white-knuckled, at his sides, and the muscles of his jaw bunched as he ground his teeth together.

"Hey," Mason said gently, tugging on his arm. "C'mon. Maybe you're just having a really wicked déjà vu, you know? Or a past-life experience."

"Just what I need. I don't even have any present-life experience," he muttered. But he let her lead him on, toward the Eighteenth Street entrance stairs that would lead them up to where the High Line stretched out, a ribbon of park floating above the streets of Chelsea. The silence stretched out between the two of them until it seemed like Fennrys couldn't stand it any longer.

"So," he said finally. "You used to come here with your dad, huh?"

Mason got the feeling that he really was actually taking a stab at making conversation. She nodded. "My dad is kind of a big cheese in the shipping industry. He has a bunch of warehouses over there." She pointed toward the docks. "At least, he used to. I don't really know if he does anymore. I don't keep track of the family biz—not like he'd let me. That's Roth's job. But he used to bring me down here with him sometimes when I was really little. Before it started to get all hipsterfied. I remember when it used to be pretty rough and pretty scary."

"I remember when it used to be mud flats and ship docks and not much else . . . and . . ." Fennrys's footsteps faltered to a stop. "There was a newspaper seller on that corner. I remember . . ."

Mason watched, fascinated, as he squeezed his eyes shut in sudden, fierce concentration.

"I can see the front page of a paper in my head. From October . . . in 1912." Fenn's eyes snapped open, and he turned and gazed down the street toward the Hudson River. "They brought the survivors of the *Titanic* disaster in the *Carpathia* into the Chelsea docks and the papers were still talking about it in October. Mostly I remember this place in the fall. Does that make any sense?"

"No. Well, maybe." Mason tried to shrug nonchalantly, but a sudden chill crawled up her spine and made her scalp tingle. What she was about to say sounded stupid inside her own head, but she was going to say it anyway. "Fenn . . . maybe . . . I don't know. Do you think you might be reincarnated?"

He snorted. "No. I think I'm clinically insane and—wait."

"What?"

"This street . . ."

As Fennrys turned to peer down Eighteenth Street, Mason gasped—suddenly the medallion in her pocket felt almost like it was squirming in the palm of her hand. As if the knotted and twisting designs on the iron disk were writhing and twining around one another. She pulled it out and held it up, dangling from its new leather cord. It swung back and forth like a pendulum for a few moments, and Fennrys raised a questioning eyebrow at Mason but didn't say anything.

She felt herself blushing. "I was going to give it back to you when we got to the park—"

Suddenly the medallion's cord went taut as the iron disk swung east, pointing down the street in the direction that Fennrys had been looking. Mason tried to swing it in another direction, but the thing was stuck like a compass needle pointing to magnetic north. It almost felt as if it was tugging her in the direction in which it pointed. She let it guide her, walking a few steps forward with Fennrys following silently in her wake. Their trajectory took them under the High Line and past an anonymous, somewhat dilapidated two-story brick warehouse with a heavily padlocked front door—an anomaly in the gentrified area. As they passed the warehouse the disk swung as if on a fulcrum and pointed sharply back at the door. Mason and Fennrys exchanged a glance and then walked to the door.

Fennrys backed up a few steps and looked up at the building. It was stout and nondescript and stood beside the High

Line elevated railway, with a pull-down iron fire escape clinging to its face like a spindly deformity. It was two tall stories high with large, small-paned windows, most of which looked as if they had been either painted or bricked over from the inside. The loading door looked as if it hadn't been used in years. There was no way to see inside—not that such a thing was encouraged: there was a small, neatly lettered, black-and-white NO TRESPASSING, PRIVATE PROPERTY sign tacked up beside the door. The bricks on the facade of the building were painted a drab medium beige. All in all, it was exactly the kind of building that any normal person in New York City wouldn't have thought twice about when passing by.

Fennrys cautiously approached the door. It was thick and made of steel, and the padlock looked like something found on a medieval dungeon. Fenn reached out with a steady hand and pressed his fingers against the surface of the lock. Mason watched, holding her breath as he closed his eyes and the lines of his face went taut with concentration. A faint shadow of a frown appeared on his brow, and his mouth twitched. He tilted his head slightly as if listening to some voice only he could hear, and then he began to murmur under his breath.

Mason strained forward, trying to understand what he was saying. Only, as before, with Calum, she couldn't catch the sounds of the words. But this time, he was brief. The padlock body fell away from the U-shaped shackle with a loud *clank*. And Mason felt her mouth drop open. She started forward, but Fennrys thrust out a hand, warning her back. He moved his hand from the lock to the door itself, and Mason thought she felt a faint crackle of energy as he did so. The air in front of them seemed to waver slightly, as though his fingers had disrupted a heat mirage. Another murmured phrase, and suddenly the tension in the air in front of them loosened and dissipated. Fenn turned to look at Mason and raised an eyebrow at her expression. Then he shrugged and, stepping forward, shouldered the door open.

The inside of the building was murky. And empty. At least that was how it appeared at first glance. Deep gray shadows gathered in the corners of a huge, dusty space populated only by thick brick support pillars and, in the far corner, a slat-sided, ancient-looking freight elevator with a massive sliding grate instead of doors.

Neither of them called out "hello." It was, Mason thought, as if they both already sensed there was no one there to answer back. Fennrys rolled his shoulders, as if loosening up before a fight, and stalked across the concrete floor, Mason following in his wake. Fenn heaved up the grate—it screeched like a warning bell, and Mason wondered if they shouldn't heed it—and stepped inside. There was a big brass operating panel to one side with a lever instead of buttons and a large black toggle switch that, when Fennrys flipped it, caused an overhead incandescent bulb in a wire cage to slowly glow to reddish life. Mason swallowed nervously and, taking Fennrys's offered hand, stepped into the boxy conveyance. Instantly her claustrophobia started tearing at the edges of her self-control. She took a deep breath and squeezed Fenn's hand spasmodically as he threw the lever into the up position and the elevator cab lurched and began a slow ascent to the second floor.

★   ★   ★

What they found there was nothing short of astonishing.

As the elevator rose and the floor before them came into view, Fennrys heard Mason draw an astonished breath. For his part, he was way too freaked out to actually breathe in that moment. The lift cab shuddered to a stop, and soft, silvery-gold lighting from hidden sources grew to illuminate a sleek, stylish loftlike apartment. Hesitantly Fennrys stepped out onto the gleaming hardwood floor of a wide vestibule that sported a hall table and a large mirror in a polished ebony-wood frame that reflected his astonished expression back at him.

Mason's face bore an almost identical look as she drifted out into the main room, her fingers trailing along table edges and the back of a long leather couch.

"You live here," she said, winding her way from living to dining room.

"Your guess is as good as mine, Mase," he answered, turning in circles to take everything in.

"No." She shook her head. "I mean—you *live* here."

She stared at Fennrys from across the room, sapphire eyes gleaming in the artful illumination and a slight hectic flush to her cheeks.

He sighed gustily and said, "Okay. I live here. And apparently I have good taste. Maybe I'm a nineteen-year-old interior design wunderkind."

Mason grinned. "Maybe you are. So let's see if we can't find a business card or something here at La Maison Wolf that can confirm it."

For the better part of half an hour, they went through

drawers and cupboards and cabinets. Mason even started lifting the carefully hung abstracts away from the walls to see if she couldn't find a hidden safe or something. There was nothing.

Where were the photographs? Mementos? Personal effects? There was absolutely zilch. Clothes in the wardrobe, boots and jackets in the front hall closet. Expensive furniture with a slightly European flair. Rich, but not extravagant. All very cool and classy and utterly lacking any clues as to the person who lived there. Even the paintings that Mason was nosing around were just bleak landscapes splashed with crimson in a series of large canvases that marched across one long brick wall.

What kind of a person was he? Who had he been? There were no personal papers. No filing cabinets or bookshelves. No mail, not even a Chinese takeout flyer, and no wallet on the front hall table. No prescriptions in the bathroom cabinet. He was almost surprised when he found a toothbrush.

Fennrys closed the mirrored cabinet door and stared at his reflection.

Who are you?

What the hell was a nineteen/twenty/however-many-year-old doing with an apartment like this in downtown Manhattan? Maybe he was some kind of computer genius entrepreneur. Which might have made sense if there had been a computer anywhere in the place. He couldn't even find a phone. In fact, there was a minimum of electronics—no TV or stereo, not even a microwave in the kitchen. And while Fennrys had the sense that he knew *of* such things, he also suspected that he was perfectly comfortable not having them in his home. And Mason was right. This was, he knew instinctively and beyond a shadow of a doubt, his home.

Or at least, *a* home.

He wandered back out into the main living space and stood between two brick support pillars. There was a metal bar suspended between them a foot and a half above head height. He reached up and wrapped his hands around it, and the metal felt cool and familiar against the palms of his hands and he knew what it was there for. A chin-up bar.

Fenn pulled up his feet and swung his legs back and forth, launching himself into a leap and landing in a casual crouch in front of the cold, dead fireplace. Something caught at his gaze, and his eyes narrowed. There was a spot, no more than a hand's-breadth wide, on the wooden mantel where the sheen of the varnish was slightly dulled. He wouldn't have noticed from any other angle. Fenn stood up and walked over to the mantel. He placed his hand on the worn patch and pushed.

There was a whisper of sound from over his shoulder, and Fenn turned to see what he'd thought had been a decorative black-glass wall turn suddenly transparent as lights on the other side began to glow. He sucked in a breath as one panel shifted and rolled aside on a hidden track, revealing a shallow floor-to-ceiling storage cabinet that was full of . . . something really quite unexpected.

"Well. It all makes sense now," Fennrys murmured to himself, stunned by what he'd found. "I'm a ninja."

XVII

Calum Aristarchos stood in the back corner of the Rockefeller Center elevator cab as it ascended swiftly to his destination floor, high above the streets of Manhattan. When the doors slid open, there was a lovely young woman there to meet him. She wore a curve-hugging white tunic dress with a draped neckline that scooped low in both back and front, and her hair was piled in an artful cascade of ringlets on top of her head. She didn't speak, just led him down a corridor decorated with an impressive collection of paintings that any museum in the world would have killed for. Cal had been there often enough to no longer be impressed.

At the end of the corridor, a set of glass doors opened up into an expansive boardroom that offered a staggering view of the Empire State Building and a large swath of downtown Manhattan. Sitting in a thronelike leather executive chair, behind a desk carved from a single slab of giant redwood, sat

Daria Aristarchos, Cal's mother. She regarded him coolly over the tops of her steepled, immaculately manicured fingers for a brief moment before her face broke into a maternal smile.

"Come in, darling," she said in a low, musical voice, rising to walk around from behind her fortresslike desk. Cal stood patiently as his elegant mother embraced him. And then as she pushed him to arm's length and examined his face. He tried not to flinch as her gaze narrowed, raking over the scars on his face. It felt almost as if his flesh was being sliced open all over again. His mother's lips disappeared in a tight line, and he saw a fierce swell of emotion gathering behind her eyes. She opened her mouth, but before she could say anything, the sound of biker boots rang out over the granite floor behind him.

Cal turned to see the same young woman who'd escorted him down the hall leading the way for—of all people—Roth Starling. He was flanked by two burly guys in full bike leathers, who stopped just inside the entrance to the office and took up sentrylike positions as Roth continued on, stopping once he had reached the center of the room.

"Calum," Daria said, glancing in Roth's direction, "sit down, dear. We have a great deal to talk about."

"With him?" Cal gestured at Mason's brother. "I don't even know him."

"You know my sister," Roth said in a deep voice that sounded almost like the warning growl of an animal. "You were with her in the gym during the storm."

His gaze flicked to Cal's scars, and Cal struggled against a sudden surge of temper. He didn't have the faintest idea what was going on. But he knew he didn't like it.

"So?" Cal glanced nervously back and forth between his mother and Roth Starling. His first fear was that someone had spilled the actual details about what had really happened that night. Probably that little weasel Rory. And now Cal was about to get the third degree about the state of his mental health or the inappropriateness of such a ridiculous prank. Probably a tiresome lecture about not tarnishing the reputation of good old Gosforth Academy. That was what Cal was expecting. He certainly wasn't expecting them to believe such a wild story.

And he sure as hell wasn't expecting an even wilder one in return.

For a moment, though, as Roth Starling approached Cal's mother, it seemed as if they had forgotten Cal was even there. Unspoken tension crackled between them, and Cal's mother, who was tall to begin with, pulled herself up to her full height.

"The peace has been broken," Daria said finally, her tone accusatory and weirdly formal. "Gunnar Starling has broken it."

Roth shook his head. "You don't know that—"

"The draugr are certainly not in the demesne of *my* house." Daria scoffed.

"My father didn't send draugr to attack his own daughter," Roth countered.

"Gunnar's daughter seems to have come through the attack remarkably unscathed." Daria pointed at Cal with one sharp, polished nail. "The same cannot be said of my son."

Cal stepped forward. "Mom—"

"Be *quiet*, Calum!"

"We are on the same side, Daria," Roth said. "We want the same things."

"Look. I *really* hate to be a bother," Cal interjected in a sharply sarcastic voice. "But what the hell is going on here?"

"Calum—"

"*No*, Mom. Don't tell me to shut up again. I want to know what's happening, and obviously you want me to know. Otherwise you wouldn't have brought me here." Cal turned to Roth. "I was in the gym, yeah, and I know what went on. Obviously you do too, and so I guess that means we're all perfectly aware of the fact that the 'storm' was about as far from normal as a storm can get." He looked back and forth between his mother and Roth. "So can we just cut out all this cryptic BS, bring me up to speed, and deal with whatever the hell is the problem?"

Daria Aristarchos blinked at her son, looking at him for a long moment, as if seeing him for the very first time. Her hand drifted up slowly to rest on the damaged side of his face. He let her keep it there for a moment and then brushed it aside and turned to Roth.

"Well?"

"What does he know?" Roth asked Cal's mother.

"Nothing. Not the way he needs to now." She turned away, walking back to her desk, and said, "I thought it might help if I asked a mutual friend to explain the situation to him."

"Rafe?" Roth asked.

Daria nodded. "I had him wait in the boardroom." She pressed a button on an intercom. "Send in our other guest, please, Lia."

Cal stood there, waiting, trying not to lose his temper. In a few moments, a lean figure in a designer suit appeared at the far end of the hall, walking toward them with animal grace. Before the man reached the office, Roth turned to Cal.

"Do you know what Ragnarok is, Cal?" he asked in a low voice.

"No," Cal answered drily. "But I'm sure there's a cream or some pills you could get for it that would clear it right up."

The two guys who'd accompanied Roth glared at Cal balefully, as if he'd just offered up a grievous insult.

"Calum," his mom snapped. "If you can't manage to act like an adult, please at least try not to embarrass me entirely."

"I'm sorry." Cal clenched a fist so hard his knuckles popped. He turned back to Roth. "Yeah, I know what it is. It's the mythical end of the world, as foretold in Norse mythology. A kind of Viking apocalypse. They haven't changed the curriculum at Gosforth since you were there, and Comparative World Religions and Ancient Belief Systems is still a required course."

Roth's mouth quirked in a half smile. "And there's a good reason," he said. "You should know that, as far as the Gosforth founding families are concerned—of which yours is one— certain of those beliefs aren't really considered ancient."

"Why, thank you," said the man who'd just stepped in from the hall with a wide, warm grin on his handsome face.

He had a dark, honeyed complexion and wore his hair in a helmet of thin dreadlocks. To Cal, he looked a little like he might be some kind of rock star or something. "I like to think some of us have weathered the years rather well. . . ." He extended his hand to Cal. "You must be Calum. I met your father once. You look just like him."

"Lord Rafe." Daria smoothly intercepted the newcomer before he and Cal could shake hands. "Do come sit down. Can I offer you a drink?"

"Lord"? thought Cal. *What is this guy, royalty or something?*

His mother led the strange man to a chair by the window and then went to a side bar to pour him a drink from a crystal decanter. She handed it to him with a slight, graceful inclination of her head.

"You're a queen among women, Daria Aristarchos," he said, taking the glass with a smile. "Such a pity the world's about to end. Otherwise I'd be inclined to take you to dinner sometime."

Cal couldn't tell if he was joking or not. Apparently his mother couldn't either.

"You really think we are in grave danger this time?" she asked in a voice devoid of her usual icy control.

Rafe countered her question with one of his own. "You've always seemed to keep yourself well-informed, Daria. What do your sources tell you?"

The shadow of a worried frown darkened Cal's mother's brow, but she said nothing. It seemed to Cal that she was holding back, unwilling maybe to offer up any more information than she had to. It was typical of his mother—she was the kind of woman who clung tightly to every possible advantage in any given situation where she stood to gain something. The silence stretched out until finally Roth huffed in frustration and turned to Rafe.

"Why now?" he asked.

"You know that last year there was an . . . incident." Rafe raised an eyebrow at Mason's brother.

"With the Gate." Roth nodded. "Yes."

"I thought that was remedied by the Fair Folk themselves," Daria said.

"It was." Rafe sipped his drink. "But it's caused a lot of . . . for lack of a better way to put it . . . structural integrity issues. Take, for example, that storm the other night."

Cal felt as though he was standing in a room where everyone had suddenly started speaking a foreign language.

The man named Rafe seemed to recognize that, suddenly. He sighed and, in a tone that sounded almost apologetic, said to Cal, "Okay, young man. Here's the CliffsNotes version: gods and goddesses are real, realms beyond this one exist. And very few of the good citizens of New York City realize that their beloved Central Park is not, in fact, just a park. It's a gateway to another realm, the Faerie Realm—a very dangerous place also known as the Otherworld. About half a year ago, that gate was in very real danger of being blown right off its proverbial hinges. You follow me so far?"

Cal nodded, dazed. *No . . .*

"Right. Of course you don't. Anyway. Cracks have appeared in the walls between the worlds. Big ones. Big enough to let things through from the realms *beyond* the Faerie kingdoms."

"Beyond?"

"The Faerie Realm is closest to the mortal world. Beyond that lie the various realms of the gods. Olympus, Asgard, Tir Na Nog . . ."

"Oz?" Calum murmured weakly. Sarcasm was really the only mental defense he had left. His mother turned an angry glare on him, but Rafe put up a hand and laughed.

"I like this kid," he said. He leaned forward, swirling the drink in his hand, and pegged Cal with an intense, unblinking stare. "Look. Think of the Otherworld—the Faerie world—as the place that lies between *here* and *there*. Humans have always lived here. The gods, for the most part, lived there. If the gods wanted to get from there to here, they had to pass through the realm of the Fair Folk. Which meant they either had to ask very nicely—treaty with the Fae—or invade them. Both options were troublesome, but still there was coming and going." He shrugged. "Not so much now. Not anymore."

"Why not?" Cal asked, intrigued in spite of himself.

"A while back, around 1900 or so, the Faerie King decreed the worlds should be separate. The Ways should be shut. So he did just that, and as a result, the gods have been, for the most part, cut off from this world in recent times."

Cal looked back and forth from his mother to Roth and back to Rafe. "That's . . . good, right?"

Rafe shrugged. "Yes and no. Just my opinion, but I think this realm is poorer in some ways for the absence of gods and monsters walking around freely. Although it's much, *much* richer in others. Mankind is freer now than it's ever been to self-determine as a species. You can chart your own course without fear of prophecies or fate or destiny stepping in."

In the back of Cal's mind, he was vaguely aware that Rafe had said "you," not "we."

"That freedom of the mortal realm—in fact, the whole damn *fate* of the mortal realm—is in danger now," Rafe continued. "My sources tell me that the Faerie kerfuffle that caused the crack in the walls also resulted in an interesting by-product: a mortal who can walk between the worlds. Not just into the Faerie Kingdom and out again. But into the *Beyond* Realms. Into the lands of the dead." Rafe's expression turned suddenly grim, and his dark, diamond bright eyes shifted toward Roth. "And out again."

"This has something to do with my family, doesn't it?" Roth said quietly. "With my father's thwarted prophecy."

"It's not totally clear to me yet. But yeah. I think so."

"What prophecy?" Cal asked.

Roth took a deep breath and sighed it out. "My sister, Mason, was supposed to be a boy," he said.

"Which would have been a *hell* of a waste." Rafe snorted.

Cal ignored the comment, even as he felt his heartbeat increase at the mere mention of Mason Starling's name. "A boy," he said. "So what? So she turned out a girl. What's the big deal?"

Roth glanced over at Rafe before he answered. "Our father was given a prophecy that he believed meant that when his third *son* was born, the way to Ragnarok would open and the world would start down the path to its end days," he explained. "But Gunnar never had a third son. Mason was born a girl, and our mother died in childbirth. Gunnar Starling has had no more blood sons."

Cal blinked. "So . . . no apocalypse."

"There is always a way." Rafe shook his head. "With prophecies and all that crap. I have no doubt that the Norns have been handing down cryptic proclamations to generation after generation, and there's always a hitch. But there's always a work-around too. The trick is in finding it. And making it happen."

There was a sudden distant shriek from outside the window, and they all turned to see a wide-winged figure float by on an updraft. Anyone on the ground looking up might have thought it was a directionally challenged turkey vulture. But it was close enough to the office windows for even Cal to recognize the hideous creature—with the face of an ugly old woman and the body of a tatter-feathered bird—from his mythology texts.

A harpy.

In the skies over New York City.

"Great," muttered Rafe. "Carrion eaters. Harbingers of doom . . ." He tossed back the rest of his drink suddenly and stood, hurling the empty tumbler at the window in a flash of white-hot rage.

"Begone!" he roared.

The tumbler hit the glass, and Cal recoiled in shock as it burst into a ball of flame and smoke as if it had been packed with explosives. The creature outside turned its repulsive face toward the commotion and squawked in surprise before flapping away.

"We'd better figure out just exactly what the hell is going on out there." Rafe cast a dark look at Roth. "Before *your* lunatic old man gets any ideas." He turned to Daria. "And if you *do* hear anything that might be useful to yours truly, I'd suggest you think twice before keeping that information to yourself. You've got my number, Daria darling. Use it wisely."

Then he strode out of the office and down the hall.

In the silence left in his wake, Cal took a deep breath. "Okay. Let me get this straight." He pointed to Roth. "You're, like, a Viking. And that guy was . . ." He glanced after Rafe. "I have no idea what that guy was." He looked at his mother. "So our family is . . . what? Descended from the Greek gods or something?"

"Don't be arrogant." Daria glared at him. "We're servants. Not descendants. Charged with sacred duties that have been handed down from generation to generation."

Cal turned to Mason's brother. "You've known all about this since you were a kid."

Roth nodded.

Cal turned to his mother. "And Meredith?" Meredith was Cal's older sister. She'd been living in Greece for the past five years, and he sometimes forgot he even had a sibling.

"She knows. She will be my successor as the high priestess of the Elusinian mysteries."

Whatever the hell those are . . .

"And why am *I* only hearing about all of this now?"

"I wasn't sure that I would *ever* tell you," Daria said frankly. "I thought you might grow up to be too much like your father."

Cal winced. His father. He didn't even know what the man looked like. He hadn't been around when Cal had been born.

Daria laid a hand on Cal's arm. "I don't have that fear anymore. And, with the attack on the academy, I knew the time had come for you to learn about your legacy."

Cal shrugged off his mother's touch and turned back to Roth. "Does Mason know about any of this?" he asked.

"She does not." Roth crossed his arms over his chest, straining the leather of his jacket over his biceps. "Neither does Rory. And if you tell them, if you breathe a word of this to my sister . . . I'll tear your head off with my bare hands."

"That some sort of ritual Viking way of dealing with your enemies?"

"More of a personal preference. And you're not my enemy, Cal." Roth grinned slightly. "Yet."

"Enough," Daria rolled her eyes and stalked past her son to stand toe to toe with Mason's brother again. "I want you to go collect the haruspex. We need to keep her close."

Roth nodded.

"What the hell's a haruspex?" Cal asked.

"A seer. A prophetess," Daria explained. "She's very powerful and very rare. And I don't want anyone else finding her and using the information she provides us with. If we're going to win the coming war, we need every possible advantage."

Cal shuddered. *War.* His mother was actually serious about this. He briefly contemplated telling her about the creatures he'd encountered at home, in the water, but something made him keep silent. At least until the time came that he fully understood just what the hell was going on. And could use it to *his* advantage.

As soon as Roth left Daria Aristarchos's office, he gunned his Harley and headed south, weaving through traffic at breakneck speed. Gwendolyn Littlefield's penthouse unit was on the fifty-first floor of a Tribeca high-rise. It faced north and offered a view of almost the entire island of Manhattan, framed by the Hudson on one side and the East River on the other. Gwen's particular talents had ensured that she'd be set for life, even if it wasn't a life she wanted.

"Gwen?" Rothgar entered the apartment and walked across the living room. He knocked gently on the sliding glass door of the penthouse's balcony, where he could see the crumpled form of a willow-slender girl, pale and dark eyed, with choppy purple hair, curled up outside on a chaise. He opened the door and stepped outside.

"You okay?"

She sat up and smiled at him wanly. Roth nodded and silently opened his arms. Gwen stood and walked into the embrace.

After a moment, Roth led her back inside. In the kitchen, the counter surface of the island was covered with a sheet of painters' plastic drop cloth, held down at the edges with four smoldering pillar candles. Off to one side lay a thick stack of hundred-dollar bills and a razor-sharp silver knife. In the center was a rewrapped bulky square of brown butcher's paper. It never ceased to gall Roth that the Fates had chosen to make this frail, gentle girl a haruspex. That they had given her the ability to divine the future by way of staring at the insides of a sacrificed animal—and then, just for added irony, made her a devout vegetarian.

"How bad?" he asked.

"I might have to invent new words." She looked up at him, her gaze still haunted by the visions she'd seen. "Things have changed, Roth."

He nodded and said, "Get some things together. Essentials. I'm taking you to Gosforth."

"You're taking me to the place they kicked me out of?"

"The place you kept trying to run *away* from. They're going to be looking for you, Gwen—"

"So you want to march me right into the heart of the enemy's camp."

"It's the last likely place anyone'll search." Roth smiled grimly. "And it'll probably be the safest place in all of New York City in the coming days."

"How can you say that? The place was just overrun by—"

"Get your things, Gwen. *Now.*"

Roth watched as she turned and went into the bedroom. Then he fished a cell phone from the back pocket of his jeans and hit a speed-dial number. "The haruspex is gone," he said in a flat voice when Daria picked up. He paced back and forth, listening, and Gwen came back out into the living room with a bag.

"No, not taken," Roth said. "Fled. I found a space in the closet where a suitcase should be, but she left behind her toothbrush in her haste. She's on the run."

Gwen raised an eyebrow at Roth and fished in her bag for her toothbrush.

"Fear is a powerful motivator," Roth said, then listened again. "No, Daria. I don't think she's afraid of *you*. I think she's afraid of the end of the world. And the plain fact that, if she'd stayed here in her apartment, she'd see it coming from her living-room window." Without another word, he hit the hang-up button on his phone and held out a hand to Gwen. "Come on." He glanced over at the kitchen island as they made their way to the door. "I'll come back here later. And I'll clean up this mess."

XVIII

The hidden cabinet in Fennrys's apartment was full of weaponry.

Beautiful, gleaming, *deadly* weaponry.

Mason stumbled back until her shoulder hit one of the loft's support pillars, and she stepped around it, putting the stout brick column between herself and Fennrys, as if for a measure of protection. She'd come out of the kitchen to tell Fennrys that she'd come up empty of clues there too, only to find him standing in front of a wall full of shiny, pointy, extravagantly dangerous clues.

"What . . . *are* you?" she said in a voice gone dry and whispery. "Really?"

Fennrys's head snapped around and he glared at her, his pale eyes gleaming icily, reflecting the light that emanated from the cabinet. "What am I? What are *you*? You're the one who found this place."

He pointed to the medallion that still dangled on its

leather cord from Mason's fist. She'd forgotten all about it. When she brought it up in front of her face, the dark gray iron disk swung innocently back and forth, no longer seemingly possessed of a will of its own. Mason had made a silent wish that she could find Fennrys a home. And like a genie loosed from a bottle, the medallion had granted that wish. Fennrys belonged here. Mason had known it the second they'd stepped from the elevator, and Fenn's discovery had just confirmed it. It was the home of a warrior and felt like him. And Mason knew that the part of her that wasn't tense with fear liked it there. A lot.

Pushing aside her apprehension, she crossed the bare hardwood floor until she stood only a few inches away from him. Every muscle in Fenn's body was taut and ready for fight or flight.

She reached up and fastened the medallion around his neck. Her fingertips brushed the skin on his collarbones, and he closed his eyes. His nostrils flared, as if he were breathing in her scent, and Mason watched the muscles of his throat working as he swallowed convulsively. She put her hand on the iron disk and felt its raised design, cool against the warmth of his skin.

"I don't know how," she whispered. "I don't know what's happening here. But I know you're home. You belong here."

"Yeah," he murmured, and opened his eyes again, covering her hand with his. "But I wouldn't have found it without you. Thank you."

Mason could feel his chest rising and falling with each breath. The subtle vibration of the beating of his heart. She felt the counterpoint of her own heart beating almost double-time to his, and she wondered—not for the first time—what in the world she was doing. She pulled her hand out from under his and took a deep, quavering breath. Behind Fennrys, the wall of blades gleamed . . . beckoning.

There were long swords and short swords. A claymore that was almost as tall as she was, and another one with an ornate basket hilt padded with black leather. An exquisitely graceful, swept-hilt rapier hung in the middle of the collection, and the sight of it caused Mason to catch her breath. She would have pegged it as being from the early seventeenth century—if the slender, silvery blade hadn't been in such pristine condition. It had to be a replica. But then she looked closer and saw marks on the blade that indicated it was an original.

Beside her, Fenn ran a practiced eye over the array of deadly implements. Then he walked across the room to where he had set down the canvas bag he'd been carrying around all day. Mason hadn't called him on the fact that she recognized it from the Gosforth gym storage. She knew what it contained—the sword he'd used to save her life.

He took the long, broad blade out of the case and looked for an empty spot to hang it. There wasn't one.

"Looks like this is a new addition to the collection," he mused.

Mason held out her hand, and he passed it to her, hilt first, so she could take a good look at it. The blade tapered from a hand's-breadth wide to a slightly rounded point, and the edges gleamed razor-sharp. The hilt was bone or maybe ivory, wrapped in wire, with a short, curved cross guard and a heavy pommel, decorated in swirling, knotted patterns for counterweight.

"It's heavy," she said, extending her arm and holding it out parallel to the floor. "But it's beautifully balanced." She handed the sword back to him and waved a hand at the wall of weaponry. "That's quite a collection. Y'know . . ." She hesitated for a second, thinking. "I heard what Toby said to you in the storage room—about your . . . abilities."

"I know you did." His mouth twitched in his usual expression of dry amusement.

"Right." She ducked her head and turned back to the cabinet. "Well, I'm thinking . . . maybe you're like some kind of government operative or something. D'you think?"

"A government operative with a sword collection and no gun. Yeah—that sounds likely." He laughed briefly, and the blade in his hand wavered and dropped to his side. He gazed down at Mason, and the loneliness and confusion were back in his eyes. "Thank you for helping me find this place, Mason," he said. "But I still don't make any sense."

He turned back to the weapons cabinet and replaced the blade in its carrier, setting it down on the shelf below the displayed weapons. Then he frowned a little and ran his hand over the wood face of what looked like a set of shallow drawers under the weaponry.

Mason wondered if there was another trove of dangerous implements in there, but when Fennrys opened the top drawer, they both stood gaping at the contents. The drawer was sectioned off into compartments containing cash. A *lot* of cash, both American and a large amount of different types of what must have been foreign currency: silver, bronze, and even what looked like gold coins with a wide variety of unfamiliar markings. He left those alone and counted out a couple of hundred dollars in various denominations of U.S. bills. He fanned through the stack with his thumb and then glanced up at Mason, who was staring at him openmouthed.

"Are you hungry?" Fenn said, his mouth quirking up in that maddening half grin. He waved the wad of cash. "I'm buying."

The Boat Basin Café at Seventy-ninth Street was a favorite weekend hangout of some of the college crowd. Mason didn't really feel like running into anyone she knew while she was with Fennrys, but she figured it would be safe enough on a weekday. Also, she was craving open-air space, and the café had a great patio that overlooked the Hudson River and the boat docks, where rich boaters would tie up their yachts while they sat eating burgers and drinking beer.

To get to the café, you had to descend a hidden, sloping path that curved toward a round, colonnaded structure in a sunken circle with an open, coliseumlike space surrounded by arched stone breezeways. A hostess led them to a table with an umbrella and smiled brightly at Fennrys as she seated them. He nodded absently at her, and Mason suppressed a grin.

Fennrys slipped the strap of the sword case off his shoulder and leaned it against the table. Mason had asked him, when they were leaving his loft, why he was bringing it along, and he just looked at her as if she'd suddenly started speaking in tongues. Secretly she supposed she was glad he had the thing with him.

It's like this, she told herself. *If you take an umbrella with you, just in case—it won't rain.* Fennrys had brought his sword, just in case—and so, logically, they wouldn't be attacked by zombies.

So far it looked as though her theory was panning out. The day was beautiful and the weather perfect. Normal. No storm . . . no zombies. Draugr. *Whatever.* Still, Mason remembered what Fennrys had said earlier about needing to always have an exit strategy, and she found herself checking out the nearest exits.

Sunlight glinted off the surface of the water, hot and blinding bright, but the breeze coming off the Hudson River was cool and soft on Mason's face. Fennrys reached up to adjust their table's umbrella to shade her from the sun's glare. Then he sat opposite her and fidgeted silently as Mason sat with her hands in her lap, watching him with bemusement. He almost seemed nervous. As if this were some kind of date or something.

It seemed like forever until a bored-looking server with three lip rings and an overabundance of tattoos came over and grunted at them.

Fennrys barely glanced up as he said, "Bring us a couple of Blue Moons. Mason, what are you hungry for?"

She blinked at him. "Uh . . ."

The server made a huffing sound, and Fennrys looked back up at him.

"What?"

The server flicked his gaze at Mason and said, "I.D."

Fennrys's jaw muscles clenched slightly. "You don't need to see her I.D.," he said. "Just get the lady a beer."

Mason put a hand on Fennrys's arm. "It's okay. I'm not . . ." She trailed off as she realized he wasn't listening to her. Instead he was just staring at the waiter, unmoving, unblinking. He didn't seem to be breathing, but his hand drifted slowly up until he was resting his fingertips on the iron medallion at his throat. His arctic-blue gaze was sharp as the edge of a finely honed blade, and Mason was glad she wasn't on the receiving end of it.

The waiter looked as though he was about to get really pissy. But then, as Fenn continued to stare at him, an expression of confusion washed over the guy's face. He frowned faintly and shook his head. Then he mumbled, "Couple a Moons. Yeah. Sure . . ." And turned and wandered off.

Fennrys turned back to Mason.

"What was *that* all about?"

He blinked at her. "What?"

"Did you, like . . . hypnotize that guy?"

"Of course not." He didn't sound as though he was so sure of that. He frowned. "I just . . . I just ordered."

He hadn't *just* ordered. He'd done something, and had made the waiter do what he'd wanted. Like magic or something.

After a few short minutes, the waiter came back and set down two glasses full of pale gold liquid garnished with round slices of orange. Mason just looked at hers as Fennrys took a long pull from his and stared toward the New Jersey side of the river. The lightness of his mood earlier was gone, and he was back to inhabiting the persona of the Fennrys Wolf.

Mason didn't really want the beer. But she took a sip, if only because Fennrys really seemed to be trying hard to be nice to her. Or something. Like he was desperate to be chivalrous but just didn't quite know how. It was actually kind of endearing, if she was going to be honest with herself.

"It's . . . good," she said, nodding at the beer she'd set back down. "Thanks."

Fennrys sighed. "You don't have to patronize me, Mase. It's okay."

"I'm not. I . . . ." She paused and frowned, not knowing what to say. It was so frustrating. She'd thought about spending time alone with the mysterious Fennrys Wolf ever since he'd disappeared into the storm, and now here she was and there was all this weirdness between them. She took another sip of the beer. It wasn't bad. The orange slice perched on the side of the glass gave it a sweet flavor that softened the bite of the alcohol.

"I'm not," she said again, and waited until he looked back at her. "You're the last person I would ever even think of patronizing. I'm just . . . I don't know. Confused, I guess."

"By what?"

"You."

He laughed a little and spread his hands, leaning back in his chair. "I'm a pretty simple guy. What you see is what you get . . . 'cause that's all there is."

She smiled at him and shook her head. "All there is right

now. You can't stay a blank slate forever, Fenn. Either you'll remember who you were, or you'll become whoever you decide you want to be. That's not the confusing part."

"What is then?" he asked. "I mean, other than my rad apartment, obvious penchant for weaponry, apparent mystical gifts, and the sudden, surprising way I entered your life . . . what could possibly be confusing to you about any of this?"

Mason did laugh then. "Yeah. That. But also . . . not so much the *how* you came into my life, but the *why* you're still here." She looked, unblinking, into his face. She hadn't really meant for the conversation to go this way.

"You saved my life, Mason," he said, his voice low, gruff.

"Just returning the favor."

"You were kind to me."

"I . . ."

He ran his thumb across the marks on his wrists. "I have a feeling you might be the only one."

Mason reached out a hand and ran her fingertips lightly across the roughened skin, where old welts had turned to scar tissue and newer ones were healing over them. She felt Fennrys shiver as she touched the underside of his wrist. "I'd really like to know who did this to you," she said quietly, a slow-burning anger at the thought of him chained up like an animal building in her chest.

"I'm not so sure you do." Fennrys reached for his beer with his other hand. "Whoever they are, I don't think they play very nice."

Mason watched as emotions chased across his face. He

looked years younger suddenly, and vulnerable. And, for a moment, as though he was watching a movie only he could see.

He remembers something, she thought. *Something he doesn't want to tell me. Or doesn't want me to know. . . .*

"Do you remember where you got those?" she asked quietly.

He inhaled deeply, his chest expanding to stretch the fabric of his T-shirt. He exhaled in a gusty sigh and took another long swallow of his Blue Moon. "No." He shook his head. "But I have a delightful collection of recurring nightmares. At least I think they're nightmares. Might be memories, though. Who knows? It would be easier to tell, I suppose, if any of them made sense. But in one, I'm in a dark place. Small, like a cellar or a cave or something. I can't really see much, there are no windows, and the floor feels like dirt. The smell is . . . indescribable. Rot and dank."

Mason felt her own nose wrinkling. "You can *smell* in your dreams?"

He shrugged. "Like I said, might be a memory. I just don't know of what. But I remember . . . chains. On the wall. And a heavy door barred with iron. I think I might have spent some time there."

"It sounds horrible."

Fennrys smiled one of his awkward smiles and shook his head. "To you, yeah. You have claustrophobia. I'm sure I probably thought it was a bloody picnic."

"Sure." Mason went with him on the joke. She didn't want things to turn gloomy. "Make *me* sound like a freak, why don't you?"

"Mason . . . between the two of us, you outstrip me in the normal department by about two hundred percent." Fennrys smiled. He actually had a really great smile—when he wasn't *trying* to use it.

Mason found herself staring at him for so long that eventually he just raised an eyebrow at her. She felt herself start to blush and shifted her gaze away from Fennrys's face, turning to stare out over the river. The day was starting to cloud over. The bright blue sky had lost some of its brilliance, and the breeze off the Hudson had died to nothing. It was starting to feel cold and clammy sitting outside on the café's terrace. Mason glanced inside, trying to spot their waiter somewhere among the shadows and clusters of patrons. The grumpy server was nowhere to be seen.

"I'm sorry this is . . . weird for you," Fennrys said. "All of it."

Mason suddenly realized with a start that he was now holding her by the arm, his long fingers lightly circling the strong, lean fencer's muscles that corded her wrist. She wasn't sure if it was to reassure her or to keep her from bolting. But the warmth of his hand on her skin sent a wave of heat flowing up her arm and on toward her head and heart. It made the rest of her feel cold in comparison, and she blinked rapidly and looked away, back out over the river . . . which, she noticed suddenly, was rapidly disappearing beneath a pall of creeping fog.

"Oh . . . damn," she whispered. "Weird doesn't even begin to cover it, Fenn." She nodded her head significantly in the direction of the thickening fog bank.

Fennrys glanced over his shoulder in the direction she was looking, and his fingers tightened sharply on her arm. Several distant, shadowy shapes were gliding silently up the river toward the boat basin.

"We should go," Fennrys said.

"I thought you might say something like that," Mason said as they both stood at the same time.

"Now." The word came out as a growl.

An eerie wail pierced the strangely dusky air, joined by another and another . . . sounding to Mason like ancient war horns. From within the heart of the murky darkness, tall, curved shapes—the heads of dragons—seemed to materialize out of the thick fog. Points of flame bloomed out over the water. One of them grew large, and suddenly a massive fire-ball slammed into the sleek white hull of a yacht moored in the basin.

Fennrys swore under his breath and stepped back, knocking over his chair as he did so. One of the patrons on the patio shrieked as the yacht burst into flames. Others seemed to have only just started to notice that the day had turned to darkness—and that there were ghost ships sailing toward them out of the heart of a demon fog. Over a chorus of startled cries, howling sounds reached Mason's ears and she went instantly ice-cold. She'd heard that sound before. *Draugr.* Only this time they weren't alone.

There were things in the sky.

And things in the water.

"What the *hell*," Mason muttered as the café's patrons started to scream in real terror. The "dragons" she'd seen gliding up the river resolved themselves into the ghostly ships with tall, curved prows in the shapes of mythic beasts. She could see warriors lining the sides of the ships, holding swords like the one Fennrys had had the first time she saw him. Only many of those weapons were broken or bent, the "men" that held them twisted and slack muscled, with round, battered shields strapped to withered forearms. The dilapidated state of them, she knew from her first encounter with the draugr, didn't make them any less dangerous.

Fennrys gestured at the apparitions. "Seriously," he said drily, his voice tight. "How often does this kind of thing happen to you?"

"Funny," Mason answered through clenched teeth. "I was going to ask you the same question."

Mason glanced over her shoulder. The crowd was pushing and shoving now, screaming, heading for the exit but moving too slowly. Mason thought of the night in the gym and what those things had done to Cal. If the draugr reached the fleeing diners, it would be a massacre. Fennrys knew it too. Mason glanced over and saw him unzipping the weapon case she'd teased him about bringing. "The only chance those people have is if I buy them some time," he said, glancing over at her. "I want you to get out of here too, Mase."

Mason's mouth went dry from fear. But she lifted her chin and said, "I'm not leaving without you."

Fenn glared at her fiercely and opened his mouth, but she cut him off before he could say anything.

"Don't," she said. "Don't even think about telling me it's for my own good. I'm not leaving, Fenn. You're going to need my help and you know it."

His nostrils flared and she saw the muscles of his jaw clench. His gaze knifed into her as he stared at her for a long, silent moment. Then he said, "Fine. You can stay. But keep behind me and don't get in my way, all right?"

"Deal," Mason said.

"I don't suppose you packed an extra—"

Wordlessly he drew a short, slender sword out of the case and handed it over.

"Right. Thanks." It fit her hand nicely and, as she gripped it, she felt a thrill tingling up her arm. But then her resolve faltered for an instant and she groped blindly for her abandoned beer and took a long, nervous swallow.

"Yeah. . . ." Fennrys plucked the plastic cup from her hand and put it back down on the table. "It's gonna take more than liquid courage to get you through the next few minutes."

Mason stood staring up at him as his eyes darkened from ice blue to the color of a stormy sea. He reached up and undid the leather rope holding his iron medallion around his neck. Murmuring under his breath, he fastened it around hers, instead.

He nodded at her, and together they turned to face the river.

Gray, tattered, square sails hung like funeral shrouds from single masts, flapping and billowing in the nonexistent breeze like the wings of the dragons. From within the heavy bank of the pea-soup fog, the flares of brilliant fireballs ignited. Behind them, a mad, panicked scramble of café patrons surged toward the exits, crowding the archway leading to the path up out of the restaurant and creating a logjam. A girl fell to her knees on the stone terrace, shrieking in terror or pain, and Mason took a half step in that direction, but Fennrys shook his head.

"Don't worry about them," he said sharply. "Don't get distracted. They'll get themselves out of here, or they won't." He jerked his head in the direction of the shapes leaping into the shallow water and advancing up the banks and swarming across the docks from the river. "But you've fought these things before, and you know they're not gonna get the chance if we don't give it to them. So concentrate. If one of those things gets past me, it'll be up to you to stop it. Nothing fancy, just go for the fast kill. All right?"

"Okay . . . okay."

"You'll be fine, Mase." Fennrys stepped in front of her and dropped into a slight crouch, bouncing lightly on the balls of his feet. "It's just like a fencing match."

"Bout. Fencing bout."

"Whatever."

Mason whipped her sword through the air, feeling the weight of it. She rolled her sword-arm shoulder and made the muscles of her face and neck relax, consciously unclenching her jaw. She sank into a modified en garde stance. Her heartbeat slowed and her breathing settled into a steady, circular rhythm. Fennrys's medallion tingled sharply against her skin. A still, silent pool welled up somewhere deep inside of her, and she saw everything with startling clarity.

And everything she saw . . . was red.

XIX

The lank gray shapes of the draugr grasped the patio railings and hauled themselves up onto the terrace, heaving aside tables and brightly colored sun umbrellas as they surged forward, milk-white eyes smoldering with mindless rage. The restaurant patrons had emptied off the patio and were scrambling to make it through the bar area, under the stone archways, and out into the round open courtyard where they could get to the spiraling path and get the hell away from the nightmares swarming up from the dark river.

Fennrys and Mason readied themselves. The odds were going to be overwhelmingly against them—at least, that's what Fennrys thought, but then he suddenly noticed that there was a thrashing in the water. The flat pewter surface of the Hudson River foamed white . . . and then reddish-black. Whatever was lurking just below the surface of the waves was actually *attacking* the advancing draugr as they dropped over the sides of the dragon boats. And that wasn't all. Huge dark shapes appeared in the skies overhead, circling on enormous wings—creatures that would repeatedly dive out of the sky to snatch up one of the fallen draugr in taloned claws and tear it limb from limb, flinging pieces of the monstrous warriors into the river, where they disappeared.

They had allies, it seemed.

The first wave of attackers hit. Teeth and claws and ragged-edged blades came at Fennrys in frenzied volleys, and he found himself parrying and slashing as if the blade in his hand was a living, breathing extension of his body.

His mind slipped effortlessly into a dark, charged place—a deep crimson-tinged reservoir of primal rage and viciously seductive whispering thoughts of mayhem and unfettered violence.

Disregarding his instructions to hang back, Mason suddenly stepped up beside Fennrys as the draugr reached him. He shouted angrily at her to get back, but she ignored him. And she more than held her own, hacking and hewing with the kind of skill that transcended raw desperation. It seemed as if she was drawing upon the same kind of pure, berserker urge to fight that Fennrys himself felt. It was as though, in those few desperate moments, Mason was possessed by a force outside herself. His sudden impulse to lend her his medallion had been right on the money, he thought. The power of the thing seemed to feed a kind of soul-deep fury in her, augmenting and unleashing it on the draugr to devastating effect. While it was enormously useful under the circumstances, a small, separate corner of Fennrys's mind sounded an alarm at that thought.

Twisted gray bodies had begun to clog the flagstones as the two of them carved out enough time and space with their blades for the bulk of the café's panicked customers to make it through the restaurant to the exit path. The terrified screams faded in Fennrys's ears, and at the same time, the draugr backed off, regrouping after their initial wave was decimated by such unexpectedly fierce opposition.

In that moment of breathing space, Fennrys turned to Mason.

"Head through the restaurant. Fall back to the courtyard," he urged her. "There's more room there to fight if they come at us again. And if they don't, then we can just keep going and get the hell out of here."

Wild-eyed and panting, Mason leaped over one of the sprawled, black-bleeding forms and ran through the maze of tumbled furniture in the restaurant, heading for an archway that led to the open-air courtyard beyond. Fennrys followed in her wake. But once they reached the coliseumlike rotunda, something happened. Fennrys saw Mason suddenly falter and fade, the berserker rage falling away as swiftly as it had come upon her. He saw her shy away from a draugr instead of pressing her attack. Her shoulders crept forward into a defensive, almost cowering, posture, and her eyes rolled wildly. She seemed to wilt right in front of him. It didn't make any sense. They were winning. What was *wrong* with her?

And then he glanced up and realized what was wrong.

A thick, heavy fog had lowered over the open circle of the café's central courtyard like an impenetrable ceiling, a smoky-black shroud that blotted out the sky. It hung like heavy velvet curtains everywhere, and the effect was disorienting, suffocating. It was suddenly impossible to tell which archway led up out of the courtyard. If they chose the wrong one, they'd be trapped and they'd never battle their way back out.

It was a neat trick—and specifically designed to target Mason's "spatial boundary" issues. It was pretty damned clear to Fennrys in that moment that someone knew a whole lot more about Mason Starling than was healthy for her. Or, at the moment, for him. Whoever was behind the attack was using Mason's fear against them.

"Aw . . . crap . . . ," Fenn muttered.

The draugr had them completely encircled.

"C'mon," Fennrys said, grabbing Mason by the hand and pulling her into the center of the rotunda. He pointed to the now-identical arches. "Which way do we go, Mase?"

"No way," she gasped.

He glanced over and saw that Mason had gone incredibly pale. The palm of her hand was clammy with cold sweat against his as he tightened his grip on her fingers.

"There's no way out! No escape! I—I don't know how to get out. Fenn . . . oh, god . . . we're trapped. . . ."

"No such thing," he snarled, and kicked a charging draugr in the chest with his heavy-soled boot, grinning savagely at the satisfying snap of the thing's sternum as he felt its ribcage cave in toward its dead, unbeating heart. "Find a way or make one, Mase," he urged her. "Use the medallion. I mean really *use* it."

It had worked for Mason before—whatever kind of power the iron disk possessed. Fennrys had to make her use it again, to find a way out of the deathtrap that had been specifically designed to prey upon her greatest fear.

"I can't. I can't . . ."

"Yes. You *can*." Fennrys turned and gripped her by the shoulders, forcing her to look into his eyes. "Make a hole in your mind, Mason. Find the escape inside of you and then make it real. Make it *happen*." He turned her back around to face the archways that were swirling with darkly sparkling sinister fog. "That's how magick works."

"I'm not—I don't . . ."

"Which one?" he said gently. "Don't worry about the path topside. Just get us to the river, sweetheart. Find a hole. Open the door and I'll follow you through, alive and kicking."

He half turned and beheaded a draugr with almost casual contempt. But that was largely show, for Mason's sake. He wasn't going to be able to keep it up much longer—his arm muscles seared with fatigue, and there were more of the gray-skinned demons pouring through the arches on all sides, lurching and shambling their way toward them. But there were friendlies in the water—at least, that's what he hoped they were—who might help them escape. It was worth a shot. Mostly because it was the only bullet they had left.

"Get us *out* of here, Mase," he whispered urgently.

The temperature was dropping precipitously, and icicles were forming on all of the arches, like sharp teeth bared in open, hungry mouths. Fennrys let go of Mason's hand, and her shoulders stiffened. But she inhaled sharply through her nostrils and turned outward, looking at each archway with an expression of fierce, arrow-sharp concentration tightening her features. Fennrys saw tiny white sparks shimmer over the surface of the iron disk at her throat. Her sapphire gaze flicked back and forth between the passageways, and suddenly, a blast of warm wind poured out of one, blowing her ebony hair back away from her face like wings on either side of her head.

"This way!"

She pointed with her sword and reached back, grabbing for Fenn's hand. Together they raced forward, plunging through the thick obscuring mist. It danced like swarms of lightning bugs along their arms and faces and they ran and suddenly they burst onto the terrace, where a fierce electrical storm raged and churned the Hudson River into a frothing white cauldron.

XX

Mason ran for the docks, where the yachts burned and the dragon-prowed ghost ships bobbed silently, emptied of their warrior crews. Her feet pounded along the weathered wooden boards, and without stopping to think about what she was doing, she threw herself off the end of the dock in a long, shallow dive that carried her into the water and under the skim of blazing yacht fuel. The world shrank to fire above and deep, icy water below. Just like one of her dreams.

She started to sink, the weight of the sword she absolutely refused to let go of dragging her down into the murky depths of the river. Her other hand clenched Fennrys's in a white-knuckle death grip, even as he thrashed and kicked, fighting against the river's swift, unyielding current. Mason was a strong swimmer, and she'd faced some heavy currents swimming in Hawaii on family vacations. But this was nothing like she'd ever felt. It was no use. It was almost as if the

Hudson River had a mind of its own—and a malicious, evil-tempered mind at that. They might have escaped the draugr, but they were now in very real danger of drowning.

Mason kicked upward with all her might, squeezing her eyes shut against the sting of the spilled fuel that mixed with the water. When she opened them again, she saw several dark shapes in the water, scaly, sinewy things with seaweed-black hair drifting on the current, hovering in a circle around her and Fenn. Mason screamed, a fan of silvery bubbles escaping her mouth and shimmying upward past her face, and a rush of white suddenly overtook the dark, nightmarish things. When Mason could see again, she found herself surrounded by nine blindingly beautiful women with pearly white hair and shimmering indigo-blue skin and emerald eyes. They were all smiling at her.

And that, Mason thought as she began to lose consciousness, the simple fact that they were smiling—*that*, on top of everything else—was just unbelievably weird.

Mason didn't know how much time had passed when she woke up to find herself on the west bank of the Hudson River, on the New Jersey side, lying on a gravelly stretch of waste ground below some kind of industrial shipping facility that looked as though it was pretty much deserted. She groaned and rolled over, retching out a gulletful of evil-tasting river water, and opened her eyes to see Fennrys crouched on his haunches a few feet away from her, regarding her with a mix of curiosity, concern, and—this hurt her a little—wariness.

"Don't look at *me* like that," she muttered acidly. "At least

I'm not a monster slayer who fell out of the middle of a thunderstorm and averted a mini zombie apocalypse."

"No," Fennrys agreed readily, "no . . . *you* just chat comfortably underwater with . . . uh . . . what exactly d'you figure those blue ladies were, anyway?"

"Goddesses, I think."

"Yeah. That's kinda what I thought too."

She sat up stiffly, wringing the foul-smelling water out of her hair, and stared out over the river. The water flowed placidly by, reflecting the light from the late afternoon sun in shades of copper and gold. She turned back to Fenn.

"How did you know?"

"Know what?"

"All that stuff you said about 'make it real in your mind and it'll become real.' You know—'that's how magic works'?" She stared at him, arms wrapped protectively around her knees. Because that was exactly what had happened back in the boat basin rotunda. She'd made a hole in her mind, just like he'd told her to, that had led out to the river. And it had. Sure, maybe it was sheer blind-luck coincidence. But she really, *really* doubted it. "Just how much *do* you remember, Fennrys?"

"Somehow I know that what you did—what I told you to do—is magick." He frowned as he said the word. "And I also know that magick, in this particular case, is spelled with a K, and it's not necessarily something you want to mess with on a regular basis."

Mason blinked at him. "With a K. Right. So . . . not magic, but magick." In her ears, it sounded exactly the same,

but in her mind, it actually felt a little different. *Weird.*
"Whichever. I don't think I could do that again."

"I hope you don't have to." Fenn pointed to the medallion
at Mason's throat. "But I think maybe you should hang on to
that. Just for a bit."

"What?" Mason looked at him. "No! You need this. You
told me you do."

"I *did* need it."

He smiled at her, and she realized that, as unused to the
gesture as he might have been, the Fennrys Wolf had a gorgeous smile.

"I needed it to bring you back to me."

Oh . . . wow . . .

"You're the only girl I know in the whole world, Mase."
He laughed a little at the expression on her face. "Be a shame
if I had to go to all the trouble of finding another one."

Just before things could tip over from suddenly awesome
to suddenly awkward, Fennrys looked away. He peeled a long
strip of river weed off the leg of his jeans and held it up in
front of his face for a moment, as if looking for clues to what
had just happened to them. But it was just a piece of weed.

He tossed it aside and, gesturing at the river, said, "So . . .
what wisdom of the ages did the synchro-swim team have to
impart to you?"

"You couldn't hear them?" Mason asked.

"Nope. Girl talk, I guess."

"Oh. Uh. Should I really be telling you, then?"

"Up to you."

Mason thought about the things the river goddesses had

told her. The sound of their voices, distorted and echoing, still reverberated weirdly through her mind. She didn't see any reason not to tell him. The words pretty obviously didn't have anything to do with Fennrys.

"They said something along the lines of 'We are the daughters of the Guardian, enemy of the Devourer,'" she said. "'We bring a message. Help you we will, for a promise and price.'" Mason shrugged. "Come to think of it, they kinda sounded like Yoda."

Fennrys frowned. "That was it?"

"No. I mean, they did help us. They got us the hell out of that swarm of . . . what were those scary black reptile things, anyway?"

"Nixxie," Fennrys said absently.

Mason blinked at him. "Which are?"

He glanced back at her and his frown deepened. "Aw, hell. I *don't* know. I just know what they're called. Go on. You were saying they helped us because—" He turned to her suddenly, visibly alarmed. "Wait. You didn't *promise* them anything did you?"

"What?" Mason was startled by his sudden intensity. "Uh . . . no. I mean. Nothing specific. Why?"

Fennrys exhaled sharply through his nose, his gaze turned inward. "I'm not sure. It's just another thing I don't know, but . . . I have a bad feeling about making promises to things like those ladies. I got the impression that they're the kind who come back to collect."

"Well, it wasn't like I said I'd do anything bad," Mason muttered, feeling a bit stupid. She'd read enough folk and fairy tales growing up to know that Fennrys was probably right. Promises were dangerous things and not to be given lightly. On the other hand, she'd been pretty sure in the moment that, if she'd refused the sea maidens, they would have swum aside and let the scaly, toothy river-lizard people—what had Fennrys called them? Nixxie?—eat her and her brave blond companion. Or, easier still, just let them drown. So, yeah. She'd made a promise. "I just promised that, if the chance ever came to me, I would . . . how did they put it? . . . 'make an end of the Devourer.'"

Fenn stared at her.

"That doesn't sound like such a bad thing, right?" she asked, suddenly seriously questioning her own judgment in the moment she'd made that promise. "I mean . . . anyone nicknamed the *Devourer* sounds pretty exceptionally kill-worthy. And it doesn't even matter. I'm a high school junior, for crying out loud, not some kind of avenging angel of death. I'm sure that the Devourer, whoever he is, is pretty safe if I'm his only threat. Don't you think?"

"I don't know, Mase. I don't think I'm going to take very much for granted in the next little while. But . . . you're probably right. And you did the right thing. If you hadn't, we'd both be dead." Fennrys plucked up a smooth, flat pebble from the rock- and rubbish-strewn shingle and tossed it up in the air a few times. "Any idea just who this Devourer might be?"

"Nope." Mason sighed. "And the goddess ladies seemed to think it wasn't all that important to fill in the blanks. Like I'd just know if I came across the guy waiting in line for a latte and a bagel at Starbucks."

Fennrys shook his head and laughed. Then, with a side-ways flick of his wrist, he tossed the rock, skipping it on the surface of the now-placid river. "You really are one very special girl, Mason Starling."

"Wow." Mason swallowed, trying to ease the knot of fear that seemed to have stuck in her throat at the thought. She tried to keep her tone light, but even she could hear the tremor in her voice. "That is *exactly* what every girl wants to hear." She pushed the wet black hair back from her face, shivering, and her teeth started to chatter even though she clenched them together hard. "In exactly *any* other circumstances than these."

Fennrys stood and crossed the three feet of distance between them, sinking down beside where Mason sat. He put his arm around her and rubbed her shoulder gently, warming her.

"I'm scared, Fenn."

"I know, Mase," he said quietly. "Would it help at all if I told you I was scared too?"

She twisted around and looked up at him. "No," she said seriously. "Not even a little bit."

"Good. 'Cause I'm not." He grinned. "Not even a little bit."

She found herself answering him back with a small smile. He hugged her tighter. She buried her face in his shoulder and wondered . . . was it just her imagination, or did his lips really brush the top of her head? No . . . there it was again. She felt every inch of her skin tingle from that point of contact on her scalp, right down to the soles of her feet.

Mason melted a little into Fenn's embrace, turning to rest her head against his broad chest so she could gaze out across the water, over the cityscape of midtown Manhattan. The boat basin docks and several yachts were on fire, but there was no longer any sign of the ghost ships or the fog bank they had ridden to shore on—only a pall of sullen smoke hanging over the oily dark flames. She wondered if the bodies of the draugr she and Fennrys had left strewn all over the café had vanished along with the boats. Just like they'd disappeared from the Gosforth gym.

Mason could hear sirens wailing, coming closer, and saw a pair of police boats blasting upriver. She hoped no one had gotten seriously hurt in the mad panic to escape the café, and she wondered how this would play out on the evening news. Had anyone managed to capture images of her swinging a sword at corpse warriors on a camera phone? She wasn't quite sure how she would explain something like that to her dad.

In the far distance, past the spiraling smoke, Mason could see a couple of birds hovering on updrafts above the city. They were huge, eagles or maybe even condors, although it was hard to tell from that distance. But then she remembered the winged shapes, blurred by speed, that she thought she'd seen attacking the draugr, and she shuddered.

The hovering birds drew her eye toward where the westering sun was reflected in the glass of New York office towers, and Mason realized with a panicked start that she had fencing practice in probably less than an hour. And, insofar as she was on the western shore of the Hudson River—in *Jersey*, for crying out loud—she'd have to sprout wings and fly, herself, if she didn't leave right that minute and try to find a cab that would take her back to the Upper West Side. She stood up so fast that she bashed the back of her skull square into Fennrys's face.

"Ow!" He clutched his nose and squeezed his eyes shut.

"Oh my god, I'm so sorry!" She reached out a hand, but then snatched it back before she did any more damage. "I truly am a danger to myself and others. . . ."

Fenn opened one eye and squinted at her. "Not that, Mason," he said, grinning his slightly mad grin. "Never that."

Mason shook her head and returned his smile, but in her mind a slender, serpentine whisper of doubt snaked through Fennrys's reassurance. She thought of Calum and his scars and wondered if she'd been the one to put him in that danger in the first place. If she *was* the one who'd been the target of the monstrous attack on the gym that night—something that, in light of the attack on the café, no matter how inexplicable it might be, seemed more and more likely—then she was dangerous. And the people she cared about could get hurt because of her. In spite of what Fennrys said.

XXI

Rory reached over and switched off the TV. The news that day was all about some kind of attack on the yacht docks down on the Hudson River, and the talking heads at the news desks had all, inevitably, turned to speculating about the T word. Rory snorted. What kind of crap-assed terrorist sets fire to a bunch of tricked-out daddy's-boy sloops with stupid names like *Into the Mystic* painted on their sterns? At any rate, the excitement was over, and nobody had even shot any decent pics of the carnage with a camera phone. Manhattanites were so lame.

Maybe, he thought, Mason was fine with living there, in a boring old dorm at the academy, but Mason was a loser and never did anything all that interesting anyway. As far as Rory was concerned, it was like trading a private spa for a public pool. To say Rory Starling was jaded on the subject of the human condition was something of an understatement.

So when the opportunity came to go home, he'd jumped

at the chance. And then decided, once there, that he would extend the opportunity by pleading a wicked head cold, brought on, no doubt, by exposure to the elements during the storm. When Mason headed back to Gosforth on Monday morning, Rory bid his baby sister a faux-congested, snuffly adieu and crawled back under the crisp Egyptian cotton sheets of his king-size bed. With any luck, he could draw this out long enough to get a full week off school.

After a few token days of lying sprawled in his room, immersed in his wide selection of video games, he finally emerged and, whistling to himself, headed off to the steam room with a pilfered bottle of his dad's special reserve cognac hidden in the pocket of his plush bathrobe.

Rory knew that Top Gunn wasn't exactly overjoyed to have him home, but the place was big enough that he'd barely even seen his father, and he was content to keep it like that. Gunnar was in a particularly stormy mood anyway, these days. So Rory could spend all the time he wanted, alone, to try to sort out just exactly what the hell had happened in the gym during the storm.

The others could ignore it or forget it or sweep it under the rug as much as they wanted—Rory was perfectly happy to let them. He knew there was a reason why he'd instinctively encouraged Mason to keep her mouth shut when he'd seen which way the others were leaning. And it wasn't just because he didn't want to wind up tabloid fodder.

They didn't want to tell anyone the truth? *Good.*

That suited him just fine.

He wanted this all for himself.

He didn't even know what "this" was . . . yet. But there were strange, excited voices whispering to him in the back of his head—voices that told him *this* was what he'd been waiting for all his life. This was that beginning of something . . . extraordinary. And Rory didn't want to share it with anyone. Especially Mason.

Padding barefoot and wrapped only in a bath towel down the plushly carpeted, dark-paneled corridor and feeling pleasantly buzzed on steam heat and brandy, Rory contemplated how to spend the rest of the day. Once he'd decided, he changed into jeans and a T-shirt and, after a brief side trip to his father's unoccupied study, headed down to the enormous cellar beneath the mansion.

Back before Rory was even born, his grandfather Magnus Starling had converted the cavernous room into a space that now housed an enormous, elaborate model train set—one which had a ridiculously accurate miniature New York cityscape, with rail tracks radiating out from Grand Central Terminal and Penn Station, and included all of Manhattan and a good deal of Long Island and the Jersey Shore. It circulated real water around the sculpted islands in the East and Hudson Rivers, down into the harbor, where a little Statue of Liberty poked out of the water.

When he was a kid, Rory would sometimes disappear down there for a whole day and lose himself in the tiny cityscape, running the miniature version of the Starling private train through the secret tunnels under the city—the ones that had been built specifically for Starling family business and were largely unknown even to some of New York's public figures.

Now, thanks to Gunnar—and Magnus—there were sections of underground track that connected Westchester County and Long Island, giving Gunnar Starling easy access to the far reaches of his empire, as if he were a king.

"He *thinks* he's a bloody king," Rory muttered to himself, crouching down and crawling beneath the huge table that supported the model. There was a device that could remove all of Central Park from the middle of the cityscape so the operator could stand there, surrounded by the city on all sides as he conducted. Rory pulled the lever and the park section dropped down to slide under the table. There was a switch on the operator panel that would activate an elaborate fiber-optic system that would make the entire model glow and twinkle like the city at night. Normally, he would have turned them on, but Rory wanted the darkness. All he needed was just enough light to read by.

He sat down in the middle of the miniature city, switched on a penlight, and pulled Gunnar's old leather diary out from under his shirt. Almost instantly, something about it felt strange. For years, the diary had remained hidden away in the lockbox in Gunnar's study, untouched by anyone except Rory. But now, on the page after the last entry there was fresh ink. Rory held his breath as he read the new entry.

The Norns paid me a second visit tonight. . . .

Rory's blood turned to ice in his veins.

The storm. It was an omen, as I suspected . . . but more than

that. Both a portent, and a portal. The ways are open again.
And my long-dead dream of Ragnarok is revived.
The Fates had seen fit to give me a second chance.
The Norns offered me a cup from which to drink. For a price.
Like mighty Odin, I am now completely bereft of sight in one
*   eye.*
But the prophecy is now clear to me, and I see the errors that, in
my arrogance, I was blind to before.

Rory felt an unaccustomed stab of sympathy for his father. They'd taken half his eyesight! He wondered, for a moment, what that would be like. But then he shook himself out of the thought and scanned down the page. His father had rewritten the same prophecy the Norns had given him all those years ago in Copenhagen. The words themselves were unaltered. But Rory was shocked to see what a few changes in punctuation had done to the meaning of the phrases. He flipped back to the original entry.

One tree. A rainbow bird wings among the branches.
Three seeds of the apple tree, grown tall as Odin's spear is,
*   gripped in the hand of the Valkyrie.*
They shall awaken, Odin Sons, when the Devourer returns.
The hammer will fall down onto the earth to be reborn.

The newer version now read:

One tree. A rainbow. Bird wings among the branches.
Three seeds of the apple tree grown tall.

As Odin's spear is gripped in the hand of the Valkyrie,
they shall awaken Odin Sons.
When the Devourer returns, the hammer will fall down on the
earth,
to be reborn.

Perplexed, Rory read his father's explanation, which suddenly clarified things.

Mason reminds me so much, every day, of her beautiful mother.
My precious Yelena. My daughter has been my greatest joy . . .
and my most bitter disappointment. But now she is the key to
achieving my dream for the world. I can see to it that she becomes
a Valkyrie—a chooser of the slain. With the spear of Odin in
her hand, Mason will have the power to create a third Odin Son
to stand beside my own two boys. They shall be the harbingers of
Ragnarok, they will call forth the Einherjar, the dead
warriors—and they shall bring about the end of the world as it
exists now. This gray, grieving, tainted realm will be reborn in
splendor from its own ashes.
And all I need do is sacrifice my beloved daughter's soul. . . .

It hit Rory like a lightning bolt. Mason's gender wasn't the thwart he'd always thought it had been. She wasn't the roadblock to the prophecy . . . she was the *key*. At that moment, Rory heard voices—coming from the wine cellar on the far side of the train room—and he crouched down under the table and shoved the diary as far into a corner beneath the model as he could. Then he held his breath and listened.

"I can hardly believe it."

"It's true. And it's within our grasp, Rothgar," his father responded.

Rory strained to hear what they were saying, keeping painfully still so that he wouldn't make any noise. Even the voices that had been whispering in his head for days now quieted.

"The end of the world," Roth said in a voice full of wonder. And . . . fear?

"*No.*" Gunnar was adamant. "The beginning of it. Help me pick something appropriate to celebrate this occasion. We will toast our good fortune, and then I will tell you what I need you to do."

"I'll do the best I can," Roth said.

"Of course you will. You've never failed me yet, Rothgar," Gunnar said. "You've never disappointed me. I wish I could say the same of all my children."

Screw you, Pops, Rory though bitterly. But Gunnar wasn't talking about him.

"It's hardly Mason's fault she was born a girl, Dad," Roth said.

"I know. And I wouldn't trade her for the world. Well. I wouldn't trade her for *this* world. But for the chance for us—for humanity—to start over, Roth? I would trade my wealth, my children, my soul itself. It is what we were put here to do. This is our destiny. And now Mason will be given the chance to redeem the accident of her birth and make us all proud."

He's going to do it, Rory thought. *He's really going to try to make this thing happen.* And then he thought . . . *I'm going to help*. Rory stayed where he was, silent and cramped, listening as Gunnar told Roth what he had learned from the three Norns. All things Rory already knew. Still, he needed to arm himself with enough reasons for Gunnar to let him have a hand in what was to come. Because obviously his father didn't trust him in the same way as he trusted his brother. The fact that his father was down here discussing his grand schemes with Roth—and Roth *alone*—was more than proof enough of that. Rory heard the muted pop of a cork and the clinking of glasses.

"Are you going to join us?" Gunnar's voice floated down to him from very close by. "Or are you going to stay crouched there like a fox in a hole waiting for the hounds to pass by?"

Slowly Rory turned his head and looked up to see his father standing like a god looking down on him. And he was holding out a glass of champagne. Gunnar flipped a switch, and the miniature cityscape all around Rory lit up and began to glow and twinkle. Rory stood like a giant emerging in the middle of the city from the gaping hole where Central Park should be. Swallowing his fear, he reached over to take the offered libation from his father.

Unlike every other feature of the model city, the Hell Gate Bridge was not exactly accurate. Rory had noticed it almost immediately when he was a small boy and had always wondered about it. In reality, the bridge was painted a dark, almost foreboding, deep red color. But in the tiny model city, the bridge was left unpainted, the metal silvery with an iridescent sheen to it. Rory had always wondered about it but, until that moment, it had never occurred to him what that was supposed to represent.

Bifrost.

The rainbow bridge to Asgard, the home of the Norse gods.

"Your ancestors had the guiding hand in building this bridge, my boys," Gunnar mused quietly, sipping on the last of the celebratory champagne. He'd sat on a tall stool beside the city model, describing his prophetic epiphany to his sons—and the steps they had to take to bring it to fruition.

"This stretch of river was originally called Hellegat. It's Dutch. A word that could mean one of two things: 'Bright Passage' . . . or 'Gate to Hel.' That's *our* Hel, boys. The Norse Hell." Gunnar traced the contours of the arching bridge with one fingertip. "I suppose it's both, really. And it has stood there all this time, waiting for us to fulfill its purpose. There is deep magick woven into the very core of its construction. The design, the materials . . . are all very special. It is a wonder, hidden in plain sight. It's not just a bridge, it is a gateway to Asgard, a path to the realm of the gods. *But* . . ." He held up his hand. "That path can only be walked by the dead, and only in *one* direction. At least, that was the way of things until recently."

"What changed things?"

"Not what, Rothgar. Who."

Gunnar absently smoothed a finger over his left eyebrow, his gaze distant. He was silent for a long moment, and Roth and Rory exchanged a glance. Rory recalled the last entry in the diary, suddenly, and wondered if Gunnar had told Roth about his vision loss—the price he'd paid for the knowledge he shared with them now.

"*Who*, father?" Roth prompted finally.

Gunnar roused himself from his reverie and tossed back the dregs of his drink.

"He calls himself the Fennrys Wolf," Gunnar said. "And he is a gift to us from the very gods themselves."

XXII

This time, there was a pebble actually sitting on her windowsill when Mason got back from class that afternoon. It was smooth and sparkly and had a silver string tied around it attached to a note. Mason smiled to herself as she plucked up the pebble and folded open the piece of paper.

My place, tonight, 6:00. TFW.

She had to admit, Fenn's way of communicating did have a certain charm. It beat the heck out of texting. Mason turned the pebble over in her hand, thinking. She shouldn't go. She had a mountain of homework, a group tutorial she really couldn't afford to miss, and later that night an optional fencing practice that she knew perfectly well Toby would not consider optional. Not for her, not this close to the NACs. Also? The last time she'd found herself in proximity to TFW, she'd been attacked and almost killed by monsters. Again.

Really, she should just be a good girl and do what she was supposed to.

But she was feeling uncharacteristically rebellious. And she deserved a night off. Didn't she?

Regardless of whether she did or didn't, Mason knew perfectly well, just from the way her heart was beating rapidly in her chest, from the way she was arguing with herself, and from the way her eyes kept straying back to the pebble in her hand and the note, that she was not going to be a good girl.

Not this time.

"I have something for you," Fennrys said as she stepped out of the freight elevator and into his apartment. When she'd arrived at the warehouse, the front door had been left ajar and the elevator had been waiting with the gate open, ready to take her up to the second floor. Mason was still a little surprised at herself. No one knew where she was, no one knew who she was with or how to find her. She'd known Fenn for a grand total of a couple of days and had almost gotten killed on more than one occasion in his presence. And yet she'd never felt so safe in all her life.

Safe—but a bit on the breathless side, nonetheless. She tried not to fidget with her hair or outfit, half wishing she'd decided against dressing up and just gone with jeans and sneakers, like usual.

As she stepped into his apartment, she noticed that every one of the windows all down the long brick wall were open a few inches, framed by panel drapes that billowed gently, like a chorus line of ghosts.

Mason felt herself smiling. He'd opened the windows for *her*.

Neither of them had spoken as Fennrys walked her over to the part of the wide-open loft that was furnished as a dining room. There was a long wooden table, and on the table rested a dark leather case, long and narrow, tapering at one end. It was adorned with a wide silver ribbon, tied in a bow. Mason glanced back and forth from the case to Fennrys.

"Go ahead," he said quietly. "Open it."

Mason reached out a hesitant hand and tugged on one end of the ribbon. It fell away, and she undid the silver clasps on the long side of the case and flipped open the lid. Inside, resting on a bed of midnight blue velvet, was the breathtakingly elegant, swept-hilt rapier with the silvery blade that Mason had so admired on the day she and Fennrys first discovered the loft apartment. And the hidden weapons cache. Her breath caught in her throat as she saw the tag attached to it. It said:

For Mason. The only girl in my world.

She took a deep, shuddering breath and kept her face turned away from Fennrys, and she blinked at the sudden wetness on her lashes that turned the reflected light from the blade into starry spangles. "You want me to have this?" she asked softly.

She heard him chuckle behind her. "I figured as long as you keep getting yourself into situations you need to fight your way out of, you might as well look good doing it."

The gleam of light on the wire-wrapped hilt compelled her to reach out and grasp it. The sweeping lines of the guard wrapped around her hand like silver flourishes from a calligrapher's pen. She lifted the sword from its velvet bed and saw that there was a soft, midnight-black leather fencing glove underneath, alongside a cross-body, baldric-style scabbard—also black, with silver finishings and a blue jewel set in the buckle fastening. It was obviously not something that had been made for Fennrys—it was feminine and sleek and so, *so* her. She picked it up and slung the belt over her shoulder, so that the scabbard hung at her left hip, and picked up the gauntlet. She sheathed the sword just long enough to slide her right hand into the soft leather that fit her, well, like a glove.

"It's perfect," she said, drawing the blade as she walked into the center of the room, where the rug had been rolled away, and swept the blade from side to side in a circling, figure-eight motion, suddenly, utterly, unself-conscious. Mason was at her best, at her most peaceful, when she had a sword in her hand. All of her shyness and her reticence evaporated, and she was able to feel confident and powerful.

Fennrys was watching her as she moved through a series of fencing exercises. Of course she was used to a much lighter, whip-slender blade, but the principles weren't too dissimilar. After a few moments of Fenn standing there watching her with his arms crossed over his chest and a smile ticking at one corner of his mouth, he turned and slid the wall aside to reveal the weapons cupboard. He plucked a second rapier— one with a plainer, more masculine hilt—from its hanger on the wall and stalked in a half circle around Mason to stand in front of her in a loose-limbed, careless en garde.

His grin was an invitation, and Mason felt herself smiling in return. She gave him a small salute with her blade. Her breath slowed in her chest even as she felt the rush of blood to her head and the surge of adrenaline as Fennrys made a feinting dart with his blade that she parried easily and swept to the side. Her own exploratory attack, a diagonal cut aimed at his left shoulder, met with an equal lack of success. The two of them circled each other for a moment, and then Mason went in for a low, running sideswipe that got under Fennrys's guard and very nearly tagged his thigh right above the knee. She thought for an instant that she would have to pull the blow to avoid actually hitting him, but then his blade came down in a lightning-fast, liquid-silver circle and crashed onto hers, with enough force to make her fingers go instantly numb.

The blade flew from her hand and skittered the length of the room.

And she suddenly found herself standing with the point of Fennrys's rapier kissing the hollow at the base of her throat.

The Wolf's pale blue eyes were glittering and cold, his pupils dilated. His nostrils flared as he shifted the point of his sword slightly to one side, so that it rested on her right shoulder, almost as if he was about to knight her, and he closed the distance between them. The cool steel of the flat of the blade slid over Mason's bare skin in a chill caress, and she shivered and looked up into Fenn's face.

"I might not remember much, but I remember this. I definitely think I've done this a lot," he murmured.

"Disarm young women in your apartment?" she asked, her breath coming in shallow gasps—and not entirely because of the exertion. "Is this your idea of a date?"

Fennrys grinned down at her. "I meant fight," he said. "I think I've fought . . . a lot."

"I could have told you that when we first met. And then again at the boat basin." She smiled at him and nodded toward where her sword lay on the floor. "Now can I have my present back, please?"

He laughed in that low, dangerous-sounding way that was almost a growl and made her heart skip a beat. Then he turned and scooped up her blade from the floor and tossed it lightly through the air toward her. She caught it just under the hilt with her gloved hand.

"So." Fennrys swept his own blade through the air in front of him. "You want to have another go?"

Mason looked at him, raising an eyebrow. She thought she might have figured out what he was up to, but she asked him all the same. "Why are you doing this?"

"What?"

"All of this." She circled the tip of her sword in the air. "The fencing thing."

"It's important to you."

"And?"

"And I want to help you win at the competition next week." He took a step toward her. "I saw how upset you were after you lost that last bout. You're an amazing fighter, Mason, but I think I can help you be even better, if you'll let me. Like I said . . . I think I've done this a lot."

"I do have a coach. . . ."

"I know."

"And Calum is supposed to be mentoring me. . . ."

"But he isn't, is he?"

She shook her head silently.

"Take off your shoes," he said.

She looked down. He had a point—heels, even relatively low ones, weren't really conducive to fighting (of course, neither was the flirty little skirt she'd worn). She kicked off her shoes and stood very still as Fennrys walked around behind her and gently lifted her arms into en garde. She settled into the pose, readying herself.

"No," he said.

His voice was right in her ear. She could feel his breath lifting the stray hairs that had escaped her ponytail.

"Your fingers are too tight. Brittle. That's why I was able to disarm you so easily just now. You have to stay relaxed." He worked the edges of his fingers under hers and loosened them so that the blade rocked slightly in her grip. "Like this."

"I know how to hold a sword."

"I know you know how to *hold* one. This isn't about holding a sword. And it's not about *using* one, either. A sword isn't a tool. Not if you're doing it right," he continued in a quiet, murmuring tone. "It's an extension of your will. There is continuity and flow. This isn't about *using* a weapon. It's about *becoming* one. About making the sword a part of your hand. Your arm. Your entire body . . ."

As he spoke, Fennrys ran his own hands over the back of hers. Along the length of her arm. Across her shoulders.

Down the muscles on either side of her spine. Over her backside and the lengths of her thighs and calf muscles, all the way to the heels of her bare feet. Mason felt as though his hands had left trails of fire and ice crystals all along her skin. She struggled to keep from gasping as he knelt beside her and grasped her bare ankles in his long fingers.

"You're tense."

"I'm standing en garde. Shouldn't I be ready to fight?"

"You can't fight if you're not loose. You have no give. No room to change your mind. Relax your feet."

"How am I supposed to change my mind from my feet?"

"Your feet will know what they're supposed to do before your brain tells them. Let them. C'mon, Mase. Wiggle your toes."

He put the flats of his palms lightly on the tops of her feet, and his thumbs lightly stroked her arches. It tickled, and she had no choice but to wiggle her toes.

"Let go of your conscious control of your body," he murmured.

Mason didn't feel like she *had* any control of her body—conscious or otherwise—at the moment. She was standing there stiff as a board, wiggling her toes and breathing shallowly and rapidly. Her heart was pounding, and it felt like it had shifted from her chest into her head. She had no idea where her brain had gone to make room for it. But, yeah, her brain was definitely gone.

"Mason?" Fenn looked up at her.

"Yeah?"

"Duck."

With speed that made him almost a blur, Fennrys launched out of his crouch and whipped his own blade up in a diagonal arc toward her head. She saw it as a flash of lightning, and the air in the room went from heavy and electrically charged to vacuum light. Her own sword flashed up and across her body and parried Fenn's strike with a screech, sliding off his blade as he sprang back and swept his rapier from side to side. He backed off a step, feinted, and then ran at her, striking with blinding speed—left shoulder, right shoulder, head cut, thrust for the heart—and Mason retreated, parrying for all she was worth, not even chancing a riposte when she could have, because she knew he was expecting that.

Instead of retaliating, she allowed Fenn to chase her almost all the way back across the room and then, at the very last moment, she dropped her blade tip, beat past his guard, swooped under, and turned her rapier, hammering the flat of the blade against Fenn's flank in what was supposed to deliver a nasty sting and get him to back off. In a competition saber bout, it would have scored her a point. In this case, it got her disarmed. Again.

Fennrys spun around and reached back. He wrapped his free arm around her blade, slammed down painfully on her forearm with the pommel of his sword, and yanked the weapon from her hand. Then he advanced on her, the two swords crossed like scissor blades across Mason's breastbone.

Ice-blue eyes glittering, that maddening half smile on his face, Fennrys backed Mason across the floor until she found she could go no farther. Her shoulder blades flattened up against the rough surface of the room's long brick wall as

Fennrys leaned in toward her.

"Well?" he asked, his lips close to her ear.

She could feel his breath on her cheek, cool and steady. He wasn't even winded, while she was almost panting for breath. *Jerk . . .*

"This is against the rules," Mason said between clenched teeth.

"Yeah."

Out of the corner of her eye, she saw his grin widen and he shrugged one shoulder, as if daring her to do something about it.

"So?"

"So . . . ," she said, "you're disqualified." And brought her knee up sharply.

Fennrys flinched—not *quite* as much as she would have liked—and Mason thrust him away, ducking around to grab her blade from his fist as she went. She lunged for the middle of the room, turning to face Fennrys and expecting him to be spitting mad. But he wasn't angry. He was laughing. Doubled over in pain, teeth bared in a frightening grimace . . . and *laughing.*

"That's more like it," he said, his voice a little ragged around the edges.

Mason huffed out a breath and shook her head in disbelief. "I just canned you and you're not *mad*?"

"All's fair, sweetheart."

"This isn't love *or* war."

He raised an eyebrow at her. "I don't know which disappoints me more."

Mason felt herself going red. *Damn it.* "You said you were going to help me with my fencing. It's a *sport*."

"Right. A competition."

"Right."

"The end goal of which is to win."

"Yes."

"At all costs."

"I . . ."

"It's just war with rules." Fenn straightened up and walked toward her, limping only slightly. "You don't win a war by half-assing it. You have style and you have skill, Mase. But you don't win a war without wanting it more than anything else. You don't win if anything stands in your way. You don't win without killer instinct."

That was what Calum had told her she lacked. Mason's vision went red, and she felt her fingers tightening on the grip of the sword. She saw the corner of Fenn's mouth quirk up in that self-satisfied grin again and—just as suddenly as it had come upon her—the red mist cleared. Suddenly she knew what he was doing. Pushing her buttons. *All* of them.

And then she remembered what he had told her about tensing up. She forced herself to loosen her grip. She slowed her breathing and made herself remember all of the places on her body where Fennrys had touched her. Hand, arm, shoulder, back, leg . . . she forced herself to stand there for the seconds it took to relax all of those muscles. A tingle of heat bloomed outward from Fenn's medallion, which she still wore around her neck. Mason grinned.

And then she unleashed her killer instinct.

XXIII

Blood, a bright, blooming circle of it, seeped through his shirt.

Fennrys put his hand to his shoulder, and crimson welled up between his fingers. A single drop fell through the air—Mason's wide eyes followed it as if it was shot in slow motion. When it hit the hardwood floor, it made a small, crimson splash mark. She gasped and, as if suddenly released from a spell, dropped her sword and ran the three steps that separated her from Fennrys, who stood swaying on his feet, staring down at where she'd wounded him as if such a thing had never happened before.

"That's never happened before . . . ," he murmured.

The coldness, the damn-it-all killer instinct she'd seen in his eyes only a moment earlier, even when he was play fighting—the thing *she'd* been trying to emulate—was gone. He just stood there looking a bit confused.

"Oh, jeezus," Mason said as she dropped her sword and

rushed forward to grip him by the shoulders and help him lower himself to the floor. Her sword lay on the hardwood beside them, and the first three inches of the razor-sharp point of the blade were stained with slick, bright blood.

"Shit, shit, shit . . . ," she hissed in a panic. Mason knew that the wound was probably not life-threatening. So high up on his shoulder, she probably wouldn't have punctured his lung, and it was nowhere near his heart. Still. There was a lot of blood.

Because you just stabbed him. There's a lot of blood because you stabbed him!

She turned and ran the length of the loft toward the bathroom. "Where is your first-aid kit?" she shouted as she rifled through the linen closet and the cupboards under the sink. "Don't tell me that you have all of those weapons in this place and no freaking first-aid kit!"

"Front hall closet. Top shelf," Fenn called out, a slight breathiness to his voice. "Hey . . . I remembered that. That's a good sign, right?"

"Sure it is," she muttered as she ran from the bathroom out into the hall. "It's great. You'll probably remember everything about who you are just in time to expire from blood loss."

On the very top shelf of the front hall closet there was, indeed, a first-aid kit. An industrial-sized one. And a quick survey of the contents before she carried it over to Fennrys gave her the distinct impression that the kit was well used. *This is not the first-aid kit of someone who occasionally burns himself making an omelet or who gets the odd sliver.*

There were places sectioned off in a top tray reserved for heavy-duty bandages, the stacks of which were visibly depleted, and the large bottle of iodine was less than half full. Tubes of antibiotic cream were squeezed halfway down their length, and a spool of surgical thread was down to its last few inches.

That was disturbing enough. But the contents of a second tray, underneath the first, were even more unnerving. And perplexing. It was full of all kinds of weird stuff like dried herbs and antique-looking glass vials full of strange crystals and liquids. There were stones carved and painted with odd symbols and things wrapped in silk that she couldn't even begin to identify.

She closed the lid and hurried back to where Fenn sat looking composed and very pale, his hand still pressed to his shoulder. Mason knelt down beside him and helped him ease his arm out of his shirt sleeve. The wound was deep, but it was clean, the neat edges a testament to the sharpness of the blade. Mason cursed herself silently. She was so used to fighting with blunted blades and padded jackets. She had no business screwing around with a real weapon. She could have killed him. He could have killed her. Yet she couldn't ignore the thrill she'd experienced when they'd fought. It had been exhilarating.

"Maybe I could put a cork on the end of my blade next time we do this, okay?" she said, pressing a thick bandage pad to the still-bleeding wound, wincing when Fennrys sucked air between his teeth in pain. "I'm sorry! I'm so sorry!"

He gazed up at her, his pupils dilated so wide that his eyes were like fathomless black pools rimmed with blue ice. "You're human," he murmured, his words a little fuzzy.

"Yup. And you're delirious." Mason tore strips of tape off a roll to hold the bandage in place. She checked the back of his shoulder to make sure the blade hadn't gone all the way through and was relieved beyond measure to see that it hadn't.

"No." Fenn rolled his head from one shoulder to the other. "I mean . . . I don't think you're supposed to be able to have done that."

"What—you don't think I can fight you?"

"Oh, I think you can fight me. A lot of things can fight me. Very few of them can win."

"I'm not a thing, Fenn."

"That's why it's kind of surprising. You see?" His eyes closed. "Maybe a glaistig coulda tagged me like that back in the day—if they got real lucky. Or one of those damned Wild Hunters . . ."

"Glee-what?" Mason asked.

"Hmm?"

"You were saying something about glee-somethings and hunters."

"I was?" He blinked at her in confusion.

Mason sat back on her heels and regarded him worriedly. He sounded like he might be going into a bit of shock. "Look . . . ," she said. "Maybe I should get you to a hospital."

"Am I still bleeding?"

"Yes."

"Then I'm still alive. No hospital."

She frowned and seriously thought about calling for an ambulance in spite of his protest, but he had a point. There would be way too much to explain about the Fennrys Wolf. And his lack of identity. And his collection of scar tissue. And the fact that Mason had *stabbed* him with a sword.

"I'll be fine, Mase," he said. "Just help me up. I just need to lie down for a few minutes. Then we'll take another crack at your lessons."

Mason had given him a couple of tablets from a pill bottle labeled codeine that she'd found in the first-aid kit, and eventually the pain in his shoulder subsided to a dull throb. Once it did, Fennrys fell into a fitful, dream-ridden doze. In his dream, he was caged. Like an animal.

He wasn't the only one there.

There was someone else. He knew it, instinctively. He could feel it as if he could feel a burning stare upon him. When he closed his eyes, he could imagine the eyes that were staring at him—like two glowing embers, sullen and hungry in their glare. A wicked smile like a knife edge gleaming. He could hear whispers that sounded like lies, even though he couldn't make out the words. And, every so often, as he lay chained on the floor of his cell, Fennrys would hear distant cries of pure, unbridled agony echo through the sooty air in that same voice. . . .

And there was a woman there.

Her features were mostly hidden in the shadows cast by the deep hood of her cloak, but Fennrys could see that she had blue eyes and an expression of deep sadness on a face that was beautiful in a strong, classically sculpted way. She also had a ring of keys dangling from her slender fingers.

Suddenly, for a moment, it was as if he stood outside himself, watching. The woman spoke and he answered her, but in the dream, Fennrys couldn't hear the words either of them said. He strained to catch the sounds, but there was a fierce buzzing in his ears that just grew louder the harder he tried to hear. He saw himself nod in agreement.

Then there was the sound of a key turning in the ancient, rust-frozen lock. More clanking as the woman unlocked the manacles around his wrists and ankles. They'd been there for a long time, and the skin beneath the rough metal was tender and raw where it hadn't scabbed over. The chains fell from him with a slithering, metallic hiss as Fennrys struggled to his feet, uncaring of his nakedness, only wanting to make it out the door and onto the other side of those iron bars. He needed to get away. The floor beneath his bare feet was rough-hewn stone, sharp and chipped in places, worn smooth in others, and it sloped upward in a dark, twisting tunnel, hemmed in by jagged black rock walls that seeped moisture. The stone glistened in places with water and, in other places, with what looked like blood.

The woman who'd released him led the way swiftly and surely. She didn't hesitate as she led Fennrys through the labyrinth, although he could have sworn they were going in circles. She never wavered. It was as if she knew the place like it was her home.

In the dream, the journey seemed to take a long, long time. The woman's soft-soled boots made no sound as she walked, and the long white tunic dress she wore beneath her cloak flowed around her legs with barely a whisper.

Suddenly the passageway opened onto a rolling meadow surrounded at its perimeter by thick forest. A wide river ran through the center. The woman spun to face him. Shadowed by the deep hood she wore, her eyes were the blue of a thunderstorm over the ocean. They glittered fiercely.

"Remember," she said in a voice of steel and smoke. "Remember your promise to me."

What promise? This was important, Fenn thought. He had to remember.

"I will."

"You won't forget."

"No."

"Everything. You will do *everything* in your power."

What on earth is she talking about? he thought as he watched himself in the dream. For the life of him, he couldn't remember what the strangely familiar, startlingly intense woman wanted him to do. But he heard himself respond in a firm, sure voice.

"Yes. Everything in my power."

Everything . . .

She reached out and placed the tip of one long finger on the medallion that hung around his neck. "There is power here. I grant you what little more I can to carry with you back into the world." The iron disk grew hot . . . and then ice cold against his skin. "Now go," she said. "Cross the River Lethe. Iris will guide you."

The cloaked woman gestured to the middle of the river.

Fennrys turned back to see another figure standing there in the water, an ethereally beautiful silver-haired woman with wide white wings unfolding behind her. She stood beside a shimmering sheet of water that seemed to flow upward from the center of the river like a diamond-bright, rainbow-hued curtain. Fennrys waded out toward it. He stepped through; the rainbows shattered like glass into shards all around him, and he fell. . . .

Fenn's eyes snapped open, and he heard his own breathing loud in his ears. The air in his bedroom was cool. It was dark. And there were soft snuffling sounds coming from the leather armchair over by the window. In the shaft of moonlight that filtered through the high grid-paned window, Fenn saw a spill of midnight-black hair drifting over the armrest.

Mason.

She was still there.

That gave him an unexpectedly warm feeling in his chest. Different from the shooting pain earlier, when she had stabbed him. He struggled up into a sitting position in the bed and felt something shift on his breastbone. He reached up and realized that Mason had tied his medallion back around his neck.

"I didn't know how to make it work." Her voice was soft in the darkness.

He looked over and saw that her eyes were open. In the silver moon glow, they were a deep, enthralling sapphire. Even from the distance of the bed to the chair, he felt himself falling into the depths of that gaze.

"Sorry?"

"Your necklace. I know you used it to help Calum heal. I

didn't know how to make it work like that, but I thought maybe just wearing it again might help."

Fennrys closed his eyes and could feel the power emanating from it. He smiled a little and looked back over at Mason, who was sitting hugging her knees under a woven throw.

"Huh. Yeah. You know, it didn't even occur to me when you were running around looking for bandages and iodine. Why don't you give me a minute, okay?" His glance flicked over to the door.

Mason frowned slightly and then nodded. "Sure. Yeah, okay . . ." She got to her feet and padded over to the big sliding door that separated the bedroom from the rest of the loft. "Call me, I guess . . . um . . . if you need anything."

Mason pulled the heavy door shut behind her, trying not to stare at Fennrys lying wounded and shirtless in the bed, as she did so. Her neck was stiff from staying curled up in the chair waiting for him to wake. She was glad he had. Now she could leave. Get back to Gosforth before anyone noticed she was gone. Except she didn't want to leave. From behind the closed door, she heard the low sounds of Fenn's voice, murmuring in the same singsong way he'd done with Calum.

She contemplated leaving but didn't want to go until she was sure Fennrys would be all right by himself. Instead of standing there fidgeting, she went and gathered up the scattered supplies from the first-aid kit and packed them neatly away.

Ready and waiting for the next time I come over and stab the guy, she thought.

She went to put the kit back on the shelf in the hall closet and noticed something this time that had escaped her when she'd been frantically searching for the thing the first time. There were several similar jackets hanging in the closet. The sleeve on one of them looked as though it had been savaged by a bear. Or a lion. Or maybe a—

"Yeah."

Fenn's voice from right behind her made Mason jump. He reached around in front of her and fingered the parallel tears in the leather.

"Shame, right? It was probably my favorite jacket."

His gaze as he looked down at her was hard and sharp. It silently dared her to say what was on her mind. Mason swallowed the knot of fear in her throat and lifted her chin.

"Are you a werewolf?" she blurted out.

Fenn squeezed his eyes shut and sighed. Mason noticed his color had improved and he looked to be regaining his strength. *Terrific. All the better to kill and eat you with.*

"Mason," he said gently. "How likely do you think that is?"

"About as likely as the existence of storm zombies. And ghost ships. And river goddesses and—"

"Right. I get it." He shook his head wearily. "Touché."

He'd put a T-shirt on, thankfully, so she could at least stare at him without blushing. She would have crossed her arms defensively over her chest if he hadn't been standing so close to her. Instead she contented herself with balling her hands into fists at her sides. She tried to remember everything he'd just taught her about staying loose before a fight. But she still felt her throat closing up.

"Are you?" she asked again. "A werewolf?"

"I don't think so."

"Except you don't *know*," she said emphatically. "But . . . I don't know . . . just look at the evidence: I mean, you drink Blue Moon beer, you heal preternaturally fast—how *is* your shoulder? Are you okay now?—and your name is the Fennrys Wolf."

"I *like* Blue Moon beer, it's feeling much better, thanks, and *maybe* it's a nickname."

"Maybe it's a description." She held out the jacket sleeve as if in irrefutable proof.

"That's *my* jacket," he countered. "What—you think I attacked myself?"

"Maybe it's from when you were bitten," Mason said stubbornly. "When you were turned. Maybe—"

"Maybe, maybe, maybe!" In frustration, Fennrys slammed his hand against the wall beside her head, and Mason flinched. "Maybe you watch too many movies!"

He must have seen the fear in her eyes then, because he backed off and turned away from her, stalking across the room toward the cavernous fireplace that yawned, dark and cold like a beastly maw, at the other end of the room. He sank down in front of it and stared hard at the remains of a blackened, ash-frosted log that lay in the grate. Almost without thinking, it seemed, he reached into the pocket of his jeans and took out a Zippo cigarette lighter. Mason watched as he lit it with the flick of his thumb and then . . . *plucked* the flame from off the lighter and, with a snap of his fingers, sent the bright little teardrop of fire arcing through the air to land on the charred log. It flared and ignited a tiny blaze that grew even as she stood there watching, openmouthed.

Finally Fenn seemed to notice her silence, and he turned to glance at her over his shoulder. Silhouetted against the firelight, his profile was starkly handsome, chiseled like a marble statue. He frowned faintly when he saw how she was staring at him.

"How . . ." Mason pointed to the lighter he still held in one hand.

Fennrys glanced down at it, that familiar look of confusion sweeping across his features for a brief instant, followed by a kind of bleak despair. He tossed the lighter down in front of him, and it hit the floor with a dull clank. His elbows resting on his knees, Fenn dropped his head in his hands and murmured, "I don't know."

Mason hesitated. She should leave. There was definitely something not right about the entire situation. Something dangerous. She knew that—had known it all along. Anyone with half a brain could see that nothing about the Fennrys Wolf was normal. But seeing him there, hunched in front of a fire he'd conjured out of thin air, Mason was struck by how completely alone he looked. How vulnerable.

She walked over and knelt down in front of him. His pale blue eyes were closed, and the lines of his face were drawn and weary looking. She put her hands on his knees, and wordlessly he leaned his forehead on hers.

"I'll help you," she said quietly. "I'll help you figure this out. I promise."

Without opening his eyes, Fenn took a deep, shuddering

breath and nodded, his head still touching hers. Mason put her arms around him and, in the firelit darkness, held him close. They stayed like that for a long time. Until shafts of light from the newly risen full moon poured in through the windows, slashed into squares by the windowpanes. Cold blue light washed over them, and Fennrys took Mason's head in his hands and lifted her face toward his. He smiled at her, and it was the most beautiful smile she'd ever seen.

He leaned forward slowly, as if half expecting her to stand and bolt, and tilted his head, kissing her fully, softly, on her mouth. The kiss seemed to turn the moonlight washing over them to electricity. Mason felt the small hairs on her arms rising, and a tingling spread out from her torso down her limbs and across her closed eyelids. She breathed deeply in through her nostrils, his signature scent of warmth and spice and leather, and let herself lean into the kiss. Just as her lips were opening under the pressure of his, she felt him smile again, and he pushed her gently away a few inches. His pale blue gaze was like moonlight itself as his eyes flicked sideways toward the window.

"See?" he said, taking her hand and running her fingertips down his cheek. "Full moonrise. And I barely even need a shave."

She laughed. And it might have been a lie to say that it wasn't half in relief. She leaned in to finish the kiss they'd started, but Fennrys put a finger to her lips, a mischievous grin playing with the corners of his mouth. His glance flicked over to the spill of moonlight, and he stood, pulling her up off the floor with him.

"Come here," he said, and walked her over to the window that opened out to overlook the High Line park that ran past the warehouse, with only seven or eight feet separating the two structures. He lifted the window, grunting a bit with the effort as the old wooden frame creaked in the age-warped tracks. Then he leaped up lightly to perch on the sill in a crouch, still wearing his boots but as sure-footed as if he were barefoot.

"C'mon," he said, beckoning her to follow.

Mason retrieved her own footwear, which Fenn had made her take off what seemed like forever ago, and ducked her head under the windowsill, but stopped short when she saw that Fennrys's muscles were coiled as if he was readying to spring from his crouch.

"Fenn?" she asked warily. "What are you doing?"

He glanced over his shoulder at her, a gleam in his eye. "When you first brought me down here, before we found this place, you said it was because you wanted to walk through the park. We never did take that walk. We should do that now."

"It's after eleven. It's closed."

"Sure it is," he said. "For anyone who's not *not* a were-wolf."

He grinned. And jumped. Mason gasped and rushed forward in time to see Fennrys clear the gap between building and park, the ornate iron barrier, and the strip of landscaping beyond, to land in what—to her—looked like a bone-crunching crouch on the paved strip of park walkway. But he popped back up to standing, rolled his previously perforated shoulder, and held out his hands to her, beckoning.

"Come on, Mason. I'll catch you," he said. "I promise."

"You're *crazy*."

"And you're still here, with me, after everything that's happened. Don't tell me *I'm* the thrill seeker. You're obviously just as crazy as I am. Now c'mon. It's just a walk in the park."

It's just a death-defying leap followed by a walk in the park, Mason thought as she found herself—utterly inexplicably—climbing up to balance precariously on the window ledge as Fennrys had done. She perched there unsteadily for a long moment, looking across the gap to where he held out his arms to her. It looked like a really far leap. And a long way down. Longer if she missed. But years of spending all of her free time lunging and crouching and standing en garde had given Mason long, lean, incredibly strong leg muscles. She took a deep breath, held it, and launched herself into the moonlit night.

For an instant, it felt like she was flying. And then falling.

Then Fennrys caught her out of the sky and pulled her in against his chest and she was back on solid ground again. Well . . . sort of. Her arms were wrapped around his neck and her feet were about three inches above the ground.

"There," he whispered in her ear. "That wasn't so hard, now was it?"

The High Line lay stretched out peacefully under the night sky, a long, winding pastoral path that meandered through steel and concrete canyons.

"My dad told me all about this stretch of track when he used to bring me down to the docks as a little girl," Mason said quietly as they strolled, drinking in the view of the Hudson River. "He was always sad about the elevated track being decommissioned. Said it was a waste of a good idea. He's kind of a train nut. And by 'kind of,' I mean 'obsessively.' I guess it's a reasonable fascination to have if you're in the business of transporting stuff, but he even has his own train and private rail lines that run in tunnels all over the place under Manhattan."

Fennrys whistled low, impressed. "At least he's got the cash to support his little habit."

"Yup. He sure does."

Fennrys gestured at the trees growing on either side of them. "What does he think about this thing being turned into a park?"

"Oh, all for it. Gunnar's big into reclamation." Mason laughed. "He thinks that we humans are horrible, wasteful, wanton creatures who don't appreciate the resources we have and mostly don't deserve them."

"Sounds a little harsh."

"I dunno. . . ." Mason shrugged, running the palm of her hand over the feathery tops of a stand of wild grasses, silvery in the moonlight. "I mean, for the most part, we haven't been very wise conservators of this planet, have we?"

"In that case, I'll refrain from gathering wildflowers for you."

As they strolled along a section of the park where the walkway narrowed to a long, straight strip, Mason pointed at the path and said, "It kind of reminds me of a piste."

"Which is?"

"The mat they lay down that defines the legal area we can fight on in fencing bouts."

Fennrys stopped walking and eyed the path. "It does, huh?"

She nodded.

"Well then, I say we use it as one. Why don't you come back tomorrow and we'll do another training session, out here under the stars?"

"Aren't you a little worried I might just kill you outright next time?"

"Death holds no fear for me," he said airily, waving a dismissive hand. "I shall conquer it as I conquer all things."

"So I can just keep stabbing you, then?" She smiled brightly up at him.

"I'd actually prefer you didn't," he said. "Not for my sake, so much as my wardrobe's. You understand."

Mason punched him playfully on the shoulder, and he winced and crumpled a bit. "Oh my god!" she gasped, reaching an arm around him to help. "I'm so sorry—"

"I'm not," he growled in her ear, as his arms suddenly wrapped around her in the kind of embrace that she could have struggled in for hours without being able to break. "Good to know that you always fall for the poor wounded-warrior act. Now I know your weakness." He grinned down at her and she punched him again, although without any leverage behind the blow, because he had her forearms pinned to his broad chest.

"You're evil," she said. At least, that's what she meant to say. Only she suddenly discovered that her lips had found other employment than speech. Fenn loosened his grip on her just enough so that she could wind her arms around his neck and pull his head down closer as they kissed under the moonlight, standing in the middle of a paradise in the sky reclaimed from what had once been an abandoned bridge to nowhere.

XXIV

In all the time she'd been at Gosforth, Mason had never had to sneak into her room after lights-out. A week ago, she wouldn't even have been able to imagine the circumstances that would necessitate such a thing. Or, for that matter, how she would even go about it.

But it turned out it wasn't so very difficult. Not after Fenn had told her how to do it. Start at the end of the maintenance shed near the back of the main stone building that housed the dining hall. Go from the stacked plastic cafeteria crates to the top of the Dumpster. From the Dumpster, it was easy—for him maybe; *she'd* had to really reach—to get to the stone ledge that ran around the perimeter of the second floor of the residence. That was how he'd gotten his pebble message to her. She smiled when she thought of the lengths he'd gone to just to see her again.

Mason dropped barefoot onto the ledge, her shoes stuffed into her purse, which was slung crosswise over her torso.

She'd left the beautiful silver sword and scabbard with Fennrys, promising that she'd come back the next night to practice—hopefully with less bloodshed, but an equal or greater amount of kissing. Which had been extraordinary and made her bare toes tingle on the cold stone ledge just thinking about it. The ledge was probably close to a foot wide, and the rough stone of the wall offered enough finger grips as she catwalked toward the window that was always open. Her window. It was with a small, only slightly weary sense of accomplishment that she threw a knee over the sill and ducked inside.

When the desk lamp flicked on behind her, she almost had a heart attack.

Mason spun around and saw Heather Palmerston sitting cross-legged and elegant in one of the room's two chairs, glaring at her.

"Yon weary traveler returns," Heather drawled. "At last."

"Jeezus, Heather!" Mason gasped. "You scared me half to death."

"Just returning the favor," she said drily. "I've spent pretty much all day covering for your perky ass, y'know. I had to tell Toby you were at math tutorial, the math tutor that you were at fencing practice, your brother that you were at the bowling alley, and your other brother you were at the library."

"Bowling alley?"

"Shut up." Heather pointed to the empty chair in the room. "Sit."

Mason did as she was told.

"I was really starting to think maybe you were dead in a ditch somewhere or something. I thought they might have *gotten* you."

"What—the draugr?"

"N . . . uh, yeah. Them too." Heather blinked as if she'd been about to say something else, but then she just shook her head, glaring fiercely at Mason. "The freaking *headmaster* stopped me in the hall today and asked me if there was something up with you lately. And my mom—my *mom*—mentioned that she'd seen your dad at the club and did I know if you were behaving yourself, because apparently he seemed, and I quote, 'troubled' when your name came up."

That wasn't good. Mason was going to have to start being more careful if she wanted to keep seeing Fenn. She looked over to where Heather was still sitting, staring at her. It was obvious that she was pretty pissed. But Mason was secretly pleased—surprised as hell, but pleased—that someone like Heather Palmerston had actually gone to the mat for her.

"I don't work this hard when *I* skip class!" Heather huffed.

"Heather?"

"What?"

"Thanks."

"You're welcome." Her eyes glittered fiercely in the lamplight. "And all I can say is, it better have been worth it."

Mason couldn't stop the grin she could feel spreading across her face. It had been *so* worth it, she thought, remembering the kissing and the moonlight—and conveniently mentally editing out the stabbing part. After a moment of silence, Heather lobbed a throw cushion at her head.

"Spill it!" Heather yelped suddenly, bounding over from the chair to the bed, where she grabbed another cushion, hugged it, and leaned forward with an expression of anticipation that was just short of salacious. "Details! All of 'em! I know you were with super-bad hot blond. What *happened*?"

Mason was shocked to her core to witness the transformation of ice queen Heather Palmerston into—apparently—Mason's gossip-hungry BFF. But she didn't sense anything the least bit insincere about it. After all, Heather had spent all day blowing smoke on Mason's behalf when she could have just ratted her out and the hell with it. Slowly it dawned on Mason that the girl she'd always thought of as the singular creature at the top of the Gosforth food chain might very well be just as lonely and friend starved as Mason herself was. But as she looked at where Heather sat staring at her expectantly, she decided it wasn't worth risking the moment of connection by psychoanalyzing the situation. Instead, she grabbed the pillow off the floor that Heather had thrown at her and flopped down on the end of the bed, facing the other girl.

She told her everything that had happened with Fennrys, including the incident at the Boat Basin Café and all that had occurred over the last few hours. Up to and including burying three inches of cold steel in Fenn's shoulder muscle.

"Ohmigod, you *stabbed* him?"

"I didn't mean to—"

"No! I *totally* would have done that too!" Heather shook her head enthusiastically. "What a great way to get his shirt off. And then you could totally be all 'oh, baby, does it hurt?' and sexy-nurse his hot blond hotness." She leered wickedly.

Mason stifled a laugh and smacked her with a pillow. "You're such a perv."

"Like you weren't all breathless and fluttery when it happened."

"More like panicking and fainty. There was a *lot* of blood." Mason shook her head. "But . . . then he used that medallion thing—like he did with Cal in the storage room—and healed himself. Almost good as new. Although I'm guessing he'll carry around another pretty impressive scar to go with all the other ones."

"Yeah. I remember those," Heather said.

"I figured." Mason snorted. "I thought you were trying to commit them all to memory, the way you were staring at him."

"It's how I cope with unmitigated terror." Heather shrugged. "I still wonder where he got them, though." She leaned back against the wall and cast a sideways glance at Mason. "He doesn't remember *any*thing?"

Mason shook her head. "Not really."

"Wow. That's weird, Starling."

"No, Heather. What's weird is that he appeared in the middle of a storm and saved us from monsters," Mason said drily. "*That* was weird. Everything else that's happened since then? I'm just kinda going with it."

"Have you kissed him yet?"

"Heather!"

"Are you gonna kiss him again?"

Mason felt herself blushing a deep crimson. But she smiled at Heather and said, "Every single chance I get."

* * *

Just outside Mason's room, Rory felt the skin on his hand and arm go from fever warm to ice-cold as he lifted his fingertips away from the polished wooden surface of the door. The instant he did so, the voices of the two girls on the other side became muffled and indistinct once again. He opened his other hand and glanced down at the tiny golden acorn in his palm. The bright glow of the rune carved on its surface dimmed as he watched, and Rory pocketed it.

He hated using the precious store of stolen magicks unless it was something important or—as in the case of the performance-enhancing charms he'd crafted and supplied to Taggert Overlea and some of the other guys on the varsity football team—*extremely* profitable. But when he'd passed by his sister's dorm room, shortcutting to the kitchen to pilfer an after-hours snack, and heard voices coming from behind her door, Rory had acted on a hunch.

After all, eavesdropping had always served him well in the past.

Drawing a tiny bit of magick from the rune-inscribed acorn, he'd augmented his own senses and *listened* . . . and every word that passed between Mason and Heather had come to him through the thick oak door with crystal clarity. His hunch had proved to be a damned good one.

Shaking the tingling chill from his hand, Rory turned on his heel and ran swiftly back down the hallway before anyone caught him lurking. He was extremely pleased with himself—that was one bout of eavesdropping that would pay off handsomely. And fulfilling Gunnar's plan just got a *whole* lot easier. Rory and Roth would no longer have to scour the entire city looking for one guy. Not when their very own baby sister had just admitted to indulging in regular make-out sessions with him.

"Holy hell." Rory chuckled as he made his way back to his own quarters in the adjacent wing of the old stone building. "Mouse has got the hots for Mister Hero."

He could hardly believe his luck. Moreover, if this Fennrys guy felt the same way about Mason—and from the sounds of things, he did—even better. Because if that was the case, when the time came, they wouldn't have to threaten him to get him to cross the Hell Gate Bridge.

They'd just have to threaten Mason.

XXV

For the next few days, late evenings were the time that Fennrys looked forward to the most. Because of Mason. They continued their sparring matches—using the after-hours High Line as their own personal piste—and Fenn refused to let Mason bring her practice blades to work with. He wouldn't know what to do with one of the whippy little things in the first place, but more importantly, he didn't want her to be afraid of the larger, sharper blade. He didn't want her to be afraid of hurting him again, and he definitely wanted to get her past her fear of the draugr.

There was also the added bonus that, once she got used to the greater weight and heft of the swept-hilt he'd given her, when she went back to the competition saber, it would be featherlight and effortless in her grip. It had been working, too, she'd told him by the end of the week. Her daytime practices had seen a marked improvement in her already impressive talents, and she seemed to be moving past her phobic responses. Apparently the change was dramatic enough that Mason seemed to think Toby might be on the verge of asking her if she was taking performance enhancers.

But it wasn't just the sparring that Fennrys looked forward to. It was the deeper joy of just spending time with the raven-haired girl, finding things to say that would make her laugh. Feeling himself smile in return. Strolling the High Line with her, sitting in the galleries that had been built into the sections of track that passed through surrounding buildings and hiding from the occasional security guard, Fennrys would hold Mason's hand as gently as if it were made of glass, even though he could feel the raw strength in the muscles and sinews under her smooth skin.

For those few nights, the High Line was their own private paradise. A ribbon of green and silver surrounded by the sparkling lights of the New York City night, it floated above the hum of the street life below. Canopied over with stars—when the sky wasn't tumbled with clouds, which seemed more nights than not these days—and Fennrys would even, if his timing was just right, steal the odd, rare kiss.

But that in itself was something that he approached as if it was a precious, gifted opportunity not to be taken lightly, or advantage of. Mason was special. And he didn't want to do anything to pressure her or make her wary of him. In the back of his mind, Fennrys had the strange, nagging sensation that he'd done that once before. With someone else special. He had the feeling that it hadn't worked out so well.

He had the feeling that a *lot* of things hadn't worked out so well in the life he couldn't remember.

As the days passed, he grew determined to find out who—and what—he was. If only because that was the only way he would ever let any kind of relationship develop further between him and Mason Starling. She was far too special to let anything happen to threaten her. Even if—maybe especially if—that something was him.

So he took it slow.

Evenings on the High Line. Nights full of dreams.

And daytimes he spent roaming the city, restlessly trying to find clues as to his own buried identity, mostly with little success. This city was his city. He knew that. Knew he'd spent significant time there. But nothing was quite how he . . . he couldn't exactly say "remembered" it. "Perceived" it, maybe, was the way to put it. It was as if there was a strange multilayered patina clinging to the places that were familiar to him. Like the way he'd told Mason that he could remember when London Terrace wasn't there. He *could*. He was sure of it.

One afternoon it finally occurred to him to investigate the only tangible thing he'd managed to tie back to his former life: the loft apartment in the anonymous, seemingly abandoned warehouse. He knew for certain that the place was his, that he lived there—but he had no way of knowing who actually owned the property. If he was paying rent to someone, Fennrys was pretty sure there would be a record of ownership somewhere. A land title maybe. Something. Some clue.

There were no signs that he had found anywhere on or in the building itself that indicated ownership. But there had to be municipal records. If there were, however, the clerk at the records office couldn't find them. And nudged perhaps by the same kind of persuasive force that Fennrys had unintentionally used on the waiter at the Boat Basin Café a few days earlier, she'd happily spent almost two hours looking.

Frustrated, Fenn returned home. It was on his way up in the freight elevator that he finally caught his first tiny break.

There was a mechanical certificate behind a sheet of glass bolted above the operator panel. It was so yellowed and faded with age that Fennrys hadn't even noticed it up to that point, and even when he peered closely, he couldn't really make out any of the words. But it was folded in half, and there was a possibility, he thought, that some bit of information on the bottom half had escaped weathering. He had no tools to unscrew the frame holding the thing to the elevator wall, so he wrapped his fist in the sleeve of his jacket and punched it, hard enough to break the glass. He worked the brittle certificate out of the frame and carried it into his living area and over to one of the windows. The typeface was ancient, from an old manual typewriter, and in the space left for Owner/Proprietor, it read "Vinterkongen Holdings." Fennrys stared at the words for a long time. They didn't exactly set any bells ringing in his head.

"Okay then," he murmured finally. "Let's see if we can't get a line on you, Mr. Vinterkongen. If that's even a real name . . ."

Fennrys figured the easiest way to access information like that would be at the New York Public Library. The day was bright as he headed toward the subway station at Twenty-third so he could make his way to Forty-second Street and then across to Fifth Avenue, where the two massive marble lions sat flanking the wide stone steps that led up to the terrace at the front of the main branch of the library.

Fennrys walked up the steps, staring at the impressive edifice in front of him. He wondered if he'd ever been there before. In some ways, it felt a little like walking into the hall of a great and powerful king, and that sensation was a strangely familiar one.

"Damn. Maybe you really are some kind of amnesiac son of a rock star," he muttered to himself. "Or maybe black-sheep royalty."

Fennrys stalked the halls until he found a reading room with public-access computer terminals. He discovered a few interesting things over the next hour and a half: among them that he couldn't type, didn't like reading off a computer screen, and found the mouse awkward to use.

"So . . . probably not a super spy, then. Or an office clerk." He sighed. "That narrows it down nicely."

Another thing, once he eventually got the hang of using the library's search interface, was that whoever it was that owned the building his loft was in had a fairly impressive portfolio of real estate holdings in and around the New York area. Besides his own outwardly dilapidated/inwardly tricked-out place, there was also an apartment on Central Park West, a turn-of-the-century music hall in the theater district, and at least a dozen other properties on the island of Manhattan itself. He found very little other information about this Vinterkongen person—if they were even a person—but where it got really interesting, not to say worrying, was when he was searching through references to old land deeds and genealogy records and stumbled across a record of a land property transfer from the early 1800s. The deal was between two parties listed as Vinterkongen and Sturlungar, an ancient family that had its origins in the Icelandic Commonwealth. A further search indicated that Sturlungar was an earlier rendering of a familial name. The more modern version of which was . . . Starling.

"What does your family have to do with my mystery landlord, Mason?" Fennrys murmured as he pushed his chair back and stared at the screen. "And just how much trouble are the two of us *really* in?"

Before he left the library, he did a search on two more terms: Iris and Lethe—the names he remembered the hooded woman saying in his dreams, after Mason had stabbed him. Iris, it turned out, according to Greek mythology, was a winged messenger of the gods, a kind of link between mortals and immortals, and a personification of the rainbow, which was also how she traveled between realms. According to several sources, she was known to spend time in the underworld. Lethe was the name of a river in that mythological underworld—and its waters induced forgetfulness in those who swam in them or drank from them.

Fennrys sat there, turning the information over in his mind, applying this new knowledge to the dream.

"It was just a dream," he murmured to himself.

But if it was . . . why then did he remember seeing a *winged woman* hovering above the fallen oak in the Gosforth gym, just after he'd crashed through a *rainbow*-colored window . . . with *no memory* of who or what he was? Why would a goddess—an ostensibly Greek goddess, at that—have taken an interest in him? Who was the cloaked woman who'd released him from imprisonment and led him to her? And exactly where in hell had he been?

That last question echoed just a little too loudly in his head.

Where *in hell* had he been?

An hour later, Fennrys sat outside on one of the many green folding chairs provided for the patrons of Bryant Park, staring up into a bright blue sky with unseeing eyes. No one gave him a second look—except for one grizzled old man in a shabby overcoat, with a ragged teddy bear stuffed under one arm, who happened to do a double take as he passed by. Fenn looked up when he noticed the man had stopped and wondered if he was going to ask for money or cigarettes.

He asked for neither and just said, "Oh. Hey."

Fennrys nodded silently at him.

"I ain't gonna have to pack up and move to another park again now, am I?" the man asked.

"Sorry?"

"Well, it's just that, last time I saw you, it was up in Central Park. Right around the time that little lady friend of yours told me to pull up stakes." He shrugged a bulky shoulder. "She told me the park wasn't safe. Nasty things there. Eat your face and all."

Fennrys felt suddenly cold—as though a cloud had passed

over the sun. "What lady friend would that be?"

"The princess, o' course."

A princess, Fennrys thought. *Right.* He tried to shake off the momentary sense of unease and smiled at the man indulgently.

"I been down here ever since," the man was saying. "I like parks." He peered at Fennrys. "You like parks, too, eh?"

"Yeah." Fennrys eyed the man warily. "I like parks fine, I guess." Except that even the *thought* of Central Park made him extremely uneasy. He stood. "But I have no idea what you're talking about, buddy."

The old man shrugged again and grinned. "You wouldn't be the first to tell me that. How've you been?"

"Do you . . . know me?" Fennrys asked.

"Don't exactly know you," he said. "Just seen ya around once in a while. Over the years. Up in Central Park. You and . . . *them.* The shiny ones."

"What shiny ones would those be, exactly?" Fennrys asked.

But the man shook his head vigorously. "Oh, no. No, no . . . I don't think I'm really supposed to talk about it." The man held up his stuffed bear—it was missing one of its button eyes—and said, "But you can ask the Major. The Major knows all about that stuff."

Damn. Fenn sighed inwardly. "That's okay. Maybe another time."

"Your call, chief."

"Listen," he said to the man and his bear. "I gotta go. You take care of yourself, old timer, all right?" He fished in his pocket for what was actually the last of Rory's roll of cash and handed it over to him.

The man's eyes bulged huge. "Dang. Thanks, buddy."

"That's for burgers. Not booze. Okay?"

"Aye-firmative, chief." The old guy made the bear salute and took the cash. Fennrys watched him go, shaking his head in bemusement. Having done his part to fill a hobo's stomach, he was still no closer to filling in the gaps in his own head.

XXVI

"**S**he's dangerous."

"Thanks, Toby." Mason rolled her eyes and pulled the laces tight on her shoe. "Just what I needed to hear."

"Oh. *I'm* sorry." Toby's sarcasm was expansive. "Did you want me to say, 'Ooh, that one's a pushover, Mase. Just like the girl you fought last week—you know, the one who whupped your butt'? Would that help?"

"No, Coach Hardass, it wouldn't." She grinned up at him.

Toby shook his head and lifted his travel mug to swallow a large mouthful of coffee. "Somebody around here seems like they've had a couple of good nights' sleeps for a change."

"Something like that." Mason switched feet and laced up her other shoe snugly. Good nights, yes. But it wasn't the sleeping that had put the smile back on her face and the sting back in her blade. It was Fennrys.

She sailed through her first three bouts. The one thing

Mason loved about fighting saber over foil or épée was that the competitors in saber tended to yell a lot. The fact that you could slash at an opponent and not just poke away at them seemed to bring out something primal in the fencers, and they hollered back and forth at each other as the flurry of attacks and ripostes sent them charging up and down the piste. She'd had to mostly keep a lid on the vocal histrionics when she and Fennrys sparred on the High Line because a lot of yelling probably would have brought the park authority—or even the cops—down on them in a heartbeat. But there in the gym, Mason could holler till she was blue in the face behind her mask.

And she did. Mostly cries of victory. She cleaned up.

"So," Toby said nonchalantly at the end of the day. "That most definitely did *not* suck. Nice to have you back, kid. And then some."

"Thanks, Tobe." Mason shook her hair out of its tail. "I guess all I needed was for you to get your boots back." She kicked one of his dilapidated steel-toes lightly. "The Birkenstocks and socks just really threw me last time."

He growled under his breath at her, and she saw a flash of apprehension in his eyes—most likely the fear that she would bring up the night of the storm again—but Mason knew better, and she kept her mouth shut. And it didn't seem so daunting anymore, keeping the terrible secret of that night. Not when she had Fennrys to share it with. After the attack at the boat basin, her strange bond with Fennrys seemed to be growing stronger day by day. All of the weirdness and the wonder that had befallen her were somehow so much easier to bear because she knew that Fennrys was there. Waiting with a sword in his hand and that crazy sexy smile on his face.

Even though almost nothing had happened between them—a kiss here, hands held there, an embrace at the end of each night before he hailed her a cab to take her home (and always opened the window for her before she got in)—Mason got breathless and light-headed just thinking about him. Like she was now.

"Hey, Mason . . ."

She spun around and, for a split second, was confused that the one who'd called her name wasn't the Fennrys Wolf.

"Oh! Uh . . . hey, Cal!" she stammered, flustered at being caught daydreaming. About the boy who was *not* the boy standing in front of her—the boy she used to daydream about only days earlier. Mason felt a sudden, stinging wash of guilt.

Calum was watching her face, and she wondered what he'd seen there, because his tentative smile wavered and a frown line ticked between his brows.

She made herself smile at him. "How are you?"

"I'm okay." His hand twitched toward his face. "Can I talk to you?"

"Yeah. Sure."

Calum gestured for Mason to follow him, and together they walked side by side in silence for a few minutes, away from the busier paths between the university buildings and toward a quiet corner of campus. Cal kept glancing sideways at Mason, as if to make sure she was still walking with him.

"You did pretty good today."

"Thanks," Mason said noncommittally. She didn't want

Cal asking about the improvement in her game, especially not when he was the one who was supposed to be helping her with that improvement. But, then again, there was no reason for her to feel bad. Cal was the one who had dropped off the face of the earth, not her. Mason knew he was hurting, but he hadn't even returned any of the texts she'd sent him in the first few days after, asking how he was. And it wasn't as if the last time they had seen each other he'd been particularly pleasant. . . .

"I'm sorry about the other day," he said, almost as if he'd heard her thoughts. "I guess I was kind of—"

"A bitch to me?" Mason asked. It was something that Heather would have said, and it felt a little weird coming out of Mason's mouth, but she was glad she'd said it. She realized that she was still pretty pissed at Cal for the way he'd treated her that day in the hallway in front of Carrie Morgan and the other Gos students. But now she worried that Calum would just turn around and forget about talking to her.

Instead Cal just smiled wanly. "Yeah. I was kind of a bitch. I've been trying to track you down to apologize, but you've been sort of scarce lately. You haven't been avoiding me or anything, have you?"

There was an almost accusatory tone to the question that, for some reason, got under her skin. She stopped short in the middle of the path. "Don't you have that the other way around?"

Mason remembered the conversation she'd had with Heather. About how Cal was—or, rather, how Heather *said* he was—in love with Mason. Casual flirting, a few movie nights with a bunch of other people . . . that did *not* equal love. Cal didn't know Mason well enough to have those kinds of feelings for her. Heather may have been convinced, enough so that she'd actually broken up with him because of it, but Mason just didn't believe it. Not for a second.

And even if she *did*, she wasn't sure she wanted that. Not anymore . . .

"What did you want to say to me, Calum?" she asked, hearing for herself the sharpness in her tone.

"Right. Yeah . . ." He took a deep breath. "Look. I think you might be the only one I can talk to about this."

The look on Cal's face melted Mason's sudden ire, and she reigned in her temper. Cal was serious. Something was deeply troubling him, and Mason couldn't help but feel badly for him. He looked really . . . lost. Alone. She wondered why he thought *she* was the only one he could talk to, and then she tried to remember the last time she'd seen him talking to anyone else at Gos. She couldn't. In fact, it seemed almost as if Cal was isolating himself from all the other students. She remembered Heather telling her that, even though he was back in class, Cal wasn't staying in the dorm. He was going home at night, and that in itself was enough to get Gosforth tongues wagging.

Mason had just assumed that he needed time away to recuperate from his injuries. But aside from the rapidly healing scars, there didn't seem to be anything wrong with Cal. Nothing physical, at least.

"What is it, Cal?" she asked. "What's bugging you?"

"Yeah, um . . ." He ran a hand through his hair, frowning. "Last night, when I was at home, I couldn't sleep. I mean—it wasn't just last night. I haven't been sleeping much since . . . you know."

Mason nodded. "I know."

"Well . . . I've been going down to the water . . ."

Cal's family owned super-swanky old-money property on Long Island, right at the very tip of Kings Point on the Gold Coast, where all the extravagant historic mansions owned by people like the Vanderbilts and the Roosevelts used to be. It was the place that F. Scott Fitzgerald had glamorously fictionalized in *The Great Gatsby*. Most of the grand old estates had been torn down or converted into public facilities, but the Aristarchos place was still standing.

She glanced over at Cal, wondering what he wanted to say to her. She saw that his gaze had become cloudy, as though his thoughts were turned inward, focusing on some memory or another.

"Cal?"

"Hmm?" His eyes snapped back up to her face. "Oh. Sorry . . ."

"So you went down to the water," Mason prompted. "What happened?"

He sighed gustily. "Look. I know that you were the one who wanted to tell people about the things that really happened in the gym that night. And I know that when the others said we should just shut up and pretend like it didn't happen, I went with that. . . ."

"Cal, it's okay. I get it. I mean, I understand. And you're right. Everyone would have thought we were just being a bunch of stupid pranking jerks. Stuff like what happened to us that night just doesn't happen to the rest of the world. You were right."

"No, Mason." His eyes glittered almost feverishly and he leaned toward her, gripping her by the shoulder, suddenly, frighteningly, intense. "*You* were. I think this kind of thing goes on more often than most people would ever admit."

"Cal . . . did something happen to you while you were home?"

He took a deep breath and spilled out an incredible story about strange creatures—frightening and beautiful—in the sound. About how, every night he'd been home since the storm, he would go down to the water's edge and watch them cavort, listen to them sing. Mason sat listening, frozen statue-still by his words. Suddenly, Cal's voice broke with emotion and she looked over at him. He was pale and his skin had an almost waxy sheen to it.

"Last night . . ." He stopped talking and swallowed convulsively.

"Last night *what*?" Mason asked.

"Last night . . . they didn't just sing to me. They called to me to go with them."

He'd said it in a whisper, but Mason still could hear the desperate, almost violent yearning in Cal's voice. He closed his eyes, the muscles in his jaw clenching at the memory, and silence stretched out between them. Mason felt herself growing pale, the blood rushing from her face as if her heart had issued a sudden recall.

"I can still almost hear their voices in my head. They were so loud. So . . . *insistent* . . ."

She reached out and took Calum's hand in her own and said, "I don't think you should go down to the water anymore, Cal."

His eyes snapped open, and he gazed at her with a razor-sharp intensity. He laughed, and his voice cracked again on the sound. "See . . . that's kind of funny coming from you, Mason. Because I have a feeling that you and I are in similar situations."

"What—"

"And I could sit here and tell you to stay away from that Fennrys guy until I was blue in the face. For your own damned good. And would you?"

Mason's mouth opened, but no sound came out.

"That's what I thought." He laughed mirthlessly and stood. "You know . . . maybe I should take my sea nymphs up on their offer. Maybe I'd find out I actually belong there. It'd be nice to belong somewhere. With some*one*."

Mason had nothing to say to that as Cal turned his back on her and walked away, but she felt his leaving like a phantom wound. A might-have-been. Calum was a dream she'd almost had. But now—and it felt like it was all *her* fault—he seemed to be living in a kind of strange and dangerous nightmare.

XXVII

Mason shivered, and Fennrys wrapped an arm around her shoulders, although he wasn't sure if the goose bumps on her arms were from the slight chill in the air or the subject of their conversation. She'd just described to him Calum's waterside encounter as they wandered along the High Line in the dark—their furtive, after-hours park strolls had become something of a ritual for them after nightly fencing practice. Fennrys cherished those moments, even when Mason found herself compelled to tell him about the problems of another guy. . . . He mentally smacked down an irrational little spark of jealousy. He would lend an ear, and then, maybe, he might find an opportunity to bring up another topic of conversation that had been ticking away at the back of his mind.

Fennrys hadn't yet broached the subject of his discoveries at the library earlier that day. He still didn't know what to make of the fact that her family and the person—or entity—

who owned his warehouse were somehow connected. . . .

He frowned and dragged his concentration back to Mason's story.

"I mean . . . it's not like it's unheard-of for weird things to be found bobbing around in the waters around New York," she was saying. "Back in the seventies or something, they found a dead giraffe in the river. A marathon swimmer collided with it—can you imagine?" She shuddered at the thought. "But . . . at least giraffes are real. They exist. What Cal was talking about, though . . ."

"Do you think they were the same ones we met?"

Mason shrugged. "I don't think so. I mean, I'm pretty sure he would have mentioned if they'd had bright blue skin. And ours weren't riding monsters. I just think it was a whole new species of weirdness."

"Why did he think you were the only one he could talk to about it?" Fennrys asked, and then immediately cursed himself silently as she turned and raised an eyebrow at him. "I mean . . . what about Heather? Didn't you tell me they were a couple?"

"Uh. Yeah. 'Were' being the operative word there."

"Oh."

"And that really wasn't the point of my story," Mason said drily.

"I know, I know . . ." He smiled down at her for a moment, but then something tugged at the edges of his awareness.

Fennrys slowed and looked around at the cityscape, glittering in the darkness, surrounding them on all sides. After a week of wildly changeable weather, the air was eerily still.

"Believe me, Mason," he said. "If I had the slightest inkling of what's going on, I'd tell you. I'd tell Calum. Hell, I'd—"

The sounds of baying animals, faint and far off, stopped Fennrys in his tracks, just inside the cavernous Chelsea Market Passage, a section of the park that ran directly through a corner of the building that housed the Chelsea Market and was home to an art installation of hundreds of panes of colored glass meant to echo the changing moods of the Hudson River. The ethereal blue, green, and red light filtering through lent an otherworldly tinge to the night. It somehow harmonized with the dissonant howling that was getting closer.

"What," Mason whispered, "is *that*?"

"I don't know," Fennrys replied. "But whatever it is . . . it's hunting."

"Hunting what?"

Fenn looked down at Mason. "Us."

"Ask a stupid question," Mason muttered under her breath.

She felt an increasingly familiar jolt of adrenaline shoot through her system. The fact that she was getting used to that couldn't be a good thing. In the far distance, coming up from the Gansevoort Street end of the park, they could see dark, loping shapes. Tall, shaggy-furred, long-legged creatures. Mason imagined she could see yellow eyes and slavering jaws, even though they were still too far away for that. But they were coming on quickly.

Fennrys was already shrugging the sword carrier off his shoulder and yanking open the flap closure. He drew Mason's swept-hilt out and handed it to her with a stern expression on his face. "That," he said fiercely, "is *only* for just in case."

"What's that supposed to mean?"

"It means you will not even think about trying to be a hero. Your job is to do one thing and to do it so well that not even I can catch up to you."

"And that is?"

"Run."

As the word left his lips, Mason's dream came flooding back to her. The one where Fennrys had told her to run . . . and then had become a monster. Before she'd even made a conscious decision, Mason had turned and was pounding north through the deserted park, following the twisting ribbon of the pathway, shining sleek and silver-gray in the light of the moon. The full moon.

There might have been people—pedestrians or club goers, maybe even a beat cop on the streets below the High Line—but because it was after hours, the park itself was, of course, utterly devoid of any living thing except her, Fennrys, and . . . whatever was chasing them. Mason didn't dare take even a moment to find a railing to look over to yell for help. And even if she could have, she didn't want to involve any innocent bystanders. She just had to run and hope that Fenn could deal with whatever it was. And if he couldn't . . . the sword in her hand flashed like molten silver in her peripheral vision as she ran.

Mason didn't look back—not even when she heard the terrible snarls and roars and skreeling yelps of pain—and she made it to the Eighteenth Street stairway in record time. She was eternally grateful that she was wearing sneakers and jeans this time. After the first fencing "lesson" with Fennrys in his apartment, Mason had foregone girly allure and opted instead for practical. It served her well in this particular instance. At Eighteenth, there was a metal grid causeway jutting out at a right angle to the park superstructure that led to a staircase, which, in turn, led to the ground. Of course, because it was after hours, the grated door at the bottom of the stairwell would be locked up tight. Mason didn't bother to try it or see if there was some way to open it from the inside. Instead, once she got to the elevated landing before the last stair flight, she threw her leg over the railing . . . and jumped.

She hit the pavement hard and tucked into a shoulder roll, trying not to decapitate herself with her own sword. Above her and to the south, she could hear the sounds of furious fighting. Half of her ached to go back and help Fennrys. The other half was consumed with the urgent need to run. Just as he'd told her. But now that she was out of the park, Mason had nowhere to go. Fenn's warehouse was right there, but Mason knew that it was guarded. Unless he himself had disabled the wards—that's what he'd called them—then there was no way for her to get into the building. She could try to hail a cab, but the streets were surprisingly deserted, and she wasn't sure what kind of cabbie would be inclined to stop for a dirt-stained, wild-eyed, sword-wielding teenage girl anyway.

Besides which, now that she was away and hidden behind the High Line stairs, she didn't want to leave Fennrys so completely alone. As she thought that, she heard a tremendous racket coming from almost directly above her. The metal stairwell grates shook and rattled violently, and peering up through the mesh and lattice of steel girders, Mason watched the battle royal as if it were staged as a shadow play. The dark shapes moved above her with lethal, muscular grace and unbridled savagery.

Suddenly Mason heard a roar of rage. She couldn't honestly tell if it came from one of the animals . . . or from Fennrys. But then a huge dog's body came slamming down out of the sky like a sack of wet cement, and Mason stifled a scream and covered her face.

Wearily, Fennrys climbed over the stair railing and dropped down onto his haunches beside Mason. He wiped the back of his hand across his brow, and it came away streaked with blood.

"It's not bad," he said, waving off her hand as Mason hissed in sympathy and went to lift the strands of blond hair that were stuck to a shallow cut leaking blood in a slow trickle down the side of his face. "Leave it," he snapped. "It'll heal."

Mason pulled her hand back. She looked startled, hurt by the angry tone of his voice, but he couldn't help it. He was so afraid for her that he was still shaking.

"I told you to run."

"I did."

"I didn't tell you to *stop* running." He could feel that his lips were still curled back in a snarl. "You should be halfway to Central Park by now, damn it!"

He turned away from Mason and looked up at where the body of another wolfhound lay still, dripping blood through the grate. The minute someone discovered the animals, there would be police and park authorities swarming all over the place asking questions. For some reason, Fennrys had half expected the things to shimmer away into nothingness after he'd killed them—like mirages. Like the draugr.

But they weren't mirages and they weren't mythical monsters. They were dogs—just dogs—and they lay there now looking mortal and pathetic in death and he felt sorry for having been the cause of it. Of course he would have felt a whole lot worse if he hadn't been. Those dogs were capable of tracking and taking down much larger prey in the wild. They could bring down boar and even bears, but they were called wolfhounds because they'd been bred specifically to kill wolves.

Only this time, it seemed, the wolf had won the fight. *This* time.

In the wake of his angry outburst, the silence stretched out between Fennrys and Mason until finally she stood and said, quietly, "Well, I guess I'd better get going, then. Like you said, I should be halfway to Central Park by now." She turned and started to walk away from him, her spine rigid.

Fennrys watched her go for a minute, something ticking away in his mind. Then he stood and jogged after her, catching up in less than half a block. He grabbed her by the wrist and slowed her down. She turned and he looked down at her. Her eyes were so blue they almost glowed in the moonlight, like a cat's.

"The next time, just keep running."

"I don't know if I can do that."

"Come on. Let's go." He took the sword gently from her hand and slipped it back into the case, along with his own.

"Where are we going now?"

"Central Park."

"Wait. I thought you were just saying that to be mean."

"I was. But I think the bear might actually be on to something. I think I might actually find some answers there."

"The *bear*?"

Mason looked up at him like he'd finally lost his marbles. Maybe he had.

"Yeah. His name's Major. I'll explain on the way." Fennrys wiped away the blood on his forehead with the sleeve of his leather jacket and waved at a cab in the distance. "Or maybe I won't."

They stood at the Columbus Circle entrance to Central Park. They'd been standing there for almost five minutes. Mason had never made it that long without being accosted by pedicab hawkers or bicycle renters or guys selling hats and T-shirts, even at that late hour. But no one bothered Fennrys or—guilt by association—*her* that evening.

"Are we going in?"

"Yeah."

"You don't look like you want to."

"I don't."

"Do you know why you don't want to?"

"Not exactly. No."

"Okay . . ."

"I think something happened to me here. Something bad."

Mason looked at Fennrys's profile. The sharp angles and planes of his face were dusted with streetlamp glow, and the pale orange light softened the contours and made him look young—like Cal or any one of her classmates at Gosforth. Mason desperately wanted to know what had happened to him to transform him from that ordinary teenage boy into the extraordinary, daunting, lonely young man at her side. She thought that she might soon find out.

Assuming he ever decides to actually enter the park, that is . . .

As if some part of him had heard her thoughts, Fenn took a sudden, lurching step forward. His nostrils flared, like he was scenting the air for danger, and his fists were knotted at his sides. But he kept going, into the park proper, veering right and heading north toward midpark. Mason followed along beside him. There was a thin veil of ground mist drifting at intervals across the paths and collecting in the hollows and vales of the park's rolling contours. In front of them, and to the sides, hidden in the deep black shadows cast by the tall trees at night, Mason thought that she could see lights dancing, like fireflies in the distance. Even though it was way too late in the year for fireflies.

She kept sneaking glances at Fennrys to see what, if anything, was going on with him. Half the time when she looked, his eyes were closed. They passed the carousel, the mall, and the lake. Heading north and east. Fennrys was utterly silent until they were almost at the Metropolitan

Museum of Art. Mason's feet were starting to ache a little, even though she was wearing her sneakers. Suddenly Fennrys stopped and tilted his head slowly, looking around. His gaze was focused on something Mason couldn't see.

"Whatever it is," he said quietly, "it's close."

"Whatever *what* is?"

"I don't know. Not exactly." He closed his eyes again, and by the orange light of a park lamp, Mason could see his eyes flicking back and forth beneath closed lids. "In my mind," he murmured, "I can see . . . lights. Like sparks or flames. It's like the whole park is laid out in front of me, and there are these pinpoints of light scattered throughout it. I think they're . . . people."

"People?"

"Not exactly. Beings . . ."

"Is this more . . . uh . . . magick?" In her mind, she added the *k* at the end. "Like some kind of mystical GPS or something?"

"I think so. It's like I can sense all the things in the park that aren't . . . human."

"Shouldn't we get *out* of the park, in that case?" Mason couldn't help but think about all of the not-human things she'd encountered lately and how she really didn't want to run into any more of them just at that moment.

But Fennrys put a hand on her arm, keeping her from bolting. "No," he said. "No . . . I don't think we're in any danger. Not here. Not tonight."

"Why not?"

"Because I've been here before. These people—things,

whatever—they're afraid of me. They won't bother us." He turned and looked north, and his gaze narrowed. Focused. "And there's someone else here. . . ."

"Who?" Mason asked in a dry whisper.

"I don't know. But they won't bother him either."

Mason quickened her pace to keep up with Fennrys. For some reason, knowing that didn't make her feel any better.

XXVIII

Fennrys warily climbed the shallow stone steps that led up Greywacke Knoll, under an arching bower of crabapple branches, and into an octagonal clearing. The open space was paved with interlocking bricks and occupied at its center by an awe-inspiring granite monument so ancient Fennrys could almost feel the history emanating from it in waves. A tall, slender, four-sided finger of stone pointing skyward, it was mounted on the backs of enormous bronze sea crabs, and its surface was covered in hieroglyphics. It was called Cleopatra's Needle, although that was a misnomer. The obelisk had actually been commissioned by the pharaoh Thutmosis III more than fifteen hundred years before that great queen had even been born.

It had taken a tremendous effort to get the thing from Egypt to New York, back in the day, but it had stood in that spot now since 1881. It drew the eye toward it and, even for someone who couldn't feel the subtle waves of power emanating from it, it would have been almost impossible to stop staring at the thing—if it weren't for the person who stood leaning on the brass rail that surrounded it. *He* drew the eye too.

The young man was fashion-model handsome, with skin that was smooth and deeply tanned to a burnished copper. His features were sharp and elegant, high cheekbones and a long nose, and the lashes rimming his eyes were so thick he looked like he might have been wearing eyeliner. His jet-black hair was dressed in uniform pencil-thin dreadlocks that swept back off his forehead and brushed his shoulders. When he smiled, it was to show off a gleaming white smile and sharply pointed canines, and his eyes were so dark brown they looked black.

They were fixed, unblinking, on Fennrys.

"You look like nine miles of bad road," he said, and laughed. It was an easy, pleasant sound . . . and it chilled Fennrys to the bone. "Could be worse, I suppose. Could be ten."

Fennrys glanced down at what he was wearing.

"No, no. The clothes are okay." He waved a hand dismissively, dressed impeccably himself in a sleek charcoal suit with an open-collared silk dress shirt underneath, midnight blue. Tiny gold hoops shone in both his ears. "I mean, personally, I would have gone for a more body-conscious jacket, but then you probably need the room. Tough to swing a weapon if you're too tailored."

Fennrys restrained himself from actually going for the sword slung across his back—he had a feeling weapons wouldn't necessarily be of much use against this one. Instead he stood in a relaxed stance, waiting to see what the stranger would do next.

"You're a clever one. And *that*"—he glanced pointedly at the sword Fennrys *hadn't* drawn—"was the right decision, Fennrys Wolf."

Fennrys didn't bother to question how the man had known what he'd been thinking. "Thought it might be," he said.

"You've been in the city for a while now," the stranger said, shifting so that he leaned one elbow on the railing in an indolent pose. His glance flicked over to Mason and then back to Fennrys. "Where've you been all this time?"

"Around," Fennrys said flatly, avoiding the urge to step protectively in front of Mason. "Today I spent a lovely few hours down at the library, and then I rounded it out relaxing in Bryant Park. Thanks for asking."

"Bryant Park. Figures." The stranger rolled his eyes skyward. "And here I am waiting for you up here, in the first place I would have thought you'd come back to. What's the matter? Too many bad memories?"

Fennrys reared back like a spooked animal.

"That's not very funny," Mason snapped.

The man's gaze narrowed, focusing on her again, and every muscle in Fennrys's body went taut with apprehension. He turned his head toward Mason without taking his eyes from the man's face.

"You know that whole 'never talk to strangers' thing, Mase?" Fennrys said in a low voice. "They don't get much stranger than this."

Mason looked up at him, her blue gaze glittering fiercely. Then suddenly, before he could stop her, she stepped around Fennrys and stalked toward the obelisk, stopping when she was only a few feet away from the stranger.

"What are you?" she demanded.

The man raised an eyebrow at her, mildly astonished. "I beg your pardon?"

"What *are* you?" she repeated. "I mean . . . so far this week I've worked my way through storm zombies, lizard mermaids, river goddesses, nasty flying things that I don't even want to know what they were, and stunt doubles for the hounds of the Baskervilles. So. What are you? Demon? Vampire?"

"Vampires don't exist." The man scoffed.

"Right. Silly me."

"I'm a werewolf."

Mason blinked and turned to Fennrys. "See? And I thought that was you!"

"Oh, please." The man snorted. "He'd need a lot more style to run with my crew. And I'm not just *a* werewolf."

Mason turned back to him.

"I'm *the* werewolf."

"Well, aren't we the lucky ones."

"You have been so far, Mason Starling," the man said sharply, and speared her with a glance that knocked the bravado right out of her. "If I were you, I'd try my very best to make sure that becomes a trend. Now I know you're freaked, and that's fine. But a little respect would go a long way. Especially considering the fact that you're standing in a park in the middle of New York City talking to a god."

"I . . . I thought you said you were a . . . a werewolf," she stammered.

All of a sudden, the man's handsome features began to blur and shift.

Fennrys lunged forward and pulled Mason away as a wash of crackling blue-black light danced over the surface of the stranger's skin—which darkened to ebony and grew sleek and shiny—as his face elongated and reshaped into a long, fiercely pointed muzzle. His ears pulled back and extended upward from the sides of his head. The muscles of his neck thickened, and a fine black pelt covered them, blurring the outlines with thick, short fur. The expensive suit disappeared, replaced by a wide golden collar that draped over his torso, extending out over his muscled shoulders almost like wings. It sparkled with precious inlaid stones and served to emphasize that the rest of him was now essentially naked except for a long, pleated linen loincloth edged in gold embroidered designs and belted with yet more gold. His hands were still . . . hands. Fennrys had almost expected paws, but no, he still had fingers and toes, like a person, only the nails were long and sharp, like claws. And painted a brilliant lapis lazuli blue. His whole body was covered in sleek black fur that shone with indigo highlights and emphasized his exquisitely sculpted physique, which— from the neck down—still looked human. Except for the fur.

His lips drew back from a long snout full of gleaming white, dagger-sharp teeth. His glittering eyes sparked with grim mirth, and he said, in a voice like the growl of a wolf, "I *was* going to ease you into the whole god thing."

* * *

Mason willed herself not to faint, even though she could practically hear the blood rushing from her head. There was absolutely no doubt in her mind that the being standing in front of her was what he said he was. Power virtually rolled off him in waves. She recognized him from books and images she'd seen online, researching a paper on ancient myths and legends. He was Anubis, the jackal-headed Egyptian god of the dead. He grinned at her again, and again his form shifted and a sleek black wolf paced a circle around where she and Fennrys stood.

And then suddenly, all around them, the shadows under the trees started to writhe and flow toward them as a half-dozen other wolves padded out into the obelisk clearing and formed a loose circle around Mason and Fennrys.

Okay, Mason thought. Maybe she *should* just faint.

Fennrys tightened his grip on her as she started to sag in his arms. She clung to him, trying not to succumb to a whole new level of fear. Then, just as suddenly as he'd shifted form, the handsome young god stood before them, once again clothed in his stylish human shape. His lupine companions sat on the ground around them, watching with eyes that held far more awareness than wolves' eyes should. Human eyes.

"I hate showing off, but I trust I've made my point?"

Mason nodded weakly.

"And I trust, also, that you understand now how I might have a bit of insight into the unusual things that have been going on in this town lately."

She nodded again.

"Good. My name, in case you didn't know, is Anubis. *You* kids can call me Rafe." His dark eyes flicked over to Fennrys. "And *we* really need to talk."

The conversation seemed, at first, like it was going to be a fairly short, utterly fruitless one. Mostly because it consisted of Rafe asking Fennrys a bunch of questions that he had absolutely no way of answering. Questions about his life before the moment when he had dragged himself out of the ruins of the Gosforth oak tree and started fighting monsters.

"You don't remember *anything*?" Rafe said eventually, the frustration evident in his voice. He shook his head, and his dreadlocks swung back and forth against his high, chiseled cheekbones.

Fennrys shrugged. "Sorry."

"Damn," Rafe murmured to himself. "The River Lethe. So *that's* how she did it. . . ."

"Can you help him?" Mason asked.

"*Help* him?" Rafe said sharply, glancing at her. "I should tear his throat out right now and be done with it. It would probably save the mortal realm a whole lot of grief!"

Mason gasped and drew back, horrified and confused.

Fennrys just stared at him, unblinking.

Rafe sighed gustily.

"What am I?" Fennrys asked.

Mason held her breath.

The Egyptian god of the dead ran a hand over his dreads and looked up, an expression of something that might have been pity in his eyes. As if he was silently apologizing for the things he was about to say. "You were born a Viking prince in the year 1003, according to the current calendar. At seven months old, you were taken away by a faerie king to be raised in a place called the Otherworld, the Faerie Realm, as a warrior and a guardian of the gateway between the worlds. That gate just so happens to exist within the confines of Central Park, so that's why I expected you'd eventually find your way back here on your return."

Mason's jaw drifted open. "F-F—"

"Faerie. Yeah." Rafe shot her a look. "At least, I assume that's what you were about to say."

"Right. Yeah." Mason swallowed nervously. "Hey, uh, I don't mean to be rude, Mister . . . Rafe. But what's an Egyptian god doing telling an ancient Viking his life story?" she asked, having a hard time reconciling the whole situation.

"Because I'm the only one kicking around these parts that knows anything about it." He shrugged. "I have connections, you see. And as for the Egyptian thing, well, there's a lot more crossover in the Beyond Realms—the realms of the gods—than you'd think. Over the millennia, the boundaries between the various regions have begun to blur. The edges between where one world ends and another begins now overlap, and it's not so very unlikely for, say, an Olympian to come into contact with an Aesir—which, I have a sneaking suspicion, is how *you* got your ass back to this realm in the first place." He glanced back at Fennrys. "I think a couple of goddesses I know are in cahoots, although I can't say for sure."

"And you?" Mason asked, wondering just how many questions she could get away with asking. "How did you get here if it's so hard to cross back and forth?"

"Me?" Rafe grinned sourly. "I was turfed out of my own underworld long before any of this happened by a brother god of mine who had the ambition—and the ego—to make it happen. I've made my home here in the mortal realm ever since. But I still get regular news updates, you know?"

"What happened to me *here*?" Fennrys asked abruptly, a tremor in his voice. "In the park?"

Rafe turned to look directly at him. "Last year there was a rebellion in the Faerie Realm. It almost resulted in a major Otherworld incursion into this realm that, if it hadn't been stopped when it was, would have ended up in a big old faerie picnic in the middle of Manhattan." Rafe's mouth quirked in a mirthless grin. "And by picnic I mean death, destruction, and general Fair Folk mayhem."

Mason understood now. She'd seen Fennrys stand up against unearthly horrors and drive them back. She nodded. "So these creatures were going to invade, and Fennrys helped stop it."

Rafe turned a dark gaze on her. "Stop it? He was one of the ones who helped *cause* it."

"What?" Fennrys shook his head sharply.

Mason looked back and forth between him and Rafe. She must have heard that wrong. Fennrys wouldn't have done something like that. He was one of the good guys.

Wasn't he?

"What the hell are you talking about?" Fennrys asked, suddenly angry.

"You don't have to take my word for it," Rafe said.

He gestured at the fog that had coalesced all around them, unnoticed, while they sat on the park bench talking about impossible things. Swirling pearlescent drifts rolled aside like drawn curtains, revealing a slight young man of medium height with blue-pale skin and dark hair that fell over his forehead, partly obscuring his eyes—so dark and empty-open, Mason felt that gazing into them would be like teetering on the edge of a bottomless abyss. The young man stepped forward, hands in the pocket of his skinny black jeans. He wore a black zippered jacket with cuffs that were frayed slightly at the wrists and a black-and-gray striped scarf. He looked as though someone had built him out of smoke and ash and gray overcast days where the sun never truly shone through the clouds.

"Etienne," Fennrys murmured in a shocked whisper. *"Ghost . . ."*

"He's a . . . ghost?" Mason asked, her voice strained.

"No," Fennrys murmured. He shook his head.

Mason saw the fear and recognition crashing down on him. She could almost feel the cracks opening in Fenn's mind—cracks through which the memories poured in a flood. She could see them filling his gaze as he stared at the pale young man. "That's his name—I mean, not really. His name's Etienne. We just used to call him Ghost."

"Actually"—the pale young man's thin mouth curved in a wan smile—"you're right on both counts."

"Because you're dead," Fenn whispered in the voice of a drowning man.

Etienne nodded. "You watched me die."

"I didn't kill you. . . ."

"No." The gray young man shrugged. "You didn't. And in truth I probably deserved it anyway."

"Why? What makes you say that?" Fennrys snarled. "Is it because, at the time, you were trying to kill *me*?"

Etienne's dark, fathomless eyes flicked up, focusing on Fennrys's face. "I was wrong to do that."

"Damn straight!"

Ghost smiled at him, a little sadly. "We were both on the wrong side of things, Fennrys. You just managed to live long enough to have the opportunity to reexamine your choices."

"I'm surprised to hear you say that."

Ghost shrugged, his black eyes glittering. "Death tends to give one a unique perspective on things." He raised a hand, and the fog bank started to shape itself into the image of another place, another time. "But then . . . *you'd* know all about that, wouldn't you, Fennrys?"

ead. I'm dead. . . .

Fennrys had died. He had sacrificed his life to save another's—to make amends for his betrayal—and, in doing so, had hoped to find glory in the beyond, in the halls of his ancestors. A welcome home to Valhalla for the weary warrior.

It hadn't quite worked out as he'd hoped.

As Ghost conjured a vision of his last moments on earth, the memories came crashing down on him, and Fennrys clutched at the sides of his head in an agony of remembering and dropped hard to his knees on the paving stones. It couldn't be true. But it was.

He remembered with shockingly painful clarity the moment when he offered to take the place of another man in the carriage of a Valkyrie. He knew that he would be forsaking the mortal realm. He would, for all intents and purposes, die. Still, he'd done it. And he'd done it largely for the sake of the red-haired, green-eyed girl who, in his memories, he could see standing there, at the edge of the Jackie Onassis Reservoir. So that, in her eyes, he could redeem himself. Regain some measure of honor in her esteem, knowing full well, by then, that he could never have anything else with her.

Fennrys heard himself cry out—a sound that was half sob torn from deep in his chest—and he squeezed his eyes shut in pain. If the damned Faerie had never stolen him, he would have lived and died as a warrior prince among his people. He would have been a hero and he would have gone to Valhalla after his death in a glorious battle. But they had. And Fennrys had grown up, full of anger and a simmering resentment at having been denied his destiny.

When he'd climbed into the carriage of the Valkyrie, Fennrys had expected that once he arrived in Valhalla—in the realm of the gods of Asgard—there would be feasting and glorious battles to be fought over and over again. Olrun, the Valkyrie, had assured him that was what it would be like. Of course she hadn't been back to Asgard in some time. Things had changed.

And someone didn't want Fennrys there.

"What are you doing? Stop!" Mason cried.

Rafe held her tightly by the wrist, his expression grim.

Fennrys was on his hands and knees in front of them, eyes wide and mouth gaping in silent screams of protest. Etienne stood before him, rigid with the effort of conjuring the vision. Etienne's black eyes tracked back and forth, watching the images of the memories he'd helped draw forth, a transparent veneer of regret washing his features. All around Fennrys, Mason could make out shapes and shadows, scenes playing out—phantom projections of the memories flooding back into the hollow places in Fenn's mind.

"What's happening to him?"

"Etienne is conjuring a vision of what happened to Fennrys in Valhalla. Because it's one of the realms of the dead—and Ghost is, himself, a charter member of those ranks—he can do that. That's what Fennrys is seeing right now."

"That doesn't look anything like the Valhalla in any of the stories I've ever read!" Mason said, pointing violently at the chamber of horrors Fenn had found himself in.

Rafe's gaze snapped to her, and his dark eyes went wide. "You can *see* that?" he asked in a voice like the crack of a whip.

"Of course I can. It's right in front of me." Mason turned back to where Fennrys writhed in pain. There were shadowy things attacking him. Nightmares with teeth and claws slashing open his flesh, serpentine darkness winding around him as he lay helpless, chained and bound on the earthen floor of a cell. "That's enough!" Mason snarled. "Make. It. *Stop*."

She rounded on the god-man, her hands knotted into fists.

Rafe drew back a few inches in the face of her anger, and he stared at her for a moment. Then he called, "Etienne. Enough."

Ghost brought his hands together with a sound like a thunderclap, and the vision vanished. Fennrys collapsed on the paving stones, his chest heaving. "I thought . . . ," he gasped, "I thought Valhalla would have better accommodations. . . ."

"It does," Rafe said grimly. "Looks like your reservation got switched. You wound up in the basement suite in Hel."

Hel—or Helheim—Mason knew, was the Norse mythological equivalent of the place that it sounded like. Hell. She couldn't bring herself to believe that Fennrys belonged in such a place. But if someone had set him free . . . maybe he hadn't.

She went and knelt down beside him, helping him sit up. He was shaking like a leaf, and she wrapped her arms around him as he sagged against her. One of the wolves that had sat, silently watching, whined piteously, and Rafe walked slowly over and crouched on his haunches in front of them. Mason shifted her body protectively in front of Fennrys.

"Listen," Rafe said in a voice that was almost gentle. "I know what it's like to be thrown out of the one place in all the worlds you think you belong. You thought you were being some kind of a hero. The Aesir obviously didn't see it that way. The problem now is, hero or villain, you are the most dangerous thing to happen to this realm in a long, long time."

"Why?"

"Because you can walk between the worlds. You can go *there* . . . and come *back* again. And there's a very nasty prophecy floating around about that very thing," Rafe explained.

As if something that cryptic could actually be called an explanation, Mason thought. "What about him?" she asked, nodding at Ghost, who had moved to stand just behind Rafe. "Isn't that what he does?"

"Him?" Rafe turned to the specter of the pale young man and waved a hand right through him. Etienne's expression soured, but other than that, it didn't seem to affect him. He was utterly incorporeal. "Not really much of a threat, see? The thing about Fennrys is that he stayed *alive* when he died." Rafe shook his head in wonder. "And because he exists, there are those who think it makes him a harbinger. And there are those who would seek to use him as a means to an end."

"What end?"

"*The* end," Rafe said. "Ragnarok. The apocalypse. The end of the world."

Mason and Fennrys exchanged an uncertain glance. As hard to believe as everything else had been up to that point, the idea of a supernatural apocalypse was just too far beyond the pale. Mason couldn't wrap her head around it.

"The business with the Faerie caused a rift to open between this realm and the ones beyond it," Rafe said. "These days, most of the ancient gods from the various pantheons— you know, Greek, Roman, Celtic, what have you—want about as much to do with you mortal folk as you do with them. The Aesir, the Norse gods—well, some of them view things a little differently. They dig the idea of ending the world, and most everyone in it, and starting fresh." Rafe's expression turned fierce. "I'm *not* cool with that. I have a very sweet apartment in SoHo. I have a wardrobe that the editor of *GQ* would kill for. I have the top-rated jazz flute soloist in the world flying in from Prague next month to perform exclusively at my club. She is twenty-one, she is a redhead, and she can whisper sweet nothings in my ear in eight different languages. I don't want the world to end. I *like* the world."

"So what are you going to do about it?" Fennrys asked quietly. "How are you going to stop the Aesir from getting what they want? Kill me? Again?"

Mason tensed. She wasn't about to let that happen.

"I'd love to." Rafe shrugged. "But I'm not really allowed to do that. I'm actually not really allowed to do much of anything. I was thrown out of my very own underworld almost five thousand years ago, and I've been wandering around the mortal realm ever since. Just between you and me? A god in exile is about as useful as a gun with no bullets. I'm simply giving you information that I think could be useful to you. I'd like to see you solve this one on your own."

"You don't have to do this," Mason said. "Do you? You could just as easily hand Fenn over to someone who could do something about him. Couldn't you?"

"Yeah. I could. As a matter of fact, there are those who think I'm going to do exactly that, as soon I find you." Rafe sighed gustily. "But I think you are stuck in a tough spot through no fault of your own. I think *you*"—he looked at Fennrys—"deserve a second chance. I'd like to help you out. Despite what everyone says, in my experience, prophecies don't always come true. And even when they do, it's usually in all the ways you never expected they would. So there's always hope. Loopholes. A way around destiny." He grinned, appropriately enough, wolfishly and said, "To hell with destiny."

A couple of Rafe's wolf companions started to pace restlessly, sniffing at the air as if they sensed the coming dawn.

Rafe glanced at them and stood. When he turned back toward Mason and Fennrys, his eyes glinted in the light from the park lamp, full of ancient wisdom.

"Go on," he said in a surprisingly gentle voice. "Live your lives. Be careful, and be strong. But understand something. *Really* understand it. If this all starts to go south . . . I mean, badly, then I'm going to have no choice but to let others take care of things their way." The gleam in his eyes turned hard and sharp. "*Don't* let it get to that point."

He turned on his heel and stalked past them, the wolf pack following like silent wraiths in his wake. Ghost—Etienne—hesitated a moment. His dark, fathomless gaze was fixed, not on Fennrys, but on Mason. His look chilled her to the marrow. Then he too drifted off into the night, following in the footsteps of the god of the dead.

Fennrys climbed shakily to his feet and held out a hand to help Mason stand. "I'm so sorry," he said. "I crashed into the middle of your normal life and have done nothing but make things hell for you. Apparently quite literally."

"Don't say that." Mason was determined, for his sake—and, truthfully, for hers too—to not just put on a brave face, but to actually *be* brave. "I'm not going to let this . . . *thing* . . . this impending doom, this cosmic conflict that's nothing more than a *stupid* game of gods and monsters and mayhem, interfere with my life." She took him by the hand and led him toward the steps that would lead back down to the park path. "You heard what Rafe said. I'm not going to run and I'm not going to hide. I'm going to live my life. And so are you."

It isn't every day that second chances like that come along, right? she thought. And even an ancient god of the dead had just said Fennrys deserved it.

Walking beside her, his head down and his features drawn tight with anguish, Fennrys said in a ragged voice, "I don't deserve—"

Mason turned suddenly and reached up to pull Fenn's head violently down toward her. She stopped him with a kiss that tore the words from his mouth before he could say them.

Startled, Fennrys hesitated a moment. But Mason's arms wound tightly around his neck, and he was suddenly kissing her back hungrily, lifting her off the ground and crushing her to him in a fierce embrace. Mason clung to him, her fingers gripping the back of his head.

"Don't *ever* say that, Fennrys," she said. "I don't ever want to hear you say that you don't deserve or you aren't worthy. You do. You *are*." Her forehead pressed against his, and they stayed locked in that embrace for a long moment until Mason said, with regret, "But you have to let me go now."

Fennrys looked stricken for an instant, until Mason started to quiver with laughter.

"No," she said, gasping. "I just meant put me down! I can't breathe. . . ."

"Oh! Sorry . . ." He immediately loosened his rib-breaking hold on her, putting her gently down on the ground. Stepping back, he brushed the hair from her face and smiled that awkward, beautiful smile of his. And, for the first time that night since the dogs had attacked them on the High Line—for the first time, really, since the attack at the school—Mason felt as if everything was going to turn out just fine.

"Now walk me the rest of the way home," she said. "I have a major competition to win tomorrow. You've put a lot of time and effort into helping me prepare for this, and I don't intend to let you down. Looming apocalypse or no looming apocalypse."

Fennrys threw back his head and laughed. "That's the spirit, sweetheart."

"Yup." Mason grinned up at him. "Screw Ragnarok. We've got more important things to do."

XXX

Mason reached up and tightened the elastic band on her thick ponytail. Her right shoulder made a cracking pop as she did so, and she groaned a bit and swung her arm in circles, testing her range of motion. She was fine, it seemed, in spite of everything she'd gone through over the last few days. Banged up but not broken. She reached down into her bag and pulled out her white padded jacket and the fine gray metal mesh lamé that went over top. Because she fought saber, the lamé covered her torso and arms. It was attached to a wire that registered hits from the electrified saber blade during bouts. As sore as she was from her recent encounters, Mason knew that any residual aches and pains would be left behind, forgotten, once she was connected to the electronic scorekeeper and facing off against her opponent, ready to compete. She half turned and reached for where she'd left her gauntlet and metal overglove on the bench beside her, but they weren't there. She turned all the way around and saw Calum, leaning against the wall, holding the protective gear out to her.

"Hi," he said.

The sound of his voice made Mason's breath catch a bit in her throat. She looked up into his eyes, trying to read in them what he was thinking. The scars on the side of his face were healing cleanly. But they would never disappear entirely. The draugr had marked Cal for life.

"I wanted to come by and wish you luck," he said, and smiled at her.

"Oh . . ."

Two weeks earlier, and Calum Aristarchos seeking her out like that would have meant the world to Mason. Now she wasn't sure what to think. He wasn't competing—his arm was still in a light sling—and she hadn't really even been expecting him to show up that night. But there he was, with that same devastating smile he always had, only marred now by the way the scar tugged at the corner of his mouth. Mason tried her best to smile back.

Cal lowered his eyes for a moment and then looked back up at her from under the shock of sun-kissed bangs that fell in front of his forehead. She'd always wanted to reach up and brush them back from his face. For as long as she'd known him. She wanted to do it now.

"I'd really like to see you win tonight, Mase."

"Thanks, Calum," she said. "That means a lot to me, you know."

"And I thought that maybe, after the competition, I could take you somewhere. You know . . . just the two of us."

Mason felt the blood rushing to her face. "I . . ."

I can't. Fenn is here. She knew that Fennrys would be somewhere, waiting for her. Watching her compete. He'd promised that he'd be there for her, and they'd already planned on going somewhere together after.

"I can't, Cal."

Mason had to look away from the flash of hurt in his eyes. She dropped her own gaze and busied herself with shrugging out of the pullover kangaroo hoodie she'd been wearing over her athletic tank. When she glanced back at Cal, she saw that the look in his eyes had gone from hurt . . . to cold anger.

"Right," he said. "I get it." He was staring fixedly at the iron medallion that she wore around her neck. "I thought you were going to give that back," he said, a tightness in his voice. "To *him*."

Oh, god, Mason thought. *Here we go again . . .*

"I did," she said.

"Really. And so that's why you're wearing it around your neck."

She turned back to her gear, trying to get her temper under control. She didn't have time for this. Not with tonight's competition roaring down on her like a freight train. If she wasn't about to let the prophesied end of the world distract her, she sure as hell wasn't going to let Cal Aristarchos do it. She needed to have her wits about her, or she was going to blow another bout.

No. You aren't. Just remember the work you did. With Fennrys.

Mason took a deep breath and said calmly, "I returned it to Fennrys a couple of days ago. And then he gave it back to me for good luck tonight. Is that such a terrible thing?"

"It is if you're seeing this guy often enough to start exchanging little love tokens." Cal's face twisted in an ugly, angry sneer that was exaggerated by his scars. "That is the *only* thing you're doing with him, right?"

"Excuse me?" Mason gaped at him, eyes wide in astonishment. "What the hell do you even care, Calum? It's not like you have some sort of claim on me. As a matter of fact, you've made it pretty freaking clear that you haven't wanted anything to do with me lately. So what is *this*?"

"Mason—"

"If you really want to know what I've been doing with him," she snapped, "I'll tell you. I've been practicing. He's been helping me, Cal. You know, the way you said you were going to? Before you got all pissy and decided that I wasn't worth your time?"

"Wait—*you* weren't worth *my* time?" Cal's face flushed an angry scarlet. It made the claw marks stand out even more, and Mason winced and turned her gaze away. Cal noticed. "Yeah. Right. I think it's probably the other way around."

"You don't know what you're talking about." Mason sat on the bench and undid her street shoes, tugging angrily on the laces until one of them snapped.

"No. Of course not." Cal scoffed. "Why would I? I'm not the hero. I'm just the guy with the scars on his face."

"Oh, please, Cal—"

"No, Mason! I've *seen* it. I've seen the way you look at me. Or should I say—the way you *don't* look at me."

Mason stared at the running shoe in her hand as if her eyes

could burn a hole through the sole of it. Cal had a point. She knew it—knew that every time she looked at him now, all she saw were the draugr's claw marks—but it wasn't that she saw Cal as ugly. Rather, the scars were more of a constant reminder of what had happened that night. The night that started all of the weirdness and terror and—if she was going to be completely honest with herself—occasional bouts of wonderfulness over the last few weeks.

"Look . . . Cal . . ." She gazed back up at him and forced herself to look at him—*really* look at him—and not look away. "I'm sorry you got hurt that night, but you have to stop taking it out on me. It wasn't my fault."

"Wasn't it?" he said quietly.

So quietly she thought for a second she'd misheard him. But then she knew she hadn't by the way he was looking at her. By the dull, blunt force of the accusation in his eyes.

"What the hell is that supposed to mean?" she asked in a cold, dangerous voice. "It was *not* my fault. And you are *not* allowed to make me feel guilty about it. You're not allowed to make me feel guilty about Fennrys, either. He's not my boyfriend, Cal. And just because—"

"You hesitated."

The words stopped her dead, the rant dying on her lips. Mason felt her throat close up. "What?" she said, her voice ragged. "I *what?*"

"That . . . *thing* . . . had me in its claws," Calum hissed savagely, "but you were right there, Mason. You had time. You had a sword. You just weren't fast enough, and *I'm* the one who gets to suffer the consequences. You just couldn't handle yourself in a fight."

Mason couldn't believe what she was hearing. "A *fight*? You make it sound like it was just some kind of schoolyard brawl! That thing—"

"Got the drop on you!"

Suddenly Calum threw her gauntlets down on the bench and pointed violently toward the gymnasium. Mason had almost forgotten she was about to compete.

"And that stuff out there tonight?" Calum snarled. "It's just make-believe, but I'm betting you can't even handle that. You hide behind that fencing mask and avoid the real world and pretend everything's fine. Normal. You pretend that . . . that *guy* is normal. But he's not. And it's not. And you can't avoid what's happening, Mason."

Mason stared at Cal. Suddenly he wasn't just talking about the two of them anymore. He wasn't talking about a fizzled school romance or hurt feelings or even the competition. "Just what do you think *is* happening, Cal?" she asked.

He opened his mouth and looked like he was about to answer her. But then he just shook his head.

"What?" she asked again.

A deep frown creased his brow behind his bangs. He stepped toward Mason and grabbed her by the arm. "All I can tell you is that something bad is coming down the pipe, Starling. Something really bad. And you better grow up pretty damned fast and realize your protected, privileged 'daddy's little girl' status isn't going to keep you safe for very much longer. And neither is your barbarian tough guy."

"Shut up, Cal!" Mason tore her arm from his grip,

suddenly terrified by the fevered intensity in his eyes. And by the things he was saying. "You don't know what the hell you're talking about!"

Things were fine. She'd decided that last night—made up her mind that everything was going to be okay. Cal didn't know what he was saying, and it *wasn't* as if it was the end of the world. "Screw Ragnarok," she'd told Fennrys. She had better things to do. But this didn't feel better. This felt terrible.

"I thought you said you came here to see me win tonight," she said, her voice breaking a little.

"I did," Cal said. "I just don't know if you can."

He turned and walked away from her. Again.

A few minutes—and a lot of deep breaths—later, Mason stalked into the gym and over to the Gosforth team bench. She nodded to her teammates and then sat and tried to empty her mind of all the things Calum Aristarchos had said to her.

Tried . . . and failed.

She made it through the first two of her three five-touch pool bouts—but only just barely. She was sweating profusely behind her mask, and her whip-thin saber felt heavy as a lead pipe in her hand. All of the tension Fennrys had worked so hard with her to release out of her body came thundering back. She was stiff and jerky in her movements. Her parries were desperate and her attacks tentative. And the lights blinking on, registering touches on the scoring box, went less and less to her. Mason fought on with desperation, but her balance was all off and her aim was wonky. But what was worse . . . she was hesitating.

Just like Cal said—

With a shocking suddenness, Angie Delnorte lunged, knocking Mason's blade aside, and whipped her own around, tagging Mason's left shoulder with a stinging slash. The green light flashed, signaling a fifth point for Angie, another bout lost for Mason, and—just like that—Mason Starling was eliminated in the first round of competition. Something that had never happened to her before.

"Are you okay?" Fennrys asked again. She hadn't answered him the first two times. He put a hand on her shoulder. "Mase?"

"Oh, yeah! I'm freaking peachy!" Mason stuffed her mask into her gear bag and stripped off her overglove and the leather gauntlet beneath with sharp, angry movements. Back in the gymnasium, they could hear the sounds of cheering for the fencers who were still competing. Mason had fled the gym at the first opportunity. Fennrys had watched her go from where he'd stood hidden by the end of the bleachers and had followed in her wake.

"C'mon," Fennrys tried to soothe her. "It wasn't—"

"What?" She rounded on him. "Wasn't that *bad*? I just made a complete ass out of myself in front of most of the school *and* blew any chance I ever would have had at making the Nationals team. You know. That's *only* the thing I've been working toward for pretty much my whole life."

"Mason—"

"The only thing that was *mine*. The only thing I cared about."

"The only thing?"

"Don't." Mason turned a blazing glare on him. "Do *not*

even go anywhere *near* there, Fennrys." She pulled the elastic band savagely from her ponytail and shook her head, her midnight hair falling in a tumble all around her face. "I've wanted this since I was a kid. And then everything happened and I started to think it just wasn't important, you know? But after last night, after everything Rafe said about living our lives, I realized it was. I realized that dreams are important, and when he said what he said, I thought it was all going to be okay. I thought I could just go ahead and be normal. With this. With *you* . . ."

"There will be other competitions, Mase."

"No. Not for me there won't be." She threw her fencing jacket into her bag and tugged on a hoodie with the Gosforth crest. "Cal was right—I never should have gotten involved with you in the first place. Everything that's happened over the last few weeks has been one giant crazy-making distraction, and I am now out of the running and off the team and a giant laughingstock. Life as I know it is pretty much over for me. So if you don't mind, I'm just going to go somewhere and be sad and pissed off until the rest of the world comes crashing to an end to keep me company. Wake me up when it really *is* Ragnarok."

That said, she stalked off down the hallway and pushed through the double doors out into the back parking lot without a backward glance. Fennrys stood there, feeling as though someone had punched him in the chest with a hammer. He had no idea what had just happened, but there was no reason Mason should have been acting the way she was. Even after what had happened in the park the night before, she'd been ready for that competition. She'd been perfect. It didn't make any sense, unless . . .

"Cal was right," she'd said.

Which meant Cal, who'd apparently been actively ignoring Mason since the night in the Gosforth gym, was suddenly talking to her again. Fennrys wondered just exactly what he'd had to say. He'd seen him lurking around near the gym stage before the match had started, but at the time he hadn't thought much about it. The kid's face was still something of a mess, and Fennrys figured that he was just doing a Phantom of the Opera thing. But now he suspected that Cal had been there to confront Mason. And if he'd done it right before her bout, then *that* could have been what threw her so badly. Fennrys turned on his heel and headed off to find Calum Aristarchos to have a few choice words with him.

"Starling!" Heather called out from somewhere behind her.

Mason kept walking.

"Mason . . . wait!"

The other girl's footsteps were pounding across the pavement. Mason had never known Heather to run for anything, and so she stopped and turned, waiting in the shadows between two campus buildings for the other girl to catch up with her. It was cold, and a chill wind blew bits of trash in swirling eddies around them.

"Hey," she said dully as Heather jogged to a halt in front of her and stood there panting heavily, her cheeks flushed from exertion. "Where's the fire?"

"I don't know," Heather gasped, bending over. She braced

her hands on her knees and shook her head, her long honey-blond hair curtaining her face. "I don't think it's started just yet. But listen, I just had a very long talk with a crazy girl named Gwendolyn Littlefield, and you are in a massive heap of trouble, Starling. Or at least you will be . . ."

Mason stared, unblinking, at her, waiting until Heather could catch her breath and tell her just what exactly *that* was supposed to mean. The moment never came. Suddenly there was a rustling sound from just over Mason's shoulder, and a large canvas bag descended over her head. She heard Heather cry out, but the sound was truncated by another noise—a dull thud—and Heather went silent. Mason was too panicked to scream as the canvas bag encased her completely. The material was thick and stiff; it blocked out all light and made it hard to breathe. It stank of stale rubber and sweat. From the smell alone, Mason knew that it must have been one of the carry bags for the basketballs that were stored in the CU gymnasium—not that knowing where the bag had come from helped in any way. It wasn't enough to give her any kind of clue as to what was happening to her. But then something else did: Mason heard muffled voices and strained to make out what they were saying. She felt the blood in her veins go ice-cold when she realized who was speaking.

"What d'you wanna do with the spare?" The voice, nasal and unpleasant, was unmistakable and belonged to the captain of the CU football team, Taggert Overlea. "She's out cold."

"I don't care what you do with her," Mason's brother Rory answered. The cold cruelty in Rory's voice made Mason want to weep.

"Maybe I should bring her along. . . ." Tag sounded unsure.

"Fine. Just keep her up front with you," Rory said as Mason felt herself being unceremoniously dumped into what felt like a small, confined space. "And keep her out of my way. We've gotta get out of here."

Oh, god! Mason thought frantically as she felt a scream crawling up her throat with agonizing slowness. *No. Not this. Anything but this* . . . She heard and felt the slam of a lid and knew with devastating certainty that Rory had thrown her in the trunk of his Aston Martin. He knew all about her raging claustrophobia, and yet he had done this. To her. To his baby sister. Mason had been right all those years ago when she'd told Roth that she suspected Rory hated her. She'd been right. And now he was going to punish her by driving her mad for something she'd done wrong. She didn't even know what that was.

The scream that had been building inside her became a howl of agonizing terror. And no one, she knew, would hear it over the thunder of the Aston's engine as the car roared off into the night, with Mason stuffed in the trunk . . . for reasons she couldn't even begin to fathom.

XXXI

"I don't know what the hell you're talking about!" Calum said through clenched teeth as Fennrys slammed him back against the gymnasium wall for the second time. He was suspended several inches off the floor, and the blond, muscular young man who held him up by his jacket front didn't even look like it was a strain to keep him there.

The Fennrys Wolf glared flatly at him. "I'm pretty sure you do."

"Hey, Cal," came a voice from over Fennrys's shoulder. The voice was low and deep. Casual and yet capable of menace, if need be. "This guy bothering you?"

"No, Roth, we're old friends," Calum grunted, glancing over to see Mason's older brother. "What does it look like?"

"It looks like he's pretty pissed at you. But whatever you say, man. I don't want to come between . . . old friends." Roth shrugged, and the two guys in bike leathers standing behind him both tried unsuccessfully not to smirk. "Don't let me interrupt. I just wanted to ask you if you know where my sister is."

Suddenly Cal found himself once again standing on solid ground as Fennrys abruptly let go of him and turned to face Roth Starling. The two young men stood staring at each other like a pair of alpha wolves coming face-to-face in the forest.

"Can I help you?" Roth asked politely.

"You're Rothgar."

"You have me at a disadvantage."

"I was led to believe that doesn't happen very often."

"It doesn't. Who, might I ask, was kind enough to tell you that?"

"Your sister."

Cal watched Roth's eyes flick over Fennrys from head to toe, assessing. "You know Mason?" Roth asked, even more politely.

He asked it so politely that every instinct in Cal's body was screaming for him to dive for cover before things got truly ugly.

"I'm a friend of hers," Fennrys answered.

"You don't go to Gosforth."

"No."

Roth smiled coldly. "Mason doesn't have friends who don't go to Gos."

"Maybe just ones she hasn't told you about."

"So you're the one," Roth murmured. "Him. The Wolf."

A moment passed. Stillness. Then movement . . .

Cal hadn't looked away—hadn't even blinked—but he

still had no idea where the weapons had suddenly appeared from. The blade in Roth's hand looked like a bowie knife, huge with a wicked curved point and a serrated edge, like a row of shark's teeth. The one in the Fennrys Wolf's hand looked like a dagger out of a medieval epic, with a broad, sharply pointed blade that Cal could tell, just by the way the light glinted off the edge, was honed to a razor sharpness.

"Jeezus," he muttered to himself, a cold sweat suddenly beading his forehead. "Calm the hell down, you guys. Somebody's gonna get hurt."

"Accidents do happen," Roth said quietly. "You might want to tell your old friend to put away his toy before misfortune strikes, Cal."

Fennrys said nothing, but the grin that spread across his face in that moment was easily the most unnerving facial expression Cal had ever seen on another human being. It even seemed to give Roth pause. And Roth's two buddies—who hadn't moved a muscle since the knives came out—exchanged flicking glances.

The claw marks on the side of his face tingled as all the blood rushed from Calum's face, and he took a single step forward, holding up a hand at each of the other men. "Stow it, both of you," he said, in his best channeling-Toby-Fortier manner. He turned to Roth. "Look, I saw Mason right before the competition. And . . . we argued. I was trying to find her just now to apologize—again. But I don't think she's here. I looked everywhere."

"She can't have gone far," Fennrys said. "I was talking to her only a few minutes ago."

Roth lowered his knife and reached into his back pocket, pulling out a cell phone. He punched in a number and waited. As the rain began to fall, they heard the chorus of the *Wizard of Oz* movie theme song playing faintly, coming from the alleyway leading to the parking lot. Roth broke into a run and reached the place where Mason's cell phone lay on the ground just as the song stopped playing. The touch screen was spiderwebbed with cracks.

They could all hear her voice coming from the phone in his hand saying, "Hey, it's Mason. Leave a message and I'll catch you on the flip side."

And a violent crack of lightning overhead was followed almost immediately by a peal of thunder that shook the air as the rain began to fall in earnest. Roth swore venomously under his breath and bent down to pick up the phone. When he stood, he turned and looked back in the direction from where they'd just come. Fennrys glanced back, too. It was as if both of them had sensed the presence of the man Cal knew as Rafe, before he'd even appeared, stepping out of the shadows and walking swiftly toward them. He was breathing quickly and looked as if he'd been running. And for a brief instant, Cal thought it looked as though the edges of his form were . . . *blurred* slightly.

Roth nodded brusquely to him and said, "We have a big problem."

"Oh . . . it's bigger than you think," Rafe said, grimly. He turned to Fennrys and nodded a brisk greeting.

"Nice to see you again," Fennrys said flatly. "Or, y'know, not."

Rafe snorted. "Remember what I said to you about prophecies having a funny way of coming true in ways you don't expect? I didn't mean funny ha-ha."

"Tell me."

"Tell him, Rothgar," Rafe said.

"Gunnar, my father, believes in Ragnarok," Roth said. "The end of the world. A mythic apocalypse of—"

"I *know* what Ragnarok is, dumbass." Fennrys rolled his eyes.

"Right. Anyway. He thinks it's the only way for the world to become good again, but his belief in the prophecy had faded over time because he was missing a fundamental piece of the puzzle."

"And that is?"

"Long story short . . . it turns out that for the prophecy to be fulfilled, Gunnar needs a Valkyrie. That's to be Mason's fate—but only so long as someone could walk into Asgard and out again, carrying the spear of Odin. If Gunnar gets the spear, he can turn my sister into a chooser of the slain. After that, the rest of his plan falls into place."

Cal went cold as ice. He should have told her. He should have told Mason all about the meeting between Rafe and his mother and Roth. He'd had the opportunity—when he'd told her about the sea-monsters, or just before the competition—but he'd bitten his tongue both times and said nothing. Sure, he'd been wary about breaking his promise to Roth, but it was more than that. He'd been so angry with her. Angry and jealous. And now Mason was gone, maybe in some kind of serious trouble, and it was his fault. He should have told her to be careful or tried to protect her.

Fennrys was staring daggers at Roth. "You didn't come here looking for Mason. Your father sent you here to get me, didn't he?"

"No." Roth hesitated a moment. And then nodded. "Well . . . yes. I mean, I was supposed to find you and bring you to Bifrost—the rainbow bridge to Asgard—with the intention of forcing you to cross over and get the spear."

"And how exactly were you going to do that?"

Roth looked back and forth between Fennrys and Rafe. "The magick of Bifrost was woven into a train bridge called the Hell Gate. It spans the East River."

"Wait." Fennrys frowned, holding up a hand. "I know that bridge. I think I met the troll that lives under it."

Cal blinked at him. "Figure of speech?"

Fennrys shook his head. "I don't think so. . . . He said the island the bridge passes over is—what did he call it?—Dead Ground."

"Well, it *is* a gateway to the underworld," Rafe muttered, clearly getting impatient. He gestured for Roth to move it along.

"Right." Roth ran a hand through his hair. "Well, the plan was for Rory to get Mason after the competition and take her to the other side of the bridge. I was supposed to track you down and tell you to cross after him."

"Track me down? How were you going to do that, exactly?"

"I have my ways."

"Those ways don't include wolfhounds, do they?"

Rafe frowned in confusion. "No," he said. "They don't."

Cal took a step forward. "My mother keeps wolfhounds," he said.

Fennrys looked at him and shook his head. Then he turned back to Roth. "Why take Mason across?"

"Insurance policy. Nobody expected you to go willingly. Rory was to threaten her—threaten to hurt her—if you didn't cross on your own."

"You son of a—"

"Wait!" Roth put up his hands. "This whole thing was Gunnar's plan. And Rory's. *Not* mine! I've never wanted Ragnarok. Ask Rafe here. I've been meeting secretly with him and Calum's mother. She's a powerful woman in her own right. We've been trying to find a way to stop this madness."

"It's true." Cal nodded.

"I *didn't* come here to find you, I swear. There's no way in hell I want you anywhere near that bridge. I was just trying to get to Mason before Rory did," Roth said, a strangely helpless expression crossing his face. It didn't suit him at all.

Fennrys just sneered at him. "You didn't try hard enough."

"Hang on a second . . . ," Cal said. "What happens if one of the living tries to cross over this bridge? I mean, a regular mortal?"

"Nothing." Roth shrugged. "You cross a bridge. Just a bridge. Wind up in Queens, no harm done. Except you're in Queens."

Fennrys shook his head. "So I'm the only guy who can cross it into Asgard."

"The only *guy*, yeah," Rafe said quietly.

All eyes turned to him.

"What?"

"Remember that bigger problem I mentioned?" Rafe's gaze was troubled. "Mason Starling's not exactly . . . *living*."

"What the hell are you talking about?" Fennrys looked as if he might actually kill Rafe for saying that. "If something's happened to her, I'll—"

"No. That's not what I meant. I wasn't sure at first. Her true nature was . . . hidden from me somehow." The shadow of a frown darkened his brow. "I'm a god in exile, remember, and nowhere near as powerful as I once was. I suspected something when I realized that she could see the vision Etienne conjured for you of your time in Valhalla. She shouldn't have been able to. Etienne confirmed it for me, though. Mason has—at one time or another—passed through to the underworld and made it back out again. Roth . . . your sister *died*."

Cal didn't even pretend to understand half of what he'd just heard. He just looked at Roth, who had gone very, *very* pale.

"Oh, god . . . the game. There was a hide-and-seek game when she was little. She was trapped in a shed for three days. I never even thought that she . . . ," Roth murmured, stricken. "But we found her. She was alive!"

"Someone must have revived her," Rafe said.

Fennrys swore quietly. "I guess that explains the claustrophobia."

"Rory doesn't know!" Roth exclaimed suddenly, a frantic light growing in his eyes. "When he tries to take her over the bridge—"

"She'll cross over. Into the beyond. And if Mason some-how finds the Odin spear on her own, the touch of it will turn her into a Valkyrie," Rafe said. "She'll become a chooser of the slain whether she wants to or not. It'll drive her. Control her. We have to stop your brother before he gets to that bridge."

Roth turned to one of his silent companions. "Give him the keys to your bike," he said, nodding toward Fennrys. "Can you ride?"

"No. I've never—"

"I can," Cal said as he stepped forward and caught the tossed keys out of the air. He glanced at Fennrys. "I'll double you on the handlebars, hero," he said sardonically, and spun the key ring on his finger as he stalked past. "Let's go."

XXXII

Mason was dimly aware of a sense of movement. It penetrated the fog of panic that had wrapped itself around her mind and turned her world into a red-and-gray nightmare that she was experiencing as though it was happening to someone else. Which was probably for the best. She knew that if she could have looked into a mirror in that moment, she wouldn't have even recognized herself. She would have seen a wild-eyed, openmouthed apparition. Pale and screaming. She knew that she'd screamed her throat raw. The stale stench of canvas and rubber choked her; dirt scratched her eyeballs and gathered under her lids. Her muscles ached from thrashing wildly.

None of it mattered. All that mattered was that she was trapped. All that mattered was that she get free. She knew, in that far corner of her brain where her rational mind had gone to cower, squeezed into a tiny ball like a terrified animal, that she would do anything, say anything, become anything to escape the confinement.

The roar of an engine started up and she recognized the throaty purr as that of Rory's car. The rumble of movement indicated that they were traveling at some speed, zigzagging in and out of traffic in the typical way that Rory was used to driving. She felt herself rolling and sliding, bouncing off the walls of the trunk and jabbing her ribs painfully on the spare tire mount—from which the tire had been removed, no doubt for just this occasion. After several infinitely long minutes, she felt the sensation of the car rolling up a ramp and the engine cutting out. Doors slamming. Heather's voice raised in woozy outrage was cut short by the sound of Tag Overlea's coarse laughter, all of it fading into the distance.

There was a long moment of extended, suffocating silence. Still the pitch darkness of the canvas bag inside the trunk and the sensation of the world shrinking around Mason. Closing in on her. Any moment it would crush her.

But then there was a lurch and the car began to vibrate again, although Mason knew that the engine was turned off. Over the panicked huffing of her own breathing and the thunder of her pulse in her ears, she figured it out. She recognized the sounds, the familiar swaying and chugging motion. Rory's Aston Martin, she knew, was now sitting in the transport compartment of Gunnar Starling's private train.

Mason thrashed around and punched at the canvas that trapped her, twisting and tightening about her arms and legs like mummy wrapping—she felt as if she'd been bound for burial. Felt as if she'd already been entombed. But when her fingers touched the edges of a sewn seam in the canvas where the stitching felt like it had begun to pull away from a frayed edge, Mason felt a tiny, tenuous sliver of hope twist painfully in her heart.

After a few minutes of frantic activity, she forced herself to stop. To listen. There was nothing beyond the sound of the train rumbling along tracks. A small part of her wondered where in hell Rory was taking her. The rest of her didn't care. If he'd already done this much to her—knowing her as well as he did—whatever her brother had in mind couldn't be good. Mason managed to thrust her head and one arm out of the tear she'd opened in the canvas bag. She wriggled and struggled, drenched in sweat and sticky with dirt but exerting an almost superhuman effort to escape. She had to stay focused on that.

She already sensed, with a kind of clinical detachment that kept her from vomiting, that she'd torn away her fingernails on most of her fingers forcing her way out of the bag. She could feel the wetness of the blood flowing down to pool in the webbing between her fingers and in the palms of her hands.

She didn't care.

She had to get out. Twisting herself around so that her shoulders were wedged against the back of the trunk, Mason began to kick at the partition in between the trunk and the seat backs. Roth had always scoffed at Rory's "toy car," telling him it was a flimsy piece of James Bond-wannabe showy crap. Mason aimed to prove his assertions, even if she wasn't thinking about it as rationally as all that. She kicked and kicked until one of her shoes went straight through the particleboard and stuck in the horsehair padding and spring coils, the ends of which caught in the flesh at the back of her calf. Mason didn't even feel it. She kept kicking until the passenger seat wrenched off its moorings with a protesting screech and folded forward, leaving her with a ragged hole to crawl through.

In the darkness, she made her way over the wrecked backseat through to the front of the car. When she caught sight of her reflection in the windshield glass, it was like staring at just another monster. Pale and hollow eyed, cheeks and forehead streaked with grime, her hoodie and leggings painted with stripes of blood and grease. Her black hair hung lank around her face like a shroud, and her face looked gaunt and ghostly. She groped wildly for the door handle and tumbled out onto the floor of the train car when it opened abruptly—and her gear bag, which Tag or Rory must have thrown in the car when they'd taken her, tumbled out too. Frantically Mason pawed through it, and her hand closed on the scabbarded silver swept-hilt sword Fennrys had given her. She'd taken it with her to the competition, for luck. She almost laughed wildly at the thought. Some luck. Still, she pulled it out and slung the strap of the baldric across her body so that the sword hung from her left hip.

She didn't know why she did that.

It wasn't as if she was going to stab Rory when she found him, was it?

No. No . . . she wasn't even going to go looking for him. Whatever he was playing at, he was serious. He never would have done such a thing to her otherwise. This was no game.

The sound of her rasping breath was so loud in her ears that she was sure Rory or Tag would hear it and come running and stuff her back into the confines of the Aston Martin, making sure she couldn't get out this time. Or worse.

The very thought sent Mason scrambling, in full panic mode, scurrying into a dark corner of the train container. In the darkness, her shoulder jammed up painfully against a metal rail, and Mason realized that there was a ladder that led up to an access hatch in the roof of the container. Freedom. Air. What she would do when she got out onto the roof, she had no idea. But it didn't matter. Already it felt as if the walls of the train container were closing in on her. Out of Rory's car wasn't enough. She needed off the train.

Mason turned and started to climb.

Rory had waited his entire life for something like this to happen. He felt almost light-headed with glee as he looked over and saw Heather Palmerston cowering on the leather banquette, pale and shaking. Tag was over by the bar, pouring himself another shot of whiskey from Gunnar's private stock and pocketing cigars from the humidor. Rory wasn't even drinking, but he still felt absolutely intoxicated. This was what it was like to be his father. This was what it was like to have power. He was the linchpin in Gunnar Starling's plan, and Top Gunn was trusting Rory not to fail him. And he wouldn't. Everything so far had gone off without a hitch.

Rory had no doubt that his competent, dutiful brother Roth would do his part and Mason's wolfy boy toy would show up right on cue. Then Rory would get to put on a big show of threatening to hurt Mason if Fennrys didn't do exactly what they wanted. He was debating just how much of it would be an act. And just how much he could actually get away with torturing his poor, pure, perfect sister before his father would take exception. In the face of achieving the Odin spear, he thought he could go pretty far.

Rory was pleased with himself in that he'd already put Mason's claustrophobia to work against her. *By now,* he thought, *she's probably curled in a fetal position and catatonic.* She wouldn't give him any trouble.

He glanced out the window and saw that the train had shunted onto the tracks that led to the long, sweeping approach to the Hell Gate Bridge. The approach ramp gradually elevated for almost two miles before it joined with the bridge proper, and the train wasn't traveling fast. He couldn't yet see the bow-curve shape of the bridge where it crossed over the East River, soared above Wards Island, and on into Queens, where Rory would stop the train and wait. The sky overhead was purple and black, shot through with neon-orange and silver jagged forks of lightning. He could even hear the thunder over the noise of the train, it was so loud.

"Keep an eye on Party Girl," he said to Tag, who was leering at Heather. "I'm gonna go check on the Mouse trap."

He slid the door at the end of the passenger car open and crossed over to the transport container. He didn't bother fumbling for the light switch. Just felt his way over to the DB5 and, grinning, pounded on the trunk. *That should scare the hell out of her,* he thought.

"Hey, Mouse!" he shouted.

There was no answer.

"What . . . no squeaks?" he taunted.

But then, in the dimness, he saw that Mason's gear bag was on the floor of the container, its contents strewn about. He ran over and saw that the passenger door was ajar . . . and that the inside of the DB5's cockpit was trashed beyond belief. There was a gaping hole leading from the trunk compartment, blood everywhere . . . and no sign of his damned sister.

Fury bubbled up in Rory's chest, and he opened his mouth to scream in rage when something caught his eye. Over in the corner of the car, he saw that the access hatch above the utility ladder was banging up and down, unlatched. Rory snarled an oath and started toward the ladder. Then stopped and ran back to the Aston Martin and opened up the glove compartment, fishing around for something in the dark before he ran back to the ladder to give chase.

The wind on top of the train hit Mason like a punch to her chest, knocking the breath from her lungs and threatening to send her flying. She couldn't stand upright, and she thought that any second she would be hurled off the top of the car, where she would tumble and smash to pieces like a broken doll on the tracks. She dropped to her knees and began to crawl, working her way toward the ornate brass luggage rail that ran around the top of the antique train car.

If it hadn't all felt so real, Mason could have sworn she was caught in the depths of another one of her nightmares—the worst one ever. Or maybe it all felt so hyperreal because she'd finally, once and for all, *lost* her grip on reality.

In that state of mind, she was almost not surprised when she glanced down over the side of the train and saw two speeding Harleys and Anubis—a large black wolf—chasing after the train like a dog chasing a car.

From inside the opulent confines of the passenger car, Heather watched through the window as the two Harleys roared up beside the train, driving precariously in the narrow lane where a set of decommissioned tracks had been removed and only a strip of weedy gravel ran. Heather pressed her face closer to the window and gasped when she saw something that looked like a lean black wolf running beside them— faster than a normal wolf should have been able to. She saw that one bike carried Roth Starling, but the one in the lead carried two riders. The Fennrys Wolf sat, clinging grimly, on the handlebars. The driver wore a helmet, but Heather recognized Cal's jacket. He steered the bike perilously close to the train as Fennrys tucked first one booted foot and then the other, under him. Heather held her breath as Fennrys stood, poised for an instant in time as if for flight, and then leaped, reaching to grasp some handhold on the side of the train.

"What the shit are those two lunatics trying to prove?" Tag said from over Heather's shoulder, his voice suffused with disbelief and something approaching awe. Then he laughed gutturally as the Harley wobbled dangerously underneath Cal.

Heather gasped and pressed close to the window, her heart in her throat as Calum struggled to bring the bike back under control on the uneven surface of the approach ramp. Heather couldn't exactly tell from where she was, but she saw Fennrys's feet and legs disappear out of sight, so that she knew he must have hauled himself up a side ladder to the top of the train. Cal gunned the bike's engine to keep pace with the train as it swept around the curve that led to the Hell Gate Bridge. The gravel strip alongside the tracks must have been punishing to ride on, and Heather could see the tendons on the backs of his hands tensed like steel cables with the effort of keeping the bike steady as they swept under the massive concrete gates and the bridge girders rose up and closed in on them and they swept on, over the East River.

Heather kept her gaze fastened on Cal, as if she could pour her strength out through the window glass and into Cal's limbs. She knew that he was there to help Fennrys save Mason, not her. It didn't matter. She saw him hunch forward, helmeted head down. . . .

And then, as Heather watched, Cal twisted his head to one side, as if something had suddenly caught his attention. He shook his head, raising one hand to the side of the helmet, as if he was trying to cover his ear. He looked like he was in pain. Heather saw his shoulders ripple as the bike began to drift toward the outer railing of the bridge. Cal's head whipped violently from side to side, and he pounded on the side of his helmet. The front wheel of the bike slewed wildly left to right as he lost control, and the back of the Harley pitched forward. Heather screamed in horror as Cal was catapulted into the air. He pinwheeled wildly through the night, and the bike slammed into one of the rust-red, arching girders of the bridge, ricocheting into the path of Roth Starling, who jammed his bike into a screeching slide. Cal's body arced through the air, plummeting over the side of the bridge, falling toward the raging river far below.

Heather watched him fall, the scream dying in her throat. She slid down the window to slump senseless on the leather banquette, horror giving way to sudden, icy-cold shock. Beside her, Tag Overlea swore under his breath and drew back from the window, wide-eyed and shaken, his features stark with disbelief. The motorcycle tumbled along beside the train for a moment, then disappeared from view.

And Calum Aristarchos . . . was gone.

XXXIII

Fennrys threw his leg over the top of the train car, almost kicking Mason's feet out from under her. She gasped and threw herself wildly back away from him. Her black hair whipped around her head like an inky tornado; her sapphire eyes were wide and rolled white like a terrified animal's. They were empty of recognition. Fennrys clambered to his feet, crouching to keep from getting knocked off the top of the train by the wind, and held out a hand to her, but she shrank from him. He looked at her face and saw that she was caught in the depths of a profound, mind-fogging panic.

What did Rory do to her? he wondered with frantic bitterness.

There was blood streaking Mason's face and arms, staining the fabric of the sweatshirt she wore. Fennrys saw the Gosforth school crest, and the image of the old woman in the Laundromat punched through his mind—the tumbling red water in the washer, the same crest slapping against the glass, soaked in blood. . . .

He shook his head sharply to dispel the horror he felt.

"Mason!" he called out to her, the wind snatching the sound of his words and hurling them behind him. "It's me!" He reached out a hand. "Come take my hand. It's going to be all right, Mase. . . ."

She wanted to believe that. She truly did.

But she was caught in a nightmare.

And in her nightmares, Fennrys always told her to run.

So she ran. She turned and lurched, stumbling and falling to her hands and knees, crawling, staggering back up and leaning into the teeth of the wind as she struggled toward the front edge of the train car. Fennrys shouted for her to stop. Massive iron girders, soaring in a graceful arching curve between two monolithic concrete gates, wavered like a mirage before Mason's eyes as the train pounded up the rising track.

She heard Fennrys call her name and turned around in time to see Rory suddenly burst out of the ladder hatch in the roof of the transport car, between her and Fennrys. He looked back and forth between the two of them, and a purely wicked grin spread across his face.

"Well!" he shouted over the wind, struggling to find his balance as he climbed out to stand in the middle of the train-car roof. "This is convenient!"

Mason couldn't believe her eyes—he had a pistol clutched in one fist. What the hell was her brother doing with a gun? She could barely make out what he was saying as the gale snatched the words from his mouth.

"I was gonna have fun messing with Mouse, but . . ."

Fennrys surged forward a step and Rory whipped up his arm, pointing the muzzle of the pistol at him.

"Stay right there, hero!" Rory glared at him. "Fun's just starting . . ."

He thrust his other hand into his pocket and pulled out something small and round. Mason couldn't tell what it was, but Rory started murmuring words she couldn't hear, and whatever it was, it started to glow.

The golden light seeped like rays of sunlight through Rory's fingers, casting a widening, brightening nimbus of light all around them. The locomotive passed through the western arch of the Hell Gate, and suddenly the whole of the bridge began to shimmer. The iron struts and girders began to sparkle and dance with cascading light and color, and the entire structure began to telescope, elongating in front of them and behind . . . stretching out to bridge the gap between the mortal realm and the beyond. Mason clapped her hands over her ears at the cacophony of buzzing and tinkling, like thousands of wind chimes caught in a hurricane, assaulting her senses. The noise built until it sounded like the pounding of hammers on harp strings. It split the air around them as the prismatic light show exploded into whiplash streamers of rainbows, billowing up, up into the night sky. Even numbed as she was, wrapped in the vestiges of her claustrophobic panic, Mason felt a kind of distant awe sweeping over her.

This was Bifrost. The rainbow bridge to Asgard.

She turned and saw, at the very center of the bridge, a shimmering curtain of diamond-white light. She had an overwhelming urge to reach it, to part the curtain and see what was on the other side. She glanced ahead at the train engine, pounding away on its eight spark-churning wheels, and suddenly she didn't see a machine. She saw a horse. A coal-black giant of a war horse, thundering over the bridge on eight *legs*.

Mason skittered back from the edge, turning in time to see Fennrys rush her brother. In the split second Rory was distracted by the blinding brilliance of the Bifrost's manifestation, Fenn surged forward and tackled Rory around the middle, slamming him hard onto the ridged metal roof. Mason watched in horror as he drove his fist into her brother's face while Rory writhed underneath him. Rory twisted around and kicked Fennrys in the side of the head, sending him rolling toward the edge of the car roof. Mason screamed, but Fennrys caught himself before he went over on the rail, just as Rory aimed another kick at him. This time Fennrys caught him and, with a heave, threw Rory back down. The look in Fenn's eyes was one of pure savagery. He drove his fist into Rory's face again and slammed down on his wrist over and over, trying to get him to drop the wildly waving gun.

Mason saw Rory's arm break. His face was bloodied. Fenn kept punching even as Rory slumped away from him. Shaken out of her stupor, Mason staggered forward and grabbed Fenn's arm before he could land another blow.

"Stop!" she cried. "Stop! You're going to kill him!"

Fennrys struggled against her for an instant, and then his expression cleared and he pulled her close. "Mason . . ." He glanced over her shoulder. The train was almost at the midpoint of the bridge now. The light of the shimmering curtain had grown unbearably bright. "Come on . . ."

He pulled her to a crouching stand and helped her toward the back end of the train-car roof. There was a porter's ladder there that led from the luggage rail down the outside of the train car.

"We have to get off the train, Mase," Fenn said. "You can't go across the bridge. Bad things will happen. Do you understand?"

She nodded numbly. *Bad things . . .*

"Climb down as low as you can. I'll be right there with you. We'll jump together—off to the side where there are no tracks. Tuck yourself as close in to me as you can, and I'll protect you when we hit the ground. Just keep your arms in tight, okay?"

He went to lift the strap of her sword hanger over her head. She couldn't jump with that on. But before he could, there was a sound like a car backfiring—only louder. Mason heard it over the roaring of the train and the howling of the wind.

Another explosion of color, this one crimson and dark, burst from Fennrys's shoulder. Fenn spun around, away from Mason, a look of dull surprise in his ice-blue eyes. Mason glanced back over her shoulder to see Rory hunched against the gale, a look of pure, mindless malice on his face. His right arm hung useless at his side, but he clutched the pistol in his left hand.

Mason turned back to Fennrys . . . but he was falling away from her, drifting in slow motion as she screamed and reached for him. As if taken by the wind, he tumbled off the back of the train. Mason stood there, statue still as the train kept thundering on, carrying her forward without him.

The brightness of the bridge all around her grew to blinding, the colors of the rainbow boiling together into a glacial-white froth that stole away the sight of the world and replaced it with sudden, shocking darkness.

The impact of the bullet punched through Fennrys's body. He clutched at nothingness and fell through the air, slamming onto the bridge decking below and tumbling over railway ties. Half conscious—half *dead* almost—he lifted his head and saw the train blasting toward the wall of shimmering light that fell like a veil in the dead center of the rainbow bridge. He saw Mason's form silhouetted on top of the train car, the sword hilt at her side gleaming, her hair lifted in the wind like a winged helmet and her sapphire eyes staring back at him in terror and anguish. . . .

There was a thunderclap and a flare of lightning that split the night . . . and then darkness. The train rumbled through the shimmering curtain and on over the Hell Gate Bridge, chugging off into the distance on the other side of the river. Fennrys could see the hunched shape of Mason's brother Rory still clinging to the top of the train car.

But Mason was gone.

Fennrys's head dropped onto his forearms, and his bruised and battered ribs heaved in a desperate sob. A moment of silence in the wake of the chaos spun out all around him, and then Rafe was there, at his side. The werewolf god's shape shifted from beast to man, and he knelt and got a shoulder under Fennrys's right arm. He helped him gently to stand and led him, dazed and battered, toward the towering concrete gate, even as Fennrys tried to pull away, mumbling in protest that he had to cross the bridge. He had to follow Mason and try to get her back.

"I'm the only one who can . . ."

"You're not going anywhere," Rafe said firmly. "I don't know what happens if you actually die when you're *in* the nether realms, and I'm not so sure I want to find out. I don't think you do either. And the way you're leaking blood from that hole, you might just do that if you go charging off after her."

"But Mason . . ."

"You'll find her. Patience. The bridge isn't going anywhere."

They were almost to the concrete gate when they felt a rumbling beneath their feet. Fennrys turned, half expecting to see a train roaring down on them from the other direction. But as the vibration built, it became clear that the sound wasn't from another locomotive. A series of concussive booms built in a crescendo until the whole of the Hell Gate structure heaved wildly, and the center of the bridge truss exploded outward in an ear-bursting screech and howl of ruptured metal and shattering concrete.

Rafe tackled Fennrys, shoving him behind one of the arch pillars, and they crouched there, covering their heads as smoke and sparks swept over them and debris rained down. When the chaos subsided, Fennrys lurched to his feet and thrust himself out away from the shelter of the gate arch. The

Hell Gate Bridge still stood before him . . . some of it.

But there in the middle was a gaping, empty space. The steel girders from either side of the bridge still reached across, like the gnarled, twisted fingers of hands, desperate to clasp each other but no longer reaching. Fennrys could smell the acrid tang of explosives drifting on the breeze. Something—some*one*—had intentionally blown the hell, quite literally, out of the Hell Gate Bridge. There would be no crossing the bridge now. Not the Hell Gate . . . nor Bifrost. No crossing over into Asgard.

Smoke spiraled up into the night.

The wail of distant sirens floated on the air.

Fennrys stood gazing in despair at the ruined bridge, knowing that Mason Starling was somewhere on the other side . . . and there was now no way on earth for him to reach her.

He felt something inside him crumple and the last of his strength went out of his legs. He started to collapse, but Rafe gripped him by the arm and kept him standing.

"What did I tell you, Fennrys Wolf?"

Fennrys turned to him, numb.

"I told you 'to hell with Destiny' and I meant it," Rafe said fiercely. "There is always a way. A loophole. *Always*. You just have to find it. And you'd better start looking, because your girl is going to need that now. And so are we, if we're going to have any chance at all of getting her back."

XXXIV

The blinding white brilliance faded slowly from behind Mason's eyes.

The wind was gone. Fennrys was gone.

The rumble of the train, silenced . . .

Slowly she opened her eyes and gazed around. An endless twilight-tinted vista rolled to the horizon—unending, desolate plains . . . ringed around on all sides by thunderheads piled thick and ominous, blotting out the margins of the sky. Mason saw flashes of purple lightning licking the edges of the barren wasteland. Thunder, so distant it sounded like a tremor deep in the earth—something more felt than heard. She turned a complete circle and came face-to-face with a cloaked and hooded figure that hadn't been there a moment before.

Mason put a hand on the hilt of the sword at her side.

The figure reached up and pushed back the deep cowl of the cloak. A spill of midnight hair framed a face, corpse pale and lovely. Dark blue eyes gazed at Mason, and a shadow of a smile curved the bloodless lips of the woman's face as she took a step forward and said in a voice like a bell tolling:

"Hello, Mason. Welcome to Hel."

She held out her arms.

"I'm your mother and I've been waiting for you. . . ."

Discover the enchantment in Lesley Livingston's ravishing urban Faerie trilogy.

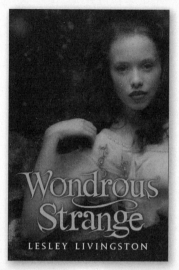